More Haunted Montana

A Ghost Hunter's Guide to Haunted Places You Can Visit

Karen Stevens

RIVERBEND PUBLISHING

More Haunted Montana

Published by Riverbend Publishing, Helena, Montana

ISBN 978-1-60639-025-2

Printed in the United States of America.

4 5 6 7 8 9 MG 20 19 18

Cover design by DD Dowden
Text layout by Barbara Fifer

Front cover image: The very haunted Dumas Brothel in Butte. Photo by Christopher Cauble.

Riverbend Publishing
P.O. Box 5833
Helena, MT 59604
1-866-787-2363
www.riverbendpublishing.com

To my dear friends and ghost-hunting companions
Pat Cody and Sue-Ellen Welfonder—
may we enjoy many more eerie adventures together!

ABOUT THE AUTHOR

Karen Stevens recently retired from Parmly Billings Library in Billings, Montana. To contact her about a haunting, email kdstevens@bresnan.net or visit her website at www.hauntedmontana.com.

CONTENTS

INTRODUCTION

From ghoulies and ghosties
and long-leggedy beasties
and things that go bump in the night
may the good Lord preserve us.
Traditional Scottish Prayer

I've always loved Halloween, with all its mystery and excitement. As a child, I would linger in the leaf-whirled darkness as long as I dared, hoping to catch a glimpse of the spirits that were said to roam the earth on All Hallows' Eve. I never saw one, but that only made me more determined to try my luck again the next year.

I never saw the "ghoulies" or "long-leggedy beasties" of the old Scottish prayer either, but things sometimes did go "bump in the night" in our family home. My folks didn't know the three story brick-and-stucco house was haunted when they bought it, but it wasn't long before we realized that we shared our house with an unseen presence. During the nineteen years I lived there, everyone in our family had experiences we couldn't explain. Doorbells rang for no apparent reason, lights turned themselves mysteriously off or on, and someone we couldn't see occasionally walked up the basement stairs. On one memorable occasion, all four of us saw the knob on the basement door begin to turn back and forth as if someone were standing on the other side. My father grabbed the knob while it was still turning and yanked the door open. There was nothing visible but the empty darkness of the stairs that led down to the basement. He was never able to explain that incident to his satisfaction—or ours.

Even as a child I was insatiably curious. *How* could something without hands turn a doorknob? Why did we hear footsteps on the stairs when no one was there? I pestered my father for answers.

Although he must have grown tired of the barrage of questions, he never discouraged me from looking for answers. When I was older, I rode my bike over to the local library and checked out every book they had on ghosts. None of them gave me the answers I needed, so I decided to conduct my own "scientific" experiments. Did ghosts leave footprints? Apparently they didn't. At least, nothing disturbed the flour I scattered at the foot of the stairs (Mom made me clean it up the next day). Then I decided to see whether ghosts could pass through a strand of yarn tacked across the stairs without breaking it. I never found out the answer, because Dad nearly tripped over it and my experiments came to an abrupt end.

Eventually we sold the house and moved on with our lives, but I never lost my childhood fascination with ghosts, whatever they may be. I still enjoy visiting haunted places and have spent many nights roaming haunted battlefields, castles, theaters and restaurants all over the United States and Britain.

For the past thirty years I've collected ghost stories here in Montana, stories that are linked to some of the most dramatic events in our state's history. My previous book, *Haunted Montana: A Ghost Hunter's Guide to Haunted Places You Can Visit,* focused on historic sites such as forts, battlefields, theaters, hotels, restaurants, museums, and railroad depots that welcome visitors. *More Haunted Montana* offers additional sites that are currently haunted, open to the public and of historic interest. Since part of the fun of visiting haunted sites is the possibility of encountering a ghost, I've once again rated each site according to the level of paranormal activity experienced by those who work or live there. A "low" rating indicates that activity is sporadic and infrequent; "moderate," that activity occurs occasionally, and "high" means that visitors have often reported ghostly experiences.

You can find stories that will send a shiver down your spine just about anywhere in this sprawling state. Do you enjoy camping? You may change your mind after you read the chapter called "Spirits of the Back Country!"At Bad Medicine campground in the Kootenai National Forest, hikers claim to have photographed a man in 19th century clothing—a man who wasn't really there.

Why not take a camera along and try your luck? Or you could rent the old U.S. Forest Service cabin at Mill Creek south of Livingston. If you need to visit the outhouse after dark, though, don't go alone. Previous campers have seen an eerie ball of light floating among the trees nearby.

You never know what you may encounter on the back roads of Montana either. Be especially watchful after dark on the Vaughan Frontage Road just out of Great Falls, where a driver narrowly avoided striking a young boy on a bicycle. Not unusual, perhaps, except that this particular youngster had been killed in a hit-and-run accident nearby years earlier.

On snowy winter nights, motorists driving along Highway 28 near Hot Springs sometimes see a young Native American woman walking beside the road accompanied by a small boy. If a well-meaning driver pulls over to offer them a ride, however, the woman and the boy promptly disappear. That stretch of Highway 28 is known locally as the "Ghost Road" because the pair were reportedly struck and killed by a pickup truck sometime in the 1990s after their car broke down during a snowstorm.

Secondary Road 446 near Rosebud can hold eerie surprises for the unwary, too. Several years ago a motorist claimed to have seen a group of mounted soldiers appear from a strange mist. They wore uniforms dating from the Indian Wars of the 1870s. One of them apparently caught sight of the automobile, and the next moment the soldiers and their horses vanished. The location was not far from the historical plaque that marks the spot where General Terry met General Gibbon and Lt. Colonel Custer aboard the steamboat *Far West* to plot strategy just before the Battle of the Little Bighorn in 1876.

Cemeteries can be haunted too, although not as often as you might imagine. There's a touching story about a pair of elderly sisters from out of state who visited an abandoned homestead in Eastern Montana, searching for the graves of their great-grandparents. They discovered to their dismay that their family's wooden grave markers had been vandalized and the site itself was littered with beer bottles and trash. The two ladies spent most of the afternoon picking up garbage and setting the markers back in place. When they finished, they stood for a few moments looking around with weary satisfaction. At that moment both of them heard a woman's disembodied voice say softly, "Thank you."

Then there's the farmer from the Roberts area who saw the glow of campfires in his pasture at night, with the shadowy forms of Indian ponies standing nearby. When he told his grandfather what he'd seen, he was told that the great Crow Chief Plenty Coups and his band used to camp in that pasture many years ago, on their summer trips to the mountains. The ghostly campfires have also been seen by people driving past late at night. Some of them actually stopped their cars and got out to beat out what they thought was a small grass fire, but when they approached, the firelight vanished, leaving no scorch marks on the earth.

A rancher and his wife from Dillon had an eerie experience when they drove to East Missoula to pick up a load of sheep a few years ago. While they were loading the sheep onto their truck, they caught sight of two young boys in 19th century clothing who were peering out at them from behind a huge cottonwood stump. As soon as the boys realized they'd been spotted, they dashed back to the cover of a grove of trees not far behind them. The "boys" had no legs. Instead, their bodies tapered off to a gray mist beneath the waist. The ranchers watched, fascinated by their first encounter with the paranormal, until the two ghosts vanished into the trees.

So many readers have told me about ghosts in their own homes that I couldn't resist including a few of their eerie true tales in the chapter called "Uninvited Guests." Be sure to read the excerpt from a chilling log kept by a couple who moved into their brand-new home—only to discover that it was already occupied.

Why should Montana have such a treasure trove of ghost stories? Most of those who made the long trek out here by steamboat, wagon train or by horse were strong-willed people, determined to be successful. Life on the frontier was rough and unpredictable, however, and all too often lives were cut short by accident, illness or violence. Scientists tell us that energy cannot be destroyed, so perhaps the energy of those who never lived to achieve their dreams lingers even now on the battlefields and in the dimly lit corridors of historic buildings and private homes across the state. Their stories deserve to be told, and their names, if known, to be remembered.

I've included stories from all over the state, from the historic Bitterroot Valley to the starkly beautiful prairies of the east. Most of the stories have never been made public. Along the way, I've met hundreds of wonderful people who graciously shared their stories with me. Many thanks to them and a special note of appreciation to "ghost researchers" Dan Damjanovich, Cynthia Berst and Dee Brown of Billings, Mary Doerk of Fort Benton and the late Robin Gerber of Miles City. Thanks also to Michelle Heberle and her crew of MAPS, the Montana Association of Paranormal Studies in Great Falls, Dustin Benner of Billings and his Montana Paranormal Research Society, and Lance M. Foster, founder of the Yahoo! group paranormalmontana and host of the popular Helena ghost walks.

By the way, if you would like to visit one of these haunted sites as many readers of my previous book have done, it's always a good idea to call ahead to verify open hours. Businesses can close without notice, and telephone numbers are also subject to change.

Please join me now as we go in search of more ghosts of the Treasure State!

THE GHOSTLY LANDLADY

GHOST RAILS INN
702 Railroad Avenue
Alberton, Montana 59820
Telephone: 406-722-4990
Webpage: www.ghostrailsinn.com

Ghostly Activity Level: High

HISTORY: The Ghost Rails Inn was built by the Milwaukee Railroad in 1909. At the time the hotel was called the Montana Hotel, and primarily housed railroad crews. The rails were pulled up in the mid-1970s when the Milwaukee Road abandoned service. The historic hotel is now a bed-and-breakfast inn owned by Grace Doyle and Thom Garrett.

PHENOMENA: A phantom brakeman is reputed to await his call in an upstairs room, while the spirit of a former landlady, Mrs. Bertha Brasch, who collapsed and died in the lobby in 1971, still bustles around making sure that everything is running well at the hotel. Guests in Room 8 report that items are sometimes moved during the night, while guests in Room 5 are occasionally awakened when Bertha sits on the side of the bed. Owner Grace Doyle caught a glimpse of a woman wearing an apron in the kitchen and spoke to her, assuming her to be the high school girl hired to help. The woman disappeared instantly. The sounds of a train have been heard arriving at the depot across the street although the tracks were removed long ago.

The historic Ghost Rails Inn is located in Alberton, about thirty miles west of Missoula. Guests from all over the world come to visit this small town in the lovely Clarks Fork River Valley. Visitors can enjoy hiking, fishing, bicycling and Montana's best white-water rafting as well as a funky used book store which stocks over 130,000 volumes. The town currently boasts 404 residents, 388 dogs, and as my friend Frank and I were to discover, at least three ghosts.

Thom Garrett and Grace Doyle never expected to purchase a bed-and-breakfast hotel when they stayed at the historic hotel in 2007, but they fell in love with the place and, a few months later, put in an offer for the old building. While negotiating the deal, they stayed in Room 5 as guests.

"That's when we had our first run-in with Bertha," Doyle told me as we sat in the comfortable lobby near the fireplace enjoying cookies and tea. "I woke up around one or two A.M. Somebody had me by the toes of my left foot. It gripped, not hard, but I couldn't pull my foot away.

"I woke Thom up and said to him, 'What are you doing? Let go of my foot!'

"He said, 'What do you think I'm doing? I'm sleeping!' I know what a Charlie horse feels like, and it was not a Charlie horse.

"Thom turned the lights on and it let me go. No one was there. We looked all around, even in the shower, and nobody was there. I thought that was just the creepiest thing. If it was a dream, it had to have been the most vivid dream I had ever had, and it even continued after I was awake. We didn't say anything to the owners next day.

"We finished negotiations in February, and when we were doing the final walk-through, Thom said to the owner, 'We know you named it Ghost Rails Inn because the railroad is gone, but is there a ghost?'

"The owner turned and looked at him dead-pan and said, 'Yes, in Room 5.' My hair just stood on end, because we'd never said anything about our experience in that room. I asked her how she knew there was a ghost, and she said, 'Because it sits on the bed. You can feel it getting up and down and see indentations where it sits.'

"Well, we opened in April and an Alaskan native who called himself 'Chief' stayed here with his wife and their adult daughter and her husband. Chief and his wife had Room 6, right across the hall from Room 5. We had not mentioned the ghost to them, because some people won't stay if you have a ghost. Others say, 'If you have a ghost, we want the haunted room.'

"Anyway, Chief came down in the morning and said, 'Do you mind if I go in Room 5 and meet your ghost?'

"I said to him, 'How do you know there's a ghost in there?' He said, 'It sat on the bed.' We had not told him anything about this, and he'd never stayed here before.

So he goes back up and is gone for half an hour. Then he comes down and says, 'Old person, I don't know if it's a man or a woman, but I don't get the sense of a man. It's awfully shy. I've been talking to it, but it just sits on the bed and won't answer my questions.'

"Another lady stayed in Room 5 and was a little spooked when she came down the next morning. 'Well,' she said, 'I woke up in the night and my husband was breathing loudly in my right ear. I lay there wondering if I should nudge him. He wasn't snoring, just breathing loudly. Then I realized my husband was on my left side! It was just this quiet breathing. I stayed awake the longest time just seeing if it would go away and too scared to move.'

"Things kind of escalated that summer. At least thirty times we've gone into Room 8 and it's smelled like old-fashioned liniment, like Bengay. At first we thought a guest must have been wearing a lot of Bengay, but we've turned on fans, opened windows, and it still comes back. Another guest in Room 8 had a different experience. She was from South Carolina. She took the teddy bear off the bed and set it on the nightstand. In the morning it was facing the other way. Someone had to have moved the bear. We hadn't told her about the ghost. She thought at first that we had come into her room and moved it.

"We smell old-fashioned peppermint in Room 6. We don't use

air fresheners or potpourris at all because some people are allergic to them. The doors all have old-fashioned latches. You have to turn the knob and flip the button. We lock the doors and leave them open so they will lock when a guest goes in. One night we went up and closed and locked the doors as usual. The next morning all the doors in every room were unlocked. We have sometimes found lights on and the radio on in unoccupied, locked rooms. We really combed through the place, thinking someone was hiding up there.

"And someone likes to squeeze our new towels and pillows."

The Inn often hosts quilting retreats, and many of the ladies who attend are frequent guests. Several of them have had eerie experiences at the Inn. Joan Contraman stayed in Room 5 during a visit in March, 2009. She was sound asleep, sleeping on her back, when suddenly she was jolted awake by someone smoothing the sheets under her. It was 2:45 A.M. by the bedside clock. She then felt hands moving along the sheets smoothing them out. Then the ghost put a hand on either side of her head and fluffed the pillow! Despite her somewhat unnerving experience, Contraman says, "I love staying at the Inn. I'm not at all afraid of being there. I actually find the ghost kind of fun. It's more like someone is caring for the Inn."

Another guest also reported an incident in Room 5. She wasn't feeling well when she sat down on the bed to go to sleep. Suddenly she felt a reassuring touch on her forearm. She said there was no mistaking it; it was as if someone was saying to her, "Get some good rest." She didn't know about the ghost stories until she read the room journal the next morning.

Owner Grace Doyle actually caught a glimpse of the ghost one busy morning when she was serving breakfast. Jasmine, the high school girl hired to help, was late that morning so Thom was helping serve. Doyle entered the kitchen to fetch something and saw a short elderly woman wearing an apron. She wore her dark hair in a bun. Assuming that Jasmine had arrived, Doyle called out, "Oh good, Jasmine, you're here!" and the figure disappeared. Doyle thinks Bertha had sensed her stress and decided to help.

By now it was getting late, and the owners had to get up

early, so Frank and I thanked them and went upstairs. We had explored all the rooms earlier and had noticed a scent of peppermint in Room 8. Room 2 had a heavy atmosphere I've learned to recognize from other haunted sites. I call it a "sense of suspended time." All the other rooms seemed perfectly normal to me. We'd chosen Room 5, the Wild Horses Room, for the night, however, since there had been paranormal activity recently in that room. It was an attractive room with an antique dresser, a Diamond Fields quilt on the brass bed, a wallpaper border featuring wild horses, and a private bath. Below the window was a pleasant flagstone-paved courtyard with a fountain. As we settled down for the night, I recalled the story about the lady who had heard someone breathing in bed next to her—the very bed we were in—and laughingly told Frank, "If I hear any breathing next to me tonight, it had better be you!"

Just in case Bertha chose to pay us a visit during the night, I set up an infrared video camera on the dresser to cover most of the room. Although I awoke several times during the night, nothing grabbed my toe, nor did I hear anything besides Frank's snoring. When I played the video back a week later, however, I heard two or three odd thuds that sounded like a heavy ceramic mug had just been set down hard next to the camera. And at one point, a dark human-shaped shadow swept across the wall behind our bed. I can't be certain that it wasn't caused by passing car lights, but I doubt it, since several other cars passed by later in the film and did not cause a similar effect. And when I started to transcribe the interview I had recorded with the innkeepers earlier that evening, I discovered that an unidentified male voice had broken into the interview and mumbled a few unintelligible words. None of us had heard anything at the time.

Perhaps the voice belonged to the phantom brakeman who is rumored to roam this lovingly-restored hotel. If so, does the spirit of landlady Bertha Brasch still roust him out in time to catch a phantom train?

If you decide to make the Ghost Rails Inn your headquarters for whitewater rafting, biking or simply enjoying this scenic area, be sure to visit Alberton's Railroad Museum, housed in authentic railroad cars. And if you need snacks or soft drinks, why not drop into Valley Grocery, just a short walk from the Ghost Rails Inn? Employees of the grocery, formerly a church, have heard coolers' doors opening and footsteps when no one was visible. It's a friendly ghost, the manager told me. "Once you get used to it, it's just part of the building."

FOOTSTEPS IN THE GUTTERS

COPPER BOWL CAFÉ, CASINO
AND BOWLING ALLEY
1500 East Park Avenue
Anaconda, Montana 59711
Telephone: 406-563-3427

Ghostly Activity Level: Low

HISTORY: The Copper Bowl Café is a 24-hour restaurant–casino–bowling alley complex built in 1959. It was purchased in 1969 by Wilbur Johnson, an avid bowler who won the state bowling singles championship in 1970. He and his son Ray won the state bowling doubles championship in 1987.

PHENOMENA: Soon after the death of owner Wilbur Johnson in 1990, staff began to see dark shadows in the bowling alley. The sounds of falling objects were heard as well as the clatter of someone running down the gutters of the bowling alley. A cook saw the figure of a woman reflected in a mirror although no one was there.

The internet abounds with ghost stories, many of which sound very convincing. A few of the stories have led me to genuinely haunted sites, while other stories do not stand up to investigation. One such story involved a supposedly haunted jail/museum and "country club" at a tiny town not far from Fort Benton. It sounded a bit too good to be true, so the next time I was in the area I decided to do some research. My initial skepticism was justified: the "country club" turned out to be a bar, the museum non-existent. The only spirits there are probably the 80-proof kind. (Nice try though, guys!)

Another story posted on the internet involved a haunting at a bowling alley in Anaconda. A woman who stated that she was a former employee of the Copper Bowl claimed that the building was haunted by a ghost called "Wilbur," who supposedly owned the Copper Bowl for many years before his death in a tragic boating accident. She also stated that the gaming machines in the casino would sometimes show credits due even though no one had been playing the machines. Although she rationalized that as a mechanical malfunction, she found it harder to explain why objects apparently moved around by themselves. When a cook who worked with her saw the figure of a woman reflected in a mirror when no one was there, she realized that another spirit had joined Wilbur.

What really alarmed the former employee, however, was the activity in the bowling alley adjacent to the restaurant. According to her, the staff sometimes heard someone walking on the lanes or in the gutters when the bowling alley was dark and deserted. They also could hear keys jingling. When they went to investigate, no one was visible. Later, the woman and the cook went into the bowling alley to smoke cigarettes and she saw a black figure walk across the alleys at the far end of the room. At the same time, both she and the cook had the feeling that they needed to leave—quickly! She quit not long afterward.

I tried to contact the woman who posted the story, but her email address was no longer valid. The story intrigued me, however, particularly since a preliminary search of newspaper archives confirmed that a man named Wilbur actually had once owned the Copper Bowl. On my next trip to Anaconda, my friend Frank and I decided to see whether there was anything to the story. We dropped in to the Copper Bowl for a late lunch. Only a few customers still lingered over meals, so I took the opportunity to introduce myself to the restaurant staff and show them a copy of the story that had been posted online. Was it true, I asked hopefully, or just another Internet tall tale?

I was quickly assured that the events mentioned in the story had actually happened. Several of the staff felt certain that they knew the identity of the poster and had actually worked with her and with the cook she had mentioned in her story.

Apparently the haunting began after Wilbur R. Johnson, who owned the Copper Bowl for many years, died unexpectedly in a boating accident on Canyon Ferry Lake on July 7, 1990. He was seventy-three at the time of his death. According to newspaper articles, Johnson and his wife Mildred had been fishing and had put into shore to catch grasshoppers for bait. There were whitecaps on the lake, and the unsecured boat began to drift away from the shore. Johnson tried to swim to it but went down about 100 yards from the shore. His body was found later that afternoon in ten feet of water.

To find out more about the alleged haunting, I spoke with one of the bowling alley staff who had worked for the Copper Bowl for seven years. The young woman agreed to tell me about her experiences but preferred to remain anonymous.

"Has anyone actually seen a ghost here?" I asked.

"One of our staff did," she replied. "He had gone upstairs to get some holiday decorations or something. We could hear him talking but thought he was just talking to himself. A couple of minutes later he came bounding downstairs, and said he thought he had seen someone wearing coveralls. He followed the person down the hall and called, 'Hey! You can't be up here! It's restricted! Hey!' The figure went around a corner and when he followed, there was no one there. And other people have seen shadows moving around the bowling alley."

She took us through the doors into the bowling alley, deserted at that time of the day. "I haven't seen anything, but sometimes I've heard loud raps on the counter. Wilbur used to do that whenever he passed the counter. And I've heard someone running down the gutters between the lanes. They're plastic, and they make a terrific crackling noise that's unmistakable. We rush in and there's no one there."

I asked her permission to walk in the gutters. Although I often bowled when I was younger, I'd never walked in the gutters and had no idea what to expect. The noise was incredible. No wonder the staff had rushed in to see who—or what—was in the bowling alley!

"Well," I commented, "no one could mistake that noise for anything else!"

We walked toward the back of the bowling alley and stopped by the pin setting machine.

"The machines were put in around 1959," she told me. "Sometimes they just don't work right. But when we get back there, we can't find anything wrong."

She indicated a photo of Wilbur in a place of honor on the back wall near the pin room. The photo appeared to have been taken in Wilbur's middle years and showed a well-dressed gentleman smiling back at us.

"After Wilbur's wife Millie died in March of 2008, the activity really increased. She passed away on a Friday morning and on Saturday afternoon the spirits just had a heyday. We could hear balls bouncing instead of being picked up by the machine and sent back to the bowler. We'd run back to pick up the ball and we wouldn't even touch it and it'd go up by itself."

I'd been taping the interview and at that point stopped to rewind the tape a bit to make sure it was recording properly. Ghosts are thought to be a form of electrical energy and have been known to interfere with cameras, tape recorders, televisions and other electrical gadgets. Sure enough, my tape recorder was running erratically, speeding up so the employee's voice was nearly unintelligible and then slowing back down to normal. Just to be on the safe side, I changed the batteries and continued the interview. When I checked again a minute or so later, I discovered that the tape had once more speeded up by itself. Parts of the interview were completely unintelligible, even when I used the multi-speed function to slow the tape.

"Wilbur," I said half-seriously, "if that's you, knock it off! I want to tell your story." Despite my appeal, the tape continued to speed up and slow down. Fortunately, my digital camera can record short bursts of film and recorded enough of the conversation to be able to piece the story together. Wilbur must have been in a playful mood that day.

I followed the young woman to a narrow room behind the pin setting machine. The room was piled six feet high with open boxes of new pins.

"This is known as the pin room," she told me. "It's always been one of the coldest parts of the bowling alley. We joke about it being Wilbur's room. One time, we had the pin boxes stacked up to the level of this shelf, and we heard a tremendous crash. We rushed back here and all the heavy boxes of pins had been tipped over at once. The pins were dumped out all over the floor." She paused, and added significantly, "There was absolutely no one here."

I tried to lift one of the boxes. They were very heavy and had been carefully stacked against the wall. It would have taken considerable force to have shifted one of them, much less all of them. I've personally seen a jar of jam sail off a countertop by itself and land upright and undamaged in the middle of a kitchen floor, but the jar weighed less than a pound. Whoever or whatever tipped the heavy pin boxes must have really wanted to make his presence known.

In September 2009 I returned to Anaconda, this time with my friend Pat Cody. We stopped at the Copper Bowl for lunch before boarding the Copper King Express excursion train. Ray Johnson, one of Wilbur's two sons, happened to be there and I asked him whether Wilbur had been known for a sense of humor. If so, he just might have been the one who had interfered with my audiotapes the previous year. Mr. Johnson described his father as a "go and do your business guy, very practical."

Murphy, who worked for Wilbur for ten years, confirmed that Wilbur was an unusually focused individual, but that "every once in a while, he did have a sense of humor. Sometimes I'll hit a switch and a machine will stay on and we joke that Willie's at it again." Murph, as he's known, has also heard the footsteps in the gutters. "Nobody's here, but you'll know who is doing it!"

I smiled, suddenly certain that Wilbur had indeed interfered with my tape recorder the previous year as a practical joke. This year I had switched to a digital recorder that uses no tape. "Well," I told Murph, "he'll have a tough time interfering with my new digital recorder!"

We were also able to confirm the anonymous online poster's claim that odd things happened in the casino. Joanne, who has worked as a waitress for the Copper Bowl for several years, was on duty at 6:30 one morning when she heard someone cough in the upper level of the casino. The bowling alley wasn't open at that hour, nor was anyone in the casino when she and another waitress checked.

Does the spirit of Wilbur Johnson still keep a watchful eye on the Copper Bowl? The employees are certain of it, and who else would be a better candidate for the ghost of the Copper Bowl than the champion bowler who had devoted so many years and so much of his energy to the business he loved? As his son Ray Johnson told me, just before he left, "I don't think retiring ever entered his mind."

And the digital recorder that I thought was immune to Wilbur's pranks? At the end of the interview with Murph, moments after I thanked him, a male voice says quietly but clearly, "Hi."

Ray Johnson was right. Wilbur Johnson is apparently still very much on the job.

If you enjoy good homemade pie, why not stop in for lunch some day? And if you decide to bowl a few lines, don't forget to give a respectful nod to the photo of Wilbur Johnson on the back wall of the bowling alley. You may even hear a loud rap on the counter nearby. It just means that Wilbur's still on duty.

Anaconda offers other attractions as well, including the Jack Nicklaus-designed Old Works Golf Course, the haunted Copper Village Museum, and the Club Moderne, an unusual bar built in 1937 in the Streamline Moderne style, a late form of Art Deco.

HIGH SPIRITS AT THE REX

REX RESTAURANT
2401 Montana Avenue
Billings, Montana 59101
Telephone: 406-245-7477
Website: therexbillings.com

Ghostly Activity Level: High

HISTORY: The Rex Hotel was built around 1910 by Buffalo Bill Cody's European chef, Alfred Heimer, with financial support from Cody. The three-story red brick building is located directly across from the railroad depot. In its heyday the Rex was considered to be the finest hotel between Minneapolis and the West Coast. During the Roaring Twenties, legend has it that "ladies of negotiable virtue" occupied the upper floors. Today those rooms are used as offices. The main floor, with its pressed-tin ceiling and handsome bar, is home to the Rex Restaurant, where superb steaks and Memphis-style barbecue may be enjoyed in surroundings reminiscent of the Old West.

PHENOMENA: Bartenders have heard the sound of men's voices and bar stools scraping on the floor when the restaurant is closed; occupants of offices on the upper floor report that objects are sometimes mysteriously moved around; a ghostly figure was seen on the stairs by restaurant staff when the building was closed; a female customer came out of a stall in the ladies' rest room to find a man staring at her. The man promptly vanished. Recently, a gentleman had a similar experience in the men's rest room. Adding machines and bar blenders sometimes turn on by themselves.

In a television interview at Halloween a few years ago, Gene Burgad, who has owned the Rex for twenty-eight years, stated that he'd never had a ghostly experience in the restaurant. He didn't discount the eerie encounters his employees claim to have had, however, and even expressed a hope that he'd have an experience some day.

He got his wish. One evening after closing, he was in the basement working when he heard bar stools scraping back in the restaurant overhead. "I thought that the bartender must have come back in," he said. "I came upstairs, checked around and found that no one had come in. The doors were still locked and nothing had been disturbed."

"Had the bar stools actually moved?" I asked curiously.

"Nope, the stools were where they were supposed to be. I remember wanting to get out of here!"

Burgad wasn't the first to hear those eerie sounds. About ten years ago, a barman gave me a chilling account of a similar experience after closing one night. He had gone down to the locked storeroom in the basement to fetch bottles of wine to replace those used that day and had only been down there a few minutes when he heard men's voices and the unmistakable scrape of bar stools from the restaurant overhead. He was certain that no one had been locked in by mistake, so he hurried back upstairs expecting to find that someone had broken into the restaurant. Nobody was there and, most puzzling of all, the bar stools were standing in their usual places. Just to be sure, he asked the police to bring one of their dogs over, and they searched the entire building. Nothing was found.

Not long afterward, a visiting psychic told him that one of the ghosts was a barman named "Buck," who had died during the Prohibition years. Newspaper indices from the 1920s and 1930s do not mention Buck, but the indices are sketchy and Buck may have been a nickname. During Prohibition the Rex was rumored to have a "floating bar" which managed to stay just a few steps ahead of the local constabulary, some of whom were said to have been good customers. The Rex may even have been linked to the underground tunnel system that once existed beneath Billings, tunnels that are said to have been used to move bootlegged cargo discreetly between buildings.

Reid Pyburn has worked for the Rex for fifteen years, the last six as bar manager. He's a calm, level-headed man, not one to jump to conclusions, but he concedes that the Rex "is a creepy building in the dark." He has good reason to think so: one night not long after he began working as bar manager, he was downstairs after closing when he too heard the sounds of bar stools scraping back and people moving around. When he mentioned what he'd heard to Bob, another bartender, Pyburn learned that Bob too experienced something similar shortly after he had begun work as bar manager. Neither man has heard the bar stools since, although others have.

"It's like the ghosts wanted to make sure we knew they were here," Pyburn said.

The two rest rooms in the basement have been the scene of many paranormal incidents. As far back as the 1970s, those rooms had an eerie reputation. A woman who worked in one of the second-floor offices at the time told me that she and her female colleagues never liked to use those rest rooms. They often felt as though they were being watched, although they never saw anyone.

Recently, the unseen watcher did make an appearance to a female guest who had gone downstairs to the ladies' rest room after dinner. No one was there when she arrived, and she didn't hear anyone come in while she was in the stall. When she came out, however, she saw what looked like a man wearing old-fashioned clothing standing a few feet away, staring at her. The figure appeared hazy rather than solid. When he realized she'd seen him, he promptly vanished! Puzzled and somewhat shaken, the woman told a waitress about her experience before leaving.

Other guests and at least one restaurant employee have also found the women's rest room a bit unsettling over the years. Pat

Cody, visiting from Texas, told me about her experience after dinner at the Rex one evening

"While I was in the stall," she told me, "I heard someone come in and go into the stall next to mine. The door slammed so hard it made the door of my own stall vibrate. When I got out and went over to the sink, I glanced over at the other stall. The door was slightly open and the stall was empty. I was the only one in the room, and I hadn't heard anyone go out."

Several of the female employees won't use the downstairs rest room in the evening. Pam Pierce, who has worked for the Rex for nine years, told me, "I was in a stall and I heard a jingling like a dangling belt. I knew I was the only one in the rest room, so I looked under the stall to see if anyone had come in. No one else was there."

The men's rest room has also had its share of incidents. One man, a longtime friend of the owner, had been washing his hands at the sink when he heard someone come in, walk behind him and go into a stall. The man dried his hands and looked around to see who had come in. Nobody was there. He hurried upstairs, white as a sheet, and left after telling Reid Pyburn, the bar manager, what had happened.

A waitress may have caught a glimpse of "Buck" one afternoon a few years ago. It was mid-afternoon, and the restaurant was closed. She started downstairs to fetch something from one of the storage rooms and saw a male figure in a white shirt disappear around the corner at the bottom of the stairs. It moved so quickly that she only saw part of a shoulder and one arm. She knew that she and one of the chefs were the only ones in the building at the time, so she and the chef hurried down the stairs after what they assumed was an intruder. Barely thirty seconds had elapsed before they reached the bottom and turned the corner but the man had disappeared. A search turned up nothing.

Pam Pierce, who had heard the sound of a jangling belt in the women's rest room, also had an unnerving experience in the bookkeeping office downstairs. "It happened about three years ago," she recalled. "I had just arrived to start work in the accounting office, helping out with the books. It was about seven or eight A.M. and there was nobody else here. I was sitting at a desk and the calculator, which was turned off, started spitting out feet of tape. When Gene Burgad, the owner, arrived, he wanted to know what had happened and I had no explanation."

"Buck" is considered a friendly if sometimes mischievous spirit, but bartender Justin encountered an entity that was decidedly unfriendly one night after closing. He was walking along a corridor in the basement that is lit by motion-detecting lights placed at strategic points. The lights are sometimes slow to come on, leaving long stretches of blackness between pools of light. Justin, a big powerful guy, had just stepped into one of those dark stretches when he felt something push him violently to the floor. He scrambled up, flailing his arms to trigger the next light, and left the building without putting the money away or turning off the lights. When Reid asked him the next day what had happened, Justin told him about his experience. Justin's wife confirmed that he had marks on his shoulders from the incident.

The ghosts have made their presence known on the main floor of the original building also. A green neon light that spells "Rex" is supposed to be turned off at closing each night. One night the bartender turned off the light, locked the building as usual, and left. As he was about to get into his truck, he noticed that the light was on again. He turned off the alarm, switched the light off, and left again. By the time he reached his truck, the light was back on. He left it on. An electrician the next day found nothing wrong with the wiring.

Since ghosts are thought to be a form of electromagnetic energy, it's not uncommon to hear reports of electrical equipment such as televisions, alarms, and cameras malfunctioning in haunted places. One such incident happened during a photo shoot just before the grand opening of the Rex's new addition. Every light in the building had been carefully turned off before the photo was taken, but when the film was developed, it showed a single light on upstairs in the hotel. No lights had been visible to the eye when the photo was taken. The photo had to be retaken.

Motion detectors at the Rex have also reacted to the presence of spirit energy in the original building. Every December, usually the night after the holiday decorations are put up, something triggers the building's alarms. When the bar manager arrives to let the police into the building, nothing appears to have been disturbed and no intruder is ever found. Perhaps the building's unseen residents have simply been inspecting the decorations.

Like most of us, ghosts enjoy being acknowledged, and will occasionally take action to convince a skeptic of their existence. Pyburn told me about a previous manager who always vehemently denied that the building was haunted. The manager was seated at the bar one evening, when a book that was displayed on a shelf above the bar fell on his head.

"It couldn't have jumped over the lip on the shelf by itself," Pyburn said. "It's happened to a couple of other men, but it happened to him twice. And that," he concluded, pointing at a copy of a biography of Rex Harrison that stood on a shelf high above the bar, "is the book that hit him on the head."

I studied the shelf for a moment. Even if we speculate that vibrations from a passing train might have caused the book to tip over, the retaining lip on the shelf should have prevented it from toppling over the edge. Just to be safe, though, a skeptic might want to sit at a different bar stool—or wear a hard hat!

The old bar room was also the location of a startling incident witnessed by assistant bar manager Jake Duenow. One evening after closing, all the furniture was removed from the restaurant and stacked in the bar so the restaurant's carpet could be cleaned. After that was done, powerful heaters were set up to help dry the carpet by morning. In the middle of the night, Duenow came down to the restaurant to check the carpet. As he entered the building, he saw something rush past him into the old bar and simultaneously all the chairs fell off the tables. He turned on all the lights, quickly checked the carpet and left, convinced that he had caught a glimpse of one of the rumored ghosts.

Tenants of a least one of the offices on the upper floors of the old building have also reported odd occurrences. They'll hear unexplained noises, or find that objects have been mysteriously moved from their places. Legend has it that "ladies of negotiable virtue" used to have rooms on the upper floors, and the Rex's maintenance man, Jerry Lease, once heard high-heeled footsteps approaching him as he worked in a corridor. No one was visible. The footsteps passed him and faded away in the distance.

Activity continues to this day. Recently a waitress told me that she was inside the basement storeroom when she caught a glimpse of someone moving past the storeroom door. Curious, she stepped out of the room to get a better look at the person, but no one was there. Only a second or two had passed, not nearly enough time for someone to reach the rest rooms or retreat back up the stairs. She had the strong impression that it was male and that it was anxious not to be seen. Perhaps "Buck" wasn't a bartender at all, but the ghost of one of the bootleggers rumored to have transported cargos of liquor through the tunnels that once ran between buildings in the downtown area.

Who haunts the Rex? Is it bootleggers? "Good time gals?" A bartender who died in the 1920s? The gambler whose coded diary was found inside a wall during renovation? We'll probably never know for sure.

Guests and ghost hunters alike will enjoy excellent meals in the Rex's historic restaurant. Be sure you pay a visit to the rest rooms in the basement—just in case! And when it's getting close to closing time and the crowd begins to thin out, don't be alarmed if you catch a murmur of men's voices in the original bar; it's likely just Buck and his ghostly cronies. For them, you see, the bar never closes.

PHANTOMS ON STAGE

ALBERTA BAIR THEATER
2nd and Broadway
Billings, Montana 59101
Telephone: 406-259-7400
Webpage: www.albertabairtheater.org

Ghostly Activity Level: Moderate

HISTORY: The Alberta Bair Theater was built in 1929 on the site of the former home of wealthy sheep rancher Charlie Bair. Originally called the Fox Theater, the building was one of the last Art Deco theaters built in the U.S. For many years, live performances as well as motion pictures were presented there, but business declined when multiplex cinemas began to be built on the west end of Billings. By 1980 the owners of the theater faced a financial crisis. A community survey determined that there was a place for a performing arts theater in Billings, so funds were raised and the theater totally renovated. It reopened in 1989 as the Alberta Bair Theater in honor of philanthropist Alberta Bair, daughter of Charlie Bair, who had grown up on the property.

PHENOMENA: The sound of doors slamming has been heard at all times of the day and night even though the doors are securely locked. On two occasions, a lighting technician saw a shimmering mass floating above the stage late at night. A second technician had just descended a staircase near the stage when he heard something jump down from the stairway and land with a loud thud behind him. No one was there. Faucets in the men's bathroom have occasionally been found running in the middle of the day even though no customers are in the building and the previous checks by maintenance staff revealed no problem.

Click.

Somewhere in the dim vastness of the Alberta Bair Theater a door closed softly.

"One of the doors at the back of the auditorium, I think," Dennis Sprankel said to me.

His colleague Randy Jordan nodded.

"We hear doors slam a lot," he added. "You know darn well they're closed. You can tell the doors in this place by the sound."

I stepped to the railing of the balcony and peered down into the auditorium. Nothing moved, yet all five of us standing in the balcony had heard the unmistakable sound of a door closing somewhere below us. No one would have remarked on it in the daytime or during evening performances, but it was nearly midnight, and we were the only souls—or so we had thought—in the otherwise deserted theater.

Rumors of a haunting at the Alberta Bair Theater had surfaced a year or two earlier. Ghost researcher Cynthia Berst contacted staff at the theater and arranged for us to tour the theater late one night in March 2003. Accompanied by my friend Frank, I arrived at the theater just after nine P.M. to find Cynthia waiting with lighting technician Dennis Sprankel and assistant facilities director Randy Jordan. The two men often worked late in the theater and were familiar with all the normal noises of the old building. They had also, over several years, experienced some of the theater's less-than-normal phenomena.

Theaters are often haunted, perhaps because so much emotion is expended within their walls. In the case of the Bair, however, the haunting is fairly recent. According to Sprankel, who has worked at the theater for 18 years, the haunting was first noticed shortly after Alberta Bair died in 1993.

Sprankel was working alone late one night, programming stage lights for a performance. The house lights were off. "About 11:30," he recalled, "I was in the lighting booth typing away, and I saw something on the stage. It looked like a hazy white cloud of some sort about fifteen feet above the stage. It drifted to the back of the stage and disappeared. It made the hair stand up on the back of my neck and I couldn't wait to get out of here." He saw it again on another occasion, and left early that night also. He has also heard footsteps in the hallways when no one is around.

Occasionally he has heard the sound of water running when walking past the men's bathroom. It's usually in the middle of the afternoon, after maintenance staff has left for the day and before customers arrive for evening performances. "I'll go in," he said, "and it's running flat out. It's always the middle of the three sinks, the hot water faucet. When I ask the janitors next day, they always tell me that nothing was running in the bathrooms when they left."

Randy Jordan has also had eerie experiences in the theater. Jordan has worked at the Bair for nine years and is often the last person to leave late at night. It's his responsibility to make sure that no one else is in the building and that everything is secure before he goes home.

"I was working late one night in the spring of 2002," Jordan said. "It was around eleven P.M. and I was the last person out of here as usual. My office is at the top of some concrete stairs that lead down to the edge of the stage. I went down the stairs, stepped onto the stage and started toward the exit door on the far side of the stage. I had just taken a few steps when I heard a loud thump right behind me. It felt like someone had jumped off the staircase from about three steps up. I turned. The house lights were off and the stage was lit only by the ghost light (a tall stand with a single bare bulb), but I could see that nothing was there.

"I thought, 'Okay, time to go.' I headed for the door, and all of a sudden it got really cold—more of an angry feeling, like I wasn't wanted there that night. It was the only time something seemed mad. I got to where the stage ends and the concrete begins, and I heard it again right behind me. I turned again, and nothing was there. Time to go!"

Jordan heard the footsteps one other time, coming up the stairs from the dressing rooms in the basement. "They seemed to be about two steps behind me, but when I looked, nobody was there."

Does Jordan think Alberta Bair haunts the Bair?

"There's a tendency to attribute a haunting to the most famous person associated with the building," he said. "It may not be Alberta at all. I heard a story about a worker who disappeared when the Fox was built back in 1929. He was supposed to have been killed and buried in the foundation. Back then, a lot of the workers were transients, so if it happened, maybe nobody missed him."

Newspaper articles about the Bair don't mention the disappearance of one of the workmen, however, so the theory remains unproven. And according to Sprankel, the haunting didn't start until after the death of Alberta Bair in 1993.

An employee whose office is on the second floor has also heard the sound of slamming doors during the daytime. The phenomenon occurs so frequently that she doesn't bother to check anymore, because no one is ever found. At least one visiting actress also was aware of the haunting. Since most of the performances at the Bair are one-night stands, few performers are there long enough to become aware of the ghost.

"She was a guest star staying at the Northern Hotel," Sprankel recalls. "She was convinced the theater was haunted.

"A woman hired from Labor Ready also had an encounter with the ghost. She had been cleaning in the balcony, and when she had finished, she said to one of the theater's employees, 'Oh, did you know you have a ghost? I was talking to her. There's nothing to worry about, she's really nice.' The startled employee didn't press the woman for a description of the ghost, so it's still not certain that the ghost is actually that of Alberta Bair."

A group of very young children who were dancing on stage apparently also saw "something" in the balcony not long afterward. The youngsters ran off stage crying and when questioned, said they saw a "monster" in the balcony. They weren't able to describe it further, but it was the same area of the balcony where the cleaner had talked to the ghost and where Dennis Sprankel had once seen an odd glimmer of light. Perhaps the children had simply been too young to distinguish between a ghost and a "monster."

The Bair's ghost also likes to interfere with the lighting system. "There was a weird thing with the light board one night," Sprankel said. "The whole thing just shut down, then came on. The old board was a piece of junk, but it was still strange."

Jordan added, "The grid is creepy too. Sometimes the ceiling lamps burn out. We see them from the stage. We go up the catwalk, up the ladder to the attic and go to replace it and it'll be working. You get back down to the deck, and it's out. That's happened a hundred times."

We followed the two men on a tour of the building from balcony down to the dressing rooms below the stage. One of them was small and claustrophobic. I shivered, and remarked, "I'll bet no one stays in here very long!"

There was nothing obviously wrong with the room, but all of us felt uneasy in it. Apparently some of the actors who had used the room did too, for almost without exception they preferred the other, larger room. Director Gerry Roe recalled that when *The King and I* was performed at the Bair, several actresses chose to dress in the inadequately lit wash room despite its rather than use that particular dressing room. The only one who would take that room, according to Roe, was the man who played the king.

There are certain stairways that Sprankel and Jordan prefer not to use unless absolutely necessary, and an area in the balcony that has a depressing atmosphere. The atrium landing seemed abnormally cold, and Jordan recounted a frightening experience he had one July evening when he decided to work late painting the atrium walls.

"It was about six or seven in the evening, still bright and hot, and everybody was gone. It was really quiet. I was going to paint for four or five hours, so I mixed up the paint and got up on the scaffold, just a couple of planks, and the door at the top of the stairs started to rattle, like something was rattling or banging on the door. I thought, 'I'm done,' and left."

Whatever haunts the Bair also played a prank on me. I had left one of my tape recorders running on stage while we toured the building. When I played it back next day, the tape was blank. I always double-check my equipment when I use it in a haunted place, and the recorder was running normally at the time.

In January 2009 the Big Sky Paranormal Investigators were granted permission to conduct an evening investigation. Dennis Sprankel gave us a tour of the entire theater, pointing out places where paranormal activity had taken place, and then turned us loose. We set up infrared video cameras in various areas and then divided the theater into stations. During the evening, all of us rotated through all six stations. Despite a battery of infrared cameras, tape recorders, dowsing rods, laser thermometers, motion detectors and EMF meters, results were inconclusive. There were a few odd noises, a glimpse of "something" moving in the balcony, and a decided reaction by dowsing rods to the area on stage where Sprankel had seen the floating cloudy mass, but nothing that definitely could be considered abnormal. The theater was "dark" that day, with no production in process. Perhaps the ghosts had taken a day off too.

Next time you enjoy one of the many fine performances at the Bair, why not linger a few minutes while the crowd thins out? If you study the balcony, particularly the area to the right of the stairs, perhaps you will catch a glimpse of the female ghost who reportedly spoke to the cleaner. Without a clear description, we can't prove that the ghost is Alberta, although people who knew Alberta well have told me that they wouldn't be surprised if she drops by from time to time. After all, the two Bair sisters were seen by friends not long after Alberta's death, seated at their favorite table at the Northern Hotel. Apparently Alberta and Marguerite, who traveled the world during their lifetimes, are still managing to get around just fine in their afterlives as well.

THE FIGURE IN THE BALCONY

ROCKY MOUNTAIN COLLEGE
15th and Poly Drive
Billings, Montana 59102
406-657-1000

Ghostly Activity Level: Low

HISTORY: Losekamp Hall was built of gray sandstone around 1917 and is one of the older buildings on the Rocky Mountain College campus. It was dedicated to the memory of John D. Losekamp, an early Billings merchant and philanthropist. Losekamp himself had only a limited education, but he believed that education was important and was a generous benefactor to Rocky Mountain College. A painting of Losekamp hangs above the hall's main door. The building is currently home to the music and drama departments.

PHENOMENA: A number of present and former students have felt as if they were being watched by an invisible presence in the auditorium. Others claim to have heard the sounds of musical instruments or a soprano voice coming from the darkened, deserted building at night. Lights have sometimes been mysteriously turned on again after security guards have shut the lights off and locked the building for the night. The sound of hurried footsteps has been heard at the back of the stage, and the stage lights have turned on by themselves on at least one occasion. The heavy front doors have opened by themselves on several occasions.

According to legend, Losekamp Hall is haunted by early Billings businessman John D. Losekamp, who supposedly murdered his wife in the building and then hanged himself on the third floor. Unfortunately for legend, Losekamp never married, and in fact died of natural causes in 1913, several years before the construction of the building named in his honor. Truth is seldom allowed to get in the way of a good story, however, so the legend has persisted despite numerous attempts to debunk it.

Another version has it that a former music student died or committed suicide in Losekamp Hall. Mysterious voices and occasionally the strains of violin music are supposedly heard coming from the locked and darkened building at night. Many campuses have similar stories, and I dismissed this one at first as typical campus folklore. Until, that is, a friend who was also a music student at Rocky in the early 1980s told me of her experience.

Sharon Raines had spent the evening painting props for an upcoming theatrical production one evening in the auditorium of Losekamp Hall. It was growing late, and she was the only one left in the building. Finished with the painting, Raines decided to go up to the balcony to see if the props would look convincingly real to the audience. The balcony was deserted, but as she stood looking down at the stage, she felt a growing sense of unease.

"I felt as if I were being intently watched by someone standing very near to me," she said. No one was visible, but her conviction that she was being watched was so overpowering that she hurriedly left the building.

"It wasn't malevolent," she assured me, "just uncomfortable. I couldn't stay there any longer."

Curious to see what I could discover for myself, I visited Losekamp Hall on a chilly afternoon in February. The auditorium was empty. I took a few photos, and then made my way up the creaky wooden stairs to the balcony where Raines had sensed a presence close to her. I sat quietly for a while, taking photos as I felt the urge, but nothing happened. I didn't sense anything unusual in the basement greenrooms that had an eerie reputation among students, either. My visit seemed to have been a waste of time.

When I looked at the photos I had taken that day, however, there were some unusual features. Several of the 35mm photos taken of the auditorium from the balcony seemed inexplicably foggy. And one of the digital photos I had taken showed an intense, glowing "orb" hovering over a row of seats.

I showed the photos to my colleague, librarian John Riffe, who was also a gifted photographer, magician, and psychic. He thought the photos were odd enough to be worth a second visit to Losekamp Hall. This time, he accompanied me.

Dense fog swirled around the electrified "gas" lights of the historic district that evening as we drove toward the campus. It was a perfect night to hunt spooks. The wooden staircase at Losekamp Hall creaked loudly as we climbed up to the balcony, adding even more atmosphere. I waited to see what John's impressions might be. I had told John nothing about Losekamp Hall except that it was reputed to be haunted.

"There's definitely someone here," John said instantly. "A male, not well educated but intelligent and interested in education."

That described Losekamp well, for he had definitely been interested in education, and twice helped the fledgling college out of financial straits. I was skeptical, however, about John's assertion that he had not been a well-educated man. Losekamp had been a well-to-do merchant and had even served a term as a state legislator. In positions like that, how could he not have been an educated man? When I checked *Progressive Men of Montana*, however, I learned to my surprise that Losekamp "had very limited educational advantages in his youth…and little opportunity was afforded for the attending of school." John's impressions had been correct on all counts!

Professor Gerry Roe actually caught a glimpse of whatever—or whoever—haunts Losekamp Hall one evening in 1993. Roe had finished rehearsing *Peter Pan*, a show he was directing for the Billings Studio Theater, and the actors had gone home. He and his friend Judy were the only ones left in the building.

"I had just shut the lights off," he recalled. "The theater was pitch black. I happened to look up, and in the balcony I saw a person. The figure was illuminated with a greenish light. There's no way it could have been lit because there was no light at all in the theater. I ran down the stairs, twisting my ankle in the darkness and got out in the lobby where my friend Judy was waiting.

`What's going on?' she asked. `You're limping!'

Roe told her what he had seen, and his friend ran into the auditorium. Nothing was there.

Does Roe believe it was the spirit of John Losekamp?

"All I know is, it was *something*," Roe said.

The haunting can be traced back at least to the late 1980s. Research uncovered a *Billings Gazette* article dated October 29, 1987. "Spooky Tales Haunt Hall," it proclaimed, and went on to interview several students who claimed to have had ghostly experiences in the building. The origin of the tales seems to focus around the picture of Losekamp that hangs above the front door. The picture, which shows Losekamp in the rather stern pose typical of his era, looked "menacing," according to some students.

The third floor seemed to be the most haunted area, according to the students interviewed by the reporter. Sandy Fox, a graduate of Rocky Mountain College, described his experience on the third floor for the *Gazette*: *"We had a ghost hunt on the third floor of Losekamp one night. We had people doing things to make people afraid. We were all holding hands, and I was on the end of the line. The hand that was free got pinched. I had a blood blister on it. When I told the others about it, they reminded me that there wasn't anyone behind me."*

Freshman Mark Bryan contributed his story: *"About a month ago, I was in the (third floor) practice room, and I felt something touch me. There was a hand on my back, and no one was there."*

Dean of Students Brad Nason believed that the stories had a more prosaic beginning, however. *"When I was a freshman in 1979," he said, "upperclassmen talked about the ghost for months. Late one night they took a bunch of freshmen up to the belfry for a ghost hunt."* They succeeded in scaring the freshmen, but found no ghosts.

Curiously enough, two ladies who stayed to talk with me after one of my "Haunted Billings" programs at Parmly Billings Library spoke in support of a haunting at Losekamp Hall. Both Kelly Grounds and her friend had had ghostly experiences in the auditorium at Losekamp Hall. Grounds told me that about seven years ago, she and four other people who were on stage rehearsing at the time saw a misty ball of light floating on the right side of the auditorium. On a separate occasion they saw people they didn't recognize walking around backstage, wearing costumes for a musical production. At the time, no such production had been put on in Losekamp Hall for at least twenty-five years.

So intriguing were the stories that in 2007 I and a dozen members of the Big Sky Paranormal Investigation group obtained permission to hold two late-night ghost hunts in the building. After searching Losekamp Hall from top floor to basement to make certain we were the only souls (living, that is) in the building, we set up video cameras with infrared capabilities, tape recorders, motion detectors, and various other pieces of equipment in the auditorium, in the balcony where Professor Roe had seen the glowing figure, and in the basement which had once been the greenroom for the actors.

As we began setting up cameras and a computer at the front of the auditorium, BSPI co-founder Eric Grider and I heard someone rush loudly down the stairs that led from the back of the stage to the basement. I hurried to the top of the stairs but saw no one and every one of our crew was accounted for. During the actual investigation nothing much happened so after several hours we turned the auditorium lights on and began to pack up our equipment. The stage lights remained off. As several of us stood in front of the stage chatting, the stage lights came on slowly, as if they were on a dimmer switch, glowing red. After about five seconds, they just as slowly turned off. We stood there stunned, hardly believing our own eyes. We knew the stage lights were not on a dimmer switch and the switch itself was stiff and required a definite effort to turn it on or off. The campus electrician thoroughly examined the lights and the electrical circuits the next day and found nothing that would explain the phenomenon witnessed by several of the group.

So who, or what, haunts Losekamp Hall? Are the ghost stories nothing more than an attempt by upperclassmen to frighten new students? Do the ghosts of former students return from time to time to recapture the heady excitement of performing on stage? Or does John Losekamp, who during his lifetime was deeply interested in the welfare of Rocky Mountain College, still make his presence known on occasion?

Losekamp was described by a *Billings Gazette* article of August 18, 1935 as a huge man, tall and heavyset, a good friend and a poor hater, an ardent fisherman and hunter. He loved children and gave gifts to dozens of needy youngsters each Christmas. If the ghost that makes its presence known from time to time is indeed John Losekamp, those who work late at night in Losekamp Hall have nothing to fear. Mr. Losekamp is no doubt just keeping a benevolent eye on the college he supported so wholeheartedly in his lifetime.

Losekamp Hall is a stately and impressive building typical of its era. It is regularly used for classes and theatrical productions and the auditorium may not be open to visitors at such times.

THE LADY IN THE NIGHTGOWN

DUDE RANCHER LODGE
415 North 29th Street
Billings, Montana 59101
Telephone: 406-259-5561
Webpage: www.duderancherlodge.com

Ghostly Activity Level: High

HISTORY: The "Dude," as it is affectionately called by locals, was built in 1950 by Annabel and Percival Goan with financial assistance from area businessmen and ranchers. The bricks used to build the Dude Rancher were salvaged from the old St. Vincent Hospital, the Russell Refinery and Washington School. The lodge was designed around a central courtyard and the low-pitched roof; weeping mortar and a branding wall give it a distinctive appearance.

Although Percival Goan died July 18, 1962, from injuries suffered in a car wreck, his wife Annabel survived and continued to manage the lodge for many years. Her health declined in her later years, and her devoted staff cared for her in an apartment at the Dude Rancher until she moved to a nursing home shortly before her death on February 2, 1983. The motel has been owned by Virginia Karlsen since 1991.

PHENOMENA: Staff and guests have encountered several spirits in the lodge. A mysterious female voice was caught on audiotape in the basement, while footsteps have been heard when no one is visible. A woman guest in Room 226 may have actually heard the spirit of Annabel Goan. Lights in that room sometimes turn on and off by themselves and the television has been known to turn itself on while housekeeping staff is working in the room. A radio crew broadcasting from Room 226 one Halloween evening reported frequent equipment malfunctions. The spirit of a former cook sometimes clatters pots and pans in the kitchen at night and children's footsteps have been heard running in an upstairs hallway when no children are present.

Want to be a guest at a haunted motel on Halloween? If so, get your reservations in early. The Dude Rancher Lodge's haunted rooms are often booked a year in advance. Staff and guests have experienced paranormal activity in rooms 226, 224 and 223, but ghostly doings have been reported from other areas as well.

Andrea Williams has been head housekeeper at the Dude for thirty-four years. "Andy" helped take care of owner Annabel when her health declined and remembers her fondly as a gracious lady who appreciated her staff and treated them like family. Andy believes that the first paranormal incidents at the lodge began shortly after Annabel's death in 1983.

"I don't tell new staff about the ghostly happenings," Williams told me, "but within a couple of weeks, the new girls will report hearing someone coming up the stairs or walking down the hall. Or they'll be in a room cleaning and hear someone knocking on all the doors. When they look, there's no one there. They all have little stories about seeing things or hearing things."

Room 226 seems to be a focus for many of the incidents. Annabel herself had no particular connection to that room, but Williams says that Annabel's grandson lived there when he took over as manager after Annabel's death. Williams' theory is that Annabel's spirit may still visit his old room on occasion.

Annabel may not be the only one to visit Room 226. "My sister was working up in 226 one day," Williams said. "She was on the bathroom floor cleaning it and all of a sudden she heard someone knock on the room door and a male voice said, 'Excuse me?' She got up and looked out the door and no one was there. She said the hair just stood up on her neck and she finished up quickly and got out of there."

Williams herself had an odd experience in Room 226 one day. The room needed to be made up for the next guest, but when she tried to unlock the door, for some unknown reason her passkey wouldn't work. Williams didn't want to walk down to the office to get a spare key, so she said aloud, "Annabel, please can you open this door for me? I tried my key again, and the door opened right up. I said, 'Thank you, Annabel!'"

Guests on the second floor sometimes hear noises in the hall late at night. A guest in Room 226 reported that she heard children running in the hallway, and then an older woman's voice said loudly from the hallway, "Shhh!" No one was there when she looked.

Another guest, this time in Room 205, asked as she checked out one morning, "Do you have ghosts here?" The desk clerk's response was a noncommittal "Um, why?'

"Because there was someone going up and down the hallway last night, maybe two, three o'clock in the morning, and nobody was there."

Perhaps the person who was heard going up and down the hallway was the elderly lady in the nightgown who was seen on the second floor of the north wing by a desk clerk one day. The clerk had gone upstairs to get something from a laundry closet and noticed a lady in a nightgown standing at the end of the corridor by the exit, looking out a window. The window glass had long ago been replaced by frosted glass. No one could see through it. As the clerk watched, the woman turned and went into one of the rooms. The clerk had thought the upper rooms were empty, so she checked when she went back downstairs. Sure enough, none of the upper rooms had been rented that night.

The kitchen has also had its share of inexplicable phenomena. Tyler, who has worked at the Dude for ten years as a maintenance man, recalls a former cook named Bob, who lived in Room 222 for many years.

"Bob would go out at night for a few beers and then come

home," Tyler said. "He always came down about a quarter to midnight to fix himself something to eat. I heard him clattering pots and pans around many times."

Eventually Bob died in a nursing home. Tyler didn't have a chance to say goodbye to his old friend. One night, however, when he was painting the steps below the kitchen, he heard pots and pans clattering and banging above him, even though the kitchen had been closed for hours.

"I looked at my clock," Tyler said, "and sure enough it was a quarter to midnight. I came up and asked the clerk, but no, she hadn't been in the kitchen."

Tyler's never heard his late friend Bob making himself a bedtime snack in the kitchen again, but he has had other odd experiences at the Dude.

"I get 'feelings' late at night. Sometimes I hear people talking and there's no one there. Of course, it could be coming through outside vents. Once I was looking for a fuse on my bench. Next thing I know there's a fuse there, not the right one but a minute ago there wasn't any fuse there. I think there're some helpful spirits here."

Bob may not have clattered his ethereal pots and pans lately, but he may be keeping a spectral eye on his old recliner. After Bob's death, the motel's manager gave the chair to Kris, one of the night clerks. Not long after the chair was delivered to Kris' house, a glass shelf fell for no apparent reason. She brushed that off, but finds it more difficult to explain how small objects seem to move around apparently by themselves since Bob's chair arrived.

The basement is another area where staff members have had encountered something odd. As Andy Williams puts it, "I was in the basement doing laundry and one of the housekeepers was wearing black that day. I saw a black shadow go by me toward where the laundry is folded on shelves, and I thought it was the other housekeeper. It went so fast that I stopped and said, 'Geez, what's your hurry?' but there was no one there."

I had an experience of my own in the basement of the Dude in October of 2000. For many years, Renee Christiansen of Montana

Fun Adventures Tours and I have put on Halloween bus tours of haunted downtown buildings, beginning at the Dude Rancher Lodge. On that particular occasion, Renee and I got there early. While we were waiting for her bus to arrive so we could begin the ghost tours, we decided to explore the basement of the Dude. I had brought a tape recorder, and as usual, invited any spirits present to speak to us. A few minutes later, I said idly, "I wonder if the bus has arrived yet?"

Renee and I went back upstairs to check. The bus had just arrived. When I played the tape back the next day, I got a shock: an unfamiliar female voice had answered my question with, "It's out back now." Renee and I were the only souls—living, that is—in the basement at the time. Whoever spoke to us had to have not only been present in the basement but to have simultaneously known that the bus had just pulled up outside. To me, that was convincing proof of a disembodied, intelligent spirit. It remains to this day one of the highlights of my adventures as a paranormal investigator.

Odd things do sometimes happen on our tours, so we encourage guests to bring cameras and tape recorders along. Some have even captured strange mists on camera. If Room 226 hasn't been rented, Renee and I usually take our groups up to the room. One evening we brought three tours through, at 7 P.M., 8 P.M. and 9 P.M. The first tour was uneventful except for an unexplained chill in Room 226. When we arrived for the 8 P.M. tour, however, the key wouldn't open the lock. The desk clerk came up with a passkey and managed to get the door open. Once inside we found that the deadbolt had been thrown—from the inside of an empty room! We had no trouble unlocking the door for the 9 P.M. tour. We always greet Annabel courteously when we enter Room 226 and thank her when we leave, but perhaps Annabel, or whatever spirit happened to be using the room that night, simply didn't feel like having company.

Recently Carol, a guest from out of state, stayed in Room 226 with a friend. "While I was lying in bed, about to fall asleep," she told me, "I sensed something above me. When I opened my eyes

I saw what appeared to be a dark figure between the beds, bending over me. I couldn't tell whether the figure was male or female, so I could not say if it was Annabel. I let out a startled gasp and it immediately disappeared. My gasp woke my friend up, but she said, 'Don't worry, it's okay. Just go back to sleep.' I lay back in bed with my eyes open but didn't experience anything else. After quite a while I managed to go to sleep, but I was restless all night."

Intrigued by the reports, the Montana Paranormal Research Society held an investigation at the Dude Rancher in December 2009. MTPRS founder Dustin Benner invited me to join them and I watched with interest as they set up cameras and strung cables all over the south wing, which had been closed off for the investigation. During the night, several of us sat in pitch darkness in the utility tunnels beneath the building. Occasionally we heard what sounded like children's voices very close to us. Whenever that happened, temperatures would fluctuate rapidly and EMF meters would also react. We knew there was a couple with an infant in a room directly above us but these voices sounded like older children, perhaps five to ten years of age. Strangely, my digital recorder did not pick up these voices.

At 11:45 P.M. I accompanied Lora, an MTPRS member, up to the deserted restaurant to see if Bob, the former cook, would make his rumored midnight appearance. Both of us heard shuffling in the kitchen and Lora's digital recorder caught a loud sigh. A few minutes later I felt something like cobwebs gently touch my left hand twice. Meanwhile, investigators stationed in the bakery downstairs heard what sounded like someone moving around nearby.

After reviewing the evidence collected that night, MTPRS decided that some of the activity is probably due to residual energies embedded in the bricks that came from the hospital and the old school. A photo taken by MTPRS member Curtis Mattox two years earlier was more difficult to explain. The photo, taken from the doorway of Room 226 after everyone had left the room, showed the image of a woman's face reflected in a window. Despite many attempts to reproduce the photo or explain it in a logical way, MTPRS was unable to do so. Their conclusion: paranormal activity does occur in certain areas of the Dude Rancher Lodge.

Virginia Karlsen has owned the Dude Rancher Lodge since 1991. Although she is not herself a believer in paranormal activity, Karlsen does feel that Annabel's spirit lives on at the Dude Rancher through the hospitable and caring attitude of the staff.

Bring your camera and tape recorder if you reserve a room at this comfortable, historic inn. You never know who may "drop in" for a visit. And be sure to try the Dude's famous homemade pies! (Pecan's my favorite) Parmly Billings Library is just across the parking lot and the Western Heritage Center is within walking distance. Why not visit both of these very haunted locations?

THE LEGEND OF SIMONE

BOULDER HOT SPRINGS INN
31 Hot Springs Road
Boulder, Montana 59632
Telephone: 406-225-4339
Website: www.boulderhotsprings.com

Ghostly Activity Level: High

HISTORY: For centuries the hot springs at the foot of the Elkhorn Mountains have been considered sacred by Native Americans in need of healing. Because they vowed not to fight in the area, the valley became known as "Peace Valley." In 1863, prospector James E. Riley claimed the land and built a tavern and bathhouse to accommodate miners. In 1890 a new owner built a large hotel on the site, naming it the Hotel May. In 1910 the hotel was enlarged and remodeled to resemble a huge Spanish mission. From 1940 to 1975 it was owned by C.L. "Pappy" Smith, who changed the name to the Diamond S Ranch Hotel and operated it as a dude ranch. In 1990, author Anne Wilson Schaef and a limited partnership bought the by-then dilapidated resort, which had once catered to presidents and wealthy ranchers. The east wing, indoor and outdoor pools and a small dining room have since been completely refurbished. The inn now offers conference facilities for groups and a bed-and-breakfast inn that is open all year. It is an alcohol, drug and smoke-free environment.

PHENOMENA: The owners have evidence that a prostitute was murdered near the old office by a mining executive from Butte. She is thought to be the woman who has been seen standing in a window of the unused west wing. Footsteps are sometimes heard in the hallways when no one is there. The scent of perfume has been noted near the Simone Suite.

Guests at Boulder Hot Springs come for many reasons: to hike in the adjoining Deerlodge National Forest, to photograph wildlife, to explore nearby ghost towns or just to relax in the hot pool beneath the stars on a warm summer's night. Others come to find physical, emotional or spiritual healing, just as Native Americans have done for centuries. In fact, Boulder seems to "call" to those in need of healing in an almost mystical way. I saw its magic at work firsthand the night I stayed there with my friends Frank Stevens and Sue Tracy.

The three of us were sitting by the fireplace in the lobby with Judy Keffer, who was volunteering at the reception desk that evening. She had just described to me the many times she had seen visitors arrive, looking bewildered by their decision to make an unplanned stop at the resort as they drove past. Not more than five minutes later I witnessed the "pull" of Boulder's unique energies myself as a man walked in and looked around for the receptionist. Keffer excused herself and rose to greet the newcomer.

"I don't know what made me stop," I heard him say to her. "I wasn't planning to stop here." He told her that he had actually made a sudden U-turn on the narrow highway to come back to the resort. Although he wasn't able to stay that night, he promised to come back and left, shaking his head in wonderment at his own actions.

"I see what you meant," I remarked to Keffer. She just smiled. "I've come back seven times myself," she said quietly. "It's like I'm called." The resort has some permanent residents, according to Keffer, and many others have returned to volunteer time after time, drawn by the healing energies of the area. I asked her about the rumored ghosts.

"About a year and a half ago," she said, "I was in my room on the third floor of the East Wing. It was around two A.M., and I heard footsteps on hardwood floors coming up to my room as I lay in bed. That happened twice. I felt frightened, but eventually I fell asleep. I realized the next day that the floor was carpeted. There's no way I could have heard footsteps on carpet."

Paranormal events have occurred on all floors, although many reports focus on the unused west wing.

"Six weeks ago," Keffer continued, "I was on the second floor of the old west wing. There is no heat, no electricity and no running water there. It was 4:30 A.M. I was meditating but quite alert when I felt someone tapping me on my right shoulder. I kept meditating, but then I began hearing someone walking up and down the old stairs, which are very creaky. At first I thought it was one of the residents. Then I thought it was the dog, and finally I thought it was the other resident, but it lasted for a half hour. It would come right up to my wall and then go back down. I asked both residents next day but neither had been up at 4:30 A.M. I don't have an explanation for that. There was no carpet so the footsteps were very loud and distinct. They sounded like an adult's, not a child's, but I couldn't tell whether they were a man's or a woman's."

Keffer is not the only staff member who has encountered something eerie on the second floor of the old wing. Another employee told us, "One time I was lying down in one of the rooms in the west wing, and I felt this energy come through the wall, walk through my bed and out the other side of the room." She sounded more intrigued than alarmed by her experience.

Frank and I had booked Room 110 (Simone's Suite) for the night, while Sue had Room 102, the Pioneer Suite. Only one other guest was in our wing that night, and she had the room closest to the stairway. The Simone Suite is large with big windows overlooking to courtyard to the hills beyond and is decorated with lively colors. It includes a spacious boudoir bath that Simone would have loved. Ironically "Simone," or whatever the ghost's name actually was, had probably never known such luxury in her lifetime. The rooms for the working girls were small and on the third floor of the old wing, which is no longer used.

As we entered our suite, we were greeted by what I can only describe as a green, herby, medicinal smell that reminded me of liniments from bygone days, similar to but not quite like Absorbine. We found nothing in the room that could have been the source of the odor, and the scent faded away after a few minutes. We slept undisturbed that night, and I woke early, around seven. I was completely awake and looking out the window toward the disused west wing when I heard a voice with a cheery British accent say, "Good aft–" and suddenly break off. It's as if someone had begun to say, "Good afternoon." I looked over to see if Frank had said something, but he was still asleep, and he doesn't have a British accent. The voice seemed to have come from somewhere near the foot of my bed. I listened intently to see if the voice might have come from outside or from the corridor, but all was quiet.

An hour later we decided to go down to breakfast. When we opened our door, we were met by a light, delicate, flowery perfume. Sue arrived just then and also noted the scent. I joked that it must be Simone, coming back to her room after a hard night's work.

After breakfast, we met with Kerri Kumasaka, the general manager. She had lived and worked at the resort for twelve years and had agreed to take us on a tour of the un-restored west wing. I hurried back upstairs to fetch my camera, only to find the perfume was still lingering outside our door. I asked Kerri whether it could have been some sort of cleaning product, but learned that the maids hadn't been through yet.

"The building was close to being demolished in the early 1990s," Kumasaka informed us as she unlocked the doors of the west wing. "There was a lot of water damage from the leaking roof and broken pipes when Anne Schaef bought it."

We stepped into what had once been the spectacular lobby of the Hotel May. The lobby has a newly upgraded electrical system, and wooden rockers line the veranda outside. Kumasaka pointed out the exquisite amber glass light globes that hung from twelve-foot ceilings, and the stencil work.

"They say that Theodore Roosevelt once sat there by the fire," Kumasaka said, indicating a huge stone fireplace, "and boxer Jim Corbett trained here. Actor Larry Hagman and General Omar Bradley have also been here.

"At one time there was a brothel upstairs and a back staircase so politicians could go up without being seen. Simone—that's probably not her real name, but it's what we call her—was one of the women who worked in the brothel, probably in the 1920s or 1930s. She got into an argument with the manager and he stabbed her to death near the office. When Anne Schaef bought the building and started to fix it up, the people who were working on the building noticed that the stove kept turning itself on. No one could figure out who was doing it. They figured that Simone probably wanted a cup of tea so they made her a cup, and the stove stopped turning itself on."

Anne Wilson Schaef herself has had several encounters with Simone. The best-selling author of Co-Dependence: Misunderstood, Mistreated and many other books. used to soak in the hot pools as a teenager and grew to love the old hotel. Soon after she bought the dilapidated property, she scheduled a men's retreat.

"When I arrived," she wrote me, "the men were crowded into the men's plunge area on pallets. 'We're not going to sleep in the hotel,' they said. 'It's scary'."

Schaef promptly moved into one of the rooms, locked the door and crawled into bed. "An icy wind hit me," she recalled. "I instantly knew that I was not alone." She had accompanied her mother on ghost-hunting excursions as a youngster and calmly greeted the ghost and asked her name. "Simone," she heard the ghost reply.

Schaef promised Simone that the building and land would be cared for and healed, and that the ghost was welcome to stay or move on whenever she was ready. "Suddenly I felt as if I was bathed in warm scented oil," Schaef said, "and I fell immediately into a deep peaceful sleep."

One day, Schaef came back to her room and could not find her favorite sheets. "Then, I noticed the door to the linen closet was closed and locked. The closet had been full of dirty, old, musty junk and we had not had time to clean it out. The door was usually left ajar as a reminder of things to do. I got the master key and went in. There, on the only freshly cleaned spot in the entire closet were my sheets, neatly folded. I could feel Simone smiling.

"After about a year and a half, I had become quite comfortable with Simone and her friends and their ghostly goings on. I never really saw anything, but I knew people who did and I envied them. Then, one evening just after dark, I was walking down the hallway to my West Wing room and I "saw" Simone. She was standing at the end of the hallway near my room. She was wearing a long black skirt and a white high-necked blouse with long fitted sleeves with lace on the edge. Her hands were overlapped at her slim waist, her hair was pulled up and piled on her head, and she was smiling at me with a mischievous, caring twinkle in her eyes. I was excited, pleased, dumfounded, curious and thrilled! Immediately I checked to make sure it wasn't just my reflection in the window. I had a black top and white pants on. Then I moved back and forth to see if there was any spot where I would get a reflection in the large window in the room at the end of the hall. There wasn't. It seems that Simone had let me see her!"

Simone may also have appeared in a photograph taken by a guest. The photograph shows a woman in a white Victorian-style dress standing in one of the windows of the west wing. But she's apparently not the only spirit to roam the old building. When I replayed my audiotape of the interview with Kumasaka later, it was obvious that Frank, Sue and I hadn't been the only ones listening. The audiotape was full of whispery voices, although the only one that could be clearly made out was a male voice that exclaimed, "Absolutely!" while Kumasaka was describing the old card room with the bright red Chinese stenciling.

In 2009 I returned, this time with my friend Pat Cody. Pat is highly sensitive to atmosphere and I was curious to see whether she would sense anything unusual. After checking into the Simone Suite late that evening, we promptly headed down to the outdoor pool, looking forward to a relaxing soak in the hot water. We spent over an hour in the pool, watching the moon rise over the nearby mountains and just enjoying the soothing warmth. Before going to bed, I set out a tape recorder and invited Simone to make her presence known during our visit. I woke in the morning amidst a cloud of perfume that seemed to be concentrated on my left index finger. The scent was as fresh and strong as if someone had touched that finger with a perfume dropper. Pat thought it was a fairly expensive scent and not one that she recognized. Neither of us wears perfume, and a search revealed no scented soaps or lotions in our room, no potpourris. Had Simone good-naturedly granted my request to make her presence known? We simply could find no natural explanation for this bizarre event.

Pat then told me about her own odd experience during the night. She had been on the verge of falling asleep when she became aware of male voices, and visualized a dark-haired man, hair slicked back with pomade, wearing a white shirt without the collar attached and suspenders holding up his trousers. He was somewhat portly and appeared to be listening to someone else in the room, although Pat saw no one else. Judging by his clothing and hairstyle, she thought he dated from the 1920's or 1930's. Only then did I tell Pat of my own experience on a previous visit, when I had heard a male voice with an English accent say "Good aft-" as if he were beginning to say, "Good afternoon."

Sandy, a young woman who has worked at the front desk for four years, told us about a ghostly sighting by two guests in 2008.

"One day a lady came to me and asked if anybody lived in the upper room of the old wing that overlooks the outdoor pool. I told her no, the wing was unused. She insisted that somebody had been up there. I told her that it might be a maintenance guy or a worker up there getting something.

"The guest said, 'She was watching me swimming in the outdoor pool She was wearing a white gown.' I took her out to the lobby and showed her the newspaper articles without telling her about Simone. Simone wears a white gown. The guest about had a heart attack when she read it.

"The exact thing happened a week later, again in broad daylight. A gentleman came to me and asked if anyone lived in the unused wing. I said 'No, but there might be a maintenance guy or something.'

"He said, 'For the whole three hours I was in the pool a woman was watching from that window.'

At that point, Pat spoke up. "While we were in the pool last night, I saw a long red bar of light in the window of that room. I thought it was some sort of emergency lighting." There was no electricity in that wing, and no source of red light. I recalled glancing up at the windows of the old wing several times during our swim but had noticed nothing, so the bar of red light will join the lady in the white dress as two more unexplained incidents in the west wing.

And the renovated east wing also has more to offer than just a presence in Simone's suite. According to Sandy, a male guest who stayed in Room 105 across the hall from Simone's Suite heard footsteps out in the hall during the night. He knew he was the only guest in that wing, so he looked out to see who was walking down the hall. No one was there. He called Sandy to tell her about it a few days later, thoroughly convinced that something odd was going on that night.

Pat and I left Boulder Hot Springs the next day with great reluctance—and not just because we'd enjoyed a delicious breakfast, the beautiful rooms, and our swim in the outdoor hot pool the night before. There's something absolutely unique about Boulder, an overwhelming sense of peace and a healing energy that I've never encountered anywhere else. Perhaps that's one of the reasons Simone—and her ghostly friends—choose to stay.

If you'd enjoy comfortable, elegant rooms, a healing atmosphere, and almost three hundred acres of natural beauty, consider making Boul-

der Hot Springs Resort your headquarters to explore the nearby radon mines, Lewis & Clark Caverns, and Elkhorn State Park. And if you try the outdoor hot pool on a warm starry night, glance occasionally up at the windows of the unused west wing. You may just catch a glimpse of a young lady in a white dress smiling back at you—before she vanishes.

THE MAN IN THE CHECKERED SHIRT

MONTANA ALE WORKS
611 East Main Street
Bozeman, Montana 59715
Telephone: 406-587-7700
Website: www.montanaaleworks.com

Ghostly Activity Level: Low

HISTORY: In 1911, the Northern Pacific Railway built a freight warehouse on Main Street to better compete with the Gallatin Valley Railroad Company. The historic industrial building was abandoned in the early 1990s and sat empty and neglected for several years until being renovated in 2000 and reopened as the Montana Ale Works, an award-winning eatery and brewpub that has become a popular Bozeman hangout.

PHENOMENA: The figure of a man in a checkered shirt has reportedly been seen floating in the pool room. The stereo system sometimes turns on by itself. Motion detectors occasionally indicate that something is moving in the empty restaurant, and potted plants have apparently moved by themselves. An unidentified male voice was picked up by a digital recorder.

My friend Pat Cody and I arrived in Bozeman on the last leg of an adventurous two-week tour of western Montana in search of ghost stories. We were eager to stop at the Ale Works for two reasons: to fortify ourselves with a good dinner before heading over Bozeman Pass to Billings, and to talk to some of the staff about paranormal activity in the building.

According to an article by Kira Stoops in the Fall 2007 issue of the magazine *Outside Bozeman*, the ghost of a man wearing a red-and-black checkered shirt had been seen a number of times in the pool room, floating in midair. The ghost sometimes made its presence known at closing time as well. Locked doors would reportedly open and close by themselves, a radio would begin to play, and the security system would indicate that someone was moving around inside the empty restaurant. One night, longtime employee Jen Dehmer became so frustrated when the security system couldn't be set that she yelled, *"We just want to leave, go away!"*

Dehmer and a fellow employee heard a resounding crash from the kitchen and quickly left. When they came to work the next morning, nothing was out of place. The ghost is assumed to be a former employee of the Northern Pacific Railway, killed in an industrial accident on the site.

The story sounded intriguing, and we arrived shortly after the restaurant opened at 4 P.M. The handsome 8,000-square-foot former warehouse is built of warm honey-colored brick and still has a loading dock at the back. It reminded me of a funky Chicago loft conversion, retaining much of the industrial atmosphere inside with high ceilings, open trusses, exposed brickwork, and ventilation tubes running the length of the building. The dinner rush had not yet begun and we headed for the handcrafted concrete bar that divided the dining areas, to talk to bartender Peter Krebs. We couldn't miss him, we were told; he was tall with curly blond hair and was the only bartender on duty. He'd been at the Ale Works for a number of years and was probably the only remaining employee who had actually witnessed some of the paranormal activity in the building.

A handful of customers already were at the bar, so we seated ourselves at the far end, where it was less noisy. When Krebs came over to take our order, we introduced ourselves and explained our project. Krebs readily acknowledged his eerie experiences while working late at night.

"I've worked here since 2001," he said, juggling our questions and patron orders with equal ease. "It was mostly just standard weird stuff. You know, things get moved, can't set the alarm, lights come on when you're at one end of the building and no one else is here.

"Probably the best one was when a gal and I were sitting right there at the end of the bar late one night. The stereo was off, but we could hear 1950s music and a couple of ladies talking over it, but you couldn't understand what they were saying. I just assumed it was the other stereo system in the back, so I wandered back there to turn it off and it wasn't on. I thought, 'Well, I'm just hearing voices from the kitchen and they're resonating through the ventilator tubes,' but the tubes don't actually go into the kitchen. That was the most dramatic one.

"There was another employee here who said he used to see things, but I never did. I did hear the intercom system come on when there was no one in the building. The only way it could come on was if somebody was up in the office. And nobody was there."

"Do you know if anything happened here that might explain a haunting?" I asked, absently stirring my Virgin Mary with the asparagus spear. Often a haunting can be traced back to an historical event, whether it occurred in the existing building or on the site prior to the building's construction.

"Well," Krebs said, "a guy came in, in about 2001, who used to work here when it was a warehouse back in the 1950 and '60s, and he said there were a couple of accidents here—and one fatality."

I wondered aloud if the fatality might have occurred in the 1950s, since Krebs had said that both he and the young woman seated at the end of the bar both heard 1950s music one night when the stereo was off. Perhaps a search of newspaper archives or railroad records would uncover the name of the man who was killed. Not everyone who dies tragically or without warning lingers as a ghost, but it would be a starting point.

"Did anyone else notice anything odd about the place?" Pat put in.

"Oh yeah," Krebs replied, and he named several other employees he had worked with since 2001. "We had stuff that would move, and everybody'd just figure someone else moved it. We have a security system in here with motion sensors, and sometimes you couldn't set the alarm. Then you'd have to come in to look around and of course it's all dark and creepy. The hair on the back of your neck would go up for no reason. We used to have big potted plants up front and sometimes we'd find that they'd been moved just enough to block the sensors so you couldn't set the alarm unless you forced it.

"The dynamics have changed, though," he continued, sounding a bit regretful. "I think we haven't noticed as much lately because we're not here as late. We used to be open a lot later, especially when there was music. As the closing manager, you'd be the only person in the place, and you'd go around and lock all the doors, then you're upstairs doing the tills and the books. You'd be in here until 2:00 or 3:00, sometimes 4:00. Sometimes the hair on the back of your neck would go up for no reason. It was enough to get your attention. It didn't happen all the time, more in the colder months. Once we stopped doing the books at night, though, we haven't noticed as much. When we close, twenty minutes later we're all of out here."

I had recorded the interview on a new digital recorder, and when I transcribed the interview several days later I found that an unseen presence had apparently been listening to our conversation. When I suggested that the fatality might have occurred in the 1950s, an older male voice can be heard clearly saying, *"Upstairs."* Later, while Pat and I were chatting over our dinner, I had asked aloud whether any spirit was present, and the same male voice said with increasing urgency, *"Yes. Yes."*

So who haunts the Ale Works? Most likely, he was a railroad worker who died either as the result of an accident on the site, or perhaps he died of a medical condition like a heart attack "upstairs." So far a search of newspaper archives has turned up nothing, but perhaps someday a former railroad worker will come forward to name the man who remains tied to the scene of his death.

The Ale Works is a great place for dinner (the crème brule is delicious!) and the scene is lively. And if you're there late at night in the colder months, throw an occasional glance at the pool room. You might be lucky enough to see a man in a red-and-black checkered shirt floating above the tables.

A HOUSE IS NOT ALWAYS A HOME

DUMAS BROTHEL
15 East Mercury Street
Butte, Montana 59701
Telephone: 406-494-6908
Website: www.thedumasbrothel.com

Ghostly Activity Level: High

HISTORY: The Dumas Brothel was built in 1890 by a pair of Canadian entrepreneurs, Joseph and Arthur Nadeau. The Dumas was known as a parlor house, where elegantly dressed women entertained Butte's wealthy businessmen and politicians. Those less well-off could choose from the older or less attractive women who worked in tiny cubicles called "cribs" in the basement. During World War II, the federal government forced the closure of brothels all over the country to help the war effort. As a result, the cribs at the Dumas were shut down immediately and the basement sealed off just as it was, a time capsule not to be opened for nearly fifty years. Prostitution continued, of course, but much more discreetly. The brothel finally closed in 1982, when its last madam was sent to prison by the IRS for tax evasion. It is now a museum, the sole survivor of Butte's once-notorious red light district.

PHENOMENA: According to current owner Rudy Giecek, the Dumas is haunted by the ghost of former madam Elinore Knott, who committed suicide in 1955. Orbs, eerie mists and transparent figures have appeared on photographs taken inside the building. A young boy bicycling past on a dark evening reported lights on in the empty building and the figure of a woman standing in an upper window. A couple who stayed overnight in the Madam's Bedroom claimed to have seen the ghost of a woman, which vanished abruptly. The strong odor of fresh cigar smoke has been noticed although smoking is forbidden in the decrepit building.

When my friend Pat Cody flew up from Texas to go ghost hunting with me, she had no idea where I planned to take her.

"A brothel? You've got to be kidding!" she exclaimed, sounding rather pleased at the notion.

"It's a museum now," I hastened to explain. "Not a working brothel. But it's haunted."

I had arranged a private tour with Rudy Giecek, the outspoken, controversial Butte antique dealer who bought the Dumas from its last madam in 1990. Giecek had been outraged to see so many of Butte's historic buildings torn down in the name of progress. Even though some residents of Butte felt strongly that the brothel was a reminder of a sordid past best forgotten, Giecek was determined to save and restore the Dumas as a museum.

From the sidewalk, the Dumas appeared imposing, a two-story red brick building with tall, narrow windows. Inside, the hallway was dim and smelled faintly musty. Giecek came out of a room to greet us.

"The Dumas was a parlor house," he informed us, gesturing toward the large windows that lined one side of the hallway. A mannequin in a scarlet dress stood in one of the windows.

"The ladies would sit there where the men could see them. It's like Amsterdam, except that Butte is cold, so they put the windows inside."

Giecek knew the building was haunted when he bought it. Ruby, the last madam, told him that the building had two ghosts, one of them mean. It wasn't long before Giecek had his first encounter with the supernatural.

"First thing that happened was when I first got the phone hooked up. It rang, and it was my dad's voice. He's been dead for years. 'All eyes are upon you, son,' was all he said, and then the line went dead, buzzing."

Visitors to the Dumas sometimes got more than they bargained for, too.

"Once, I was giving a tour and it was toward the end of the day. I had latched the door so no one else could come in. It was winter, and most of the lights were already off so it was kind of dim in here. One old guy was just laughing every time I told ghost stories. He said there were no such things and he wouldn't believe it unless he saw it. Just then the latch unlatched itself and the door opened. He didn't say anything, just walked out of there. Another time, I walked into the building, and everything looked smoky. I could hear people talking, even though I knew I was the only one there. I wasn't really scared so I decided to step into the smoke or whatever it was to see what would happen, so I did, and it all stopped right then."

Giecek's Victorian photograph studio was another place where odd things had happened. He showed us a photo he had taken of a young couple wearing old-fashioned clothing. There appears to be a third figure in the photo, that of a woman with a shawl and a big hat. The living woman appears to be transparent, while the ghostly woman appears solid.

"It raised the hair at the back of my neck," Giecek admitted. "All the weird stuff happens in this corner here. I had a lot of photographers look at that photo and they can't explain it." He has posted many of the eerie photos he and his nephew have taken on the Dumas website.

All of a sudden Pat shivered. "Is it cold in here?" she asked. I hadn't noticed a chill, just the dankness of a building no longer inhabited. Giecek unlocked the door to the basement and we followed him cautiously down the stairs to the notorious cribs.

The federal government ordered all red light districts to be shut down in 1943, Giecek told us, so Butte closed down the entire crib system and went to a waiting room system.

"There was a buzzer out back, and a little peephole where they checked the guys out," he explained, "and they'd bring 'em in to a waiting room and a lineup of girls to choose from. Then they'd go with her to her room."

The cribs were abandoned and the basement sealed off. When Giecek reopened the cribs fifty years later, he found hairnets, lipsticks, bottles of perfume and opium, empty cigarette packs and other items just as the girls had left them that January day in 1943 when the order came to close the cribs. It was like stepping into a time capsule of brothel life in 1943—in more ways than one.

"I spent some nights in the building," Giecek said matter-of-factly, "and you can hear stuff going on down the basement."

There's some indication that whoever haunts the Dumas is a protective spirit.

"During the wintertime I never come down here, but one day I was sitting upstairs writing my book and I had a weird feeling I should come downstairs. The water was already up to the top of the first step." Giecek credits the ghosts with helping to save the building. "I had no reason to go downstairs," he insists.

The girls worked round the clock in three shifts to accommodate miners coming off shift. The cribs were small, barely large enough for an iron bed. One room was particularly unsettling: the door jam had been badly damaged and a bloody handprint was still visible on one of the inside walls.

"I think something really bad happened here," Giecek said. "Maybe she tried to cheat the john, or maybe he turned bad."

The Dumas used to have forty-three working rooms as well as tunnels that led to other brothels and even, it was rumored, to City Hall. Businessmen and bureaucrats could use the tunnels for a private visit to their favorite girl.

"Burro-crats—that's what we called 'em in the good old days," Giecek joked.

We followed Giecek back upstairs. He showed us an old-fashioned refrigerator with a broken lock and airholes drilled into the back. A small French prostitute used to hide inside the refrigerator whenever there was a raid, he said. The cops never thought of looking inside. We proceeded on, up to the second floor and the Madam's Suite, with its huge bed. Strange things had happened there too.

"Six months after I opened to the public," Giecek said, "I rented some of the rooms to antique dealers. Well, one night we had a break-in and they stole a bunch of stuff. The back door was open and there was a trail of stuff leading upstairs. There was a flashlight on the floor, still burning, and broken dishes all over. I put out a reward of $400 for the return of a 1943 Coke calendar that had hung on the wall for years, and a few days later a young kid came in and said he was with some older guys and they broke in. I asked him why they broke the dishes and he said they didn't, that the dishes started flying and they ran out of the building. I never did get the calendar back."

We returned to the main floor, and Pat stood talking with Rudy while I looked around. All of a sudden I caught a whiff of cigar smoke, strong and fresh. Rudy had told us that smoking wasn't allowed in the decrepit old building, and I knew that only Rudy, Pat and I were present. Intrigued, I followed the scent of smoke into a room across from the parlor that Rudy used as a store. A number of garish costumes hung there, props for Rudy's Victorian photo business, but otherwise the room was empty.

The odor of cigar smoke grew even stronger, and I felt an uncanny conviction that I was surrounded by an invisible, milling crowd of people.

"Pat!" I called. She excused herself from her conversation with Rudy and hurried across the hall to me. "Do you smell anything?"

"Smoke!" She took another sniff. "Cigar smoke, I think." She took a photo, then another, while I stood watching her. All of a sudden I felt a small hand slip into my own left hand. It felt almost like a child's hand, friendly and confiding. Startled, I looked down but saw nothing. Then I recalled Rudy's story about the little French prostitute who had sometimes hidden in the refrigerator when the place had been raided...

It was gone a moment later.

We had an even bigger surprise when we played back the tape recording we had made of the interview with Giecek. In the photography studio, Pat had suddenly shivered and complained of the cold, which I had not noticed. On the audiotape, just moments before Pat spoke, a strange female voice whispers, "I'm cold." And later, down in the cribs, when Giecek compares the bureaucrats to donkeys—"Burro-crats—that's what we called 'em in the good old days—" a female voice says cynically, "Once and always."

Whoever she was, she ought to know.

The Dumas is now eligible for funds from the federal Landmarks at Risk program, and some repairs have been made to stabilize the building. The brothel is open during the summer and tourists are welcome.

Giecek previously allowed groups interested in paranormal research to conduct investigations in the building. During one of those investigations, a group of ghost hunters from Washington State took a photo that showed a red-haired female spirit. She appeared to be standing in front of a wall covered in red wallpaper. The wall was actually painted white. Giesick scraped some of the paint off and found red wallpaper behind it!

While you're in Butte, you might like to drop in at Club 13 to see if the "ladies" are receiving guests upstairs. Or stop in at the Vu Villa Bar and Pizzaria for the best pizza in the Mining City. Listen for footsteps upstairs—it may be the late (very late) owners, still keeping an eye on the premises.

THE LADIES UPSTAIRS

CLUB 13 BAR
13 West Broadway
Butte, Montana 59701
Telephone: 406-723-3653

Ghostly Activity Level: Moderate

HISTORY: This historic building is first mentioned in city directories in 1884-85, when the Milwaukee Beer Hall was listed at the address. Over the years, a variety of businesses have occupied the premises. Among them were a millinery shop, a carpet warehouse, and several saloons, including The Club, which was started in 1934 by former boxer Frank "Red" Riley. A historical plaque on the building states that "Blue and yellow tiles were added to the ground floor façade sometime in the early 1930s but the second story façade retains its original 1880s appearance."

The Club quickly earned a reputation as a popular cocktail lounge. The second story of the building was linked to a nearby clothier's shop by a wooden catwalk, and rumor has it that "ladies of the evening" would slip across the bridge to drink and smoke privately on the upper floor. They were not allowed to mingle with the crowds on the main floor, but gentlemen looking for entertainment could join the ladies upstairs. Although the rumors are unproven, some of the carefully-worded ads for The Club in the late 1930s do seem to hint that for patrons "in the know," The Club offered more than just fine wines, liquor and cigars. Owner

Frank Riley sold the bar in 1963 and after several changes of ownership it was bought by colorful saloonkeeper Patrick "Packey" Buckley in 1965. Buckley ran the bar until the late 1970s. It is now owned by Kandice and John Van Valkenburg, who have begun to restore the building.

PHENOMENA: Women's voices have been heard coming from the second floor pool room and the scent of perfume has been noted when no one is present. The juke box occasionally turns on by itself, usually playing the same song. Footsteps have been heard crossing the ceiling, and security cameras have captured mist swirling near one of the pool tables upstairs.

Bartenders, security staff and maintenance workers are some of the best sources of ghost stories since they often work late at night in older buildings. Frank and I decided to drop in at the Vu Villa Bar and Pizzaria one day since we both enjoy a good pizza, and the bar was rumored to be haunted. The pizza was just as good as locals had assured us it would be, and Corey, the young man who was bartending at the time, told us about the Vu's ghost—and, as a bonus, a previously unknown ghost story involving Club 13.

According to Corey, the Vu was reputed to be haunted by the ghost of Pelligrina Campagna, wife of the original owner. When her husband Rocco died in 1898, only four years after he built the bar, Pelligrina was left with twelve children to support. She did so by managing the bar until her own death in 1925. A historical plaque on the outside of the building even notes that she has reportedly been seen behind the bar on occasion, going about her work as if she were still alive.

Corey has never seen Pelligrina's ghost, but he has heard odd thumps and bangs from the apartment upstairs where the Campagnas used to live, usually at closing time. Other bartenders have told him that they occasionally find bar stools on the floor when they arrive in the morning, even though they had placed the stools on the bar as usual the night before. They assume it is in the ghost of an old timer, and sometimes leave a drink out for him.

Corey's skepticism vanished long before he came to work at the Vu. "The first one that made me a believer was the Club 13 Bar," he told us between customers. "I used to close the place at night. To do so, I had to go upstairs and across the pool room to shut off the lights and then go back down. One night I went to grab my hat and I swear I heard footsteps crossing the floor upstairs. I was out of there so fast that when I got home my wife took one look at me and said, 'What's wrong?'"

The story was intriguing, so on my next trip to Butte, my friend Pat Cody and I headed for Club 13. The two-story building with its whitewashed masonry and vivid blue and yellow tiles stood out from its red brick neighbors and must have looked ultramodern in the 1930s, particularly since its patrons could enjoy their drinks in air-conditioned comfort. The Butte Archives has preserved one of Club 13's colorful bar menus from the late 1930s that lists a wide variety of drinks including absinthe cocktails for 35¢ and imported Scotches.

We arrived at Club 13 shortly after noon, but discovered that the bar didn't open until 4 P.M., and we had an interview in Bozeman at that time. Just as we turned away, disappointed, another of the astounding coincidences that blessed our trip occurred: the owner, Kandice Van Valkenburg, arrived unexpectedly for an appointment with a supplier. I introduced Pat and myself and explained my project as she unlocked the door and motioned us in.

"We do have ghosts," she said matter-of-factly. "You can hear them moving around upstairs, mostly at night. I believe they're women because you can smell perfume at times."

The bar was long and narrow, typical of its era. The ceiling was a coppery pressed tin with a geometrical pattern. It looked almost new and seemed to glow in the subdued light. Kandice noticed us admiring it, and commented, "The ceiling's original. When we bought the place two years ago, it was covered up. We brought it all back and exposed the brick wall." After a long search, Kandice and her husband found a beautiful 105-year-old back bar in North Dakota and installed it in Club 13. The bar's arches are elegantly simple, unlike most from that rather ornate era, and fit in well with the surroundings.

The Club hadn't been well treated in the past, and Kandice acknowledged that it will take time to bring it back to its original glory. She showed us a photo of what the building looked like before the blue and yellow tiles were added in the 1930s. The original façade had been made of handsome red brick.

"We want to put the brick façade back too," she added. "We love Butte because of its history. With all we've done over the past year, I think the ladies upstairs are celebrating."

The Van Valkenburgs didn't know that the bar was haunted when they bought it, but Tanya, a bartender who had worked there for years, told them she was sure there were ghosts. "We have four security cameras that cover the pool room upstairs," Kandice said. "Tanya told us that she had seen figures up there and heard footsteps and laughter. And some really odd things started to happen when we did the remodel. We could smell perfume when no one was around. Then we found an old perfume card. It still had a little scent, an old-type perfume. And there's the jukebox. Several times it's turned itself on and played a song. It's odd, because you have to put money in it. I think it was the same song each time.

"There may be a gentleman ghost, but I think most of the ghosts are women. This was a higher-class drinking bar," she continued, "a nice place where you could get a drink in a nice glass. Women were only allowed upstairs. They came across the catwalk from the clothing store. Men could also go over to the clothing store and be fitted for a suit as well as be entertained by the women."

The afternoon was warm, and Kandice offered us a cold drink. We accepted gratefully. Kandice opened a trapdoor behind the bar and disappeared down a narrow ladder to the basement where the soft drinks were stored. While she was gone, Pat leaned over the bar to take a photo of the open trapdoor and a movement on the security monitor caught her eye.

"Is one of your cameras usually cloudy?" Pat asked Kandice when she reappeared with our ginger ale. I caught the suppressed excitement in her voice and leaned over to see what she had spotted. On one of the four security cameras, a cloud of gray mist slowly drifted from the lower right corner toward a pool table. I took a quick photo but most of the mist, or whatever it was, had already dissipated.

"That's Camera 4," Kandice said, pausing to look at the camera Pat indicated. "It's way at the back, next to the windows. The ladies used to sit where they could look out of the windows. You can go up there if you want to."

Pat didn't hesitate. "I think there's a little tea party going on up there," she said, "with maybe a 'little something' in the tea!" She hurried up the worn stairs, the railings polished by thousands of hands over more than eighty years of use. I couldn't help but wonder about the men who had slipped quietly up those same stairs so long ago to meet ladies for drinks and perhaps "a little something" extra.

The stairway opened into a long, narrow room with large windows overlooking the street. It wasn't hard to imagine the scene as it might have looked so many years ago: elegantly dressed women holding a drink or a cigarette in manicured hands, gentlemen in well-fitted suits or tuxedos, heavy drapes at the windows, light spilling onto the street from above, a haze of cigarette and cigar smoke, ladies' perfumes, the clink of glasses, laughter, music drifting up from the bar downstairs. The reality was quite different. Two pool tables occupied the center of the room, and there were a few chairs and tables along the walls. No one was visible and the mist we had seen on the monitor was gone.

Pat and I feel strongly that it's both discourteous and counterproductive to "provoke" ghostly activity as some investigators do. Civility pays off, with the dead as with the living, so I greeted the unseen ladies politely and apologized for interrupting them. Was I talking to an empty room or were there really invisible presences watching us? Perhaps Pat's photos would give us the answer. Occasionally misty figures or floating balls of energy called "orbs" can be captured on camera although they may not have been visible to the naked eye. There was no audible response to my greeting of course; I hadn't really expected one, but I did feel a sudden strong tingling sensation around my head and shoulders.

On a hunch, I turned my tape recorder on and invited the ladies to make their presence known by speaking into my recorder. As soon as Pat had finished taking photos, I thanked our unseen hostesses and added, "We won't intrude on you much longer." The audiotape at that point recorded a faint sigh, perhaps of relief, perhaps of regret because we were leaving.

Only later, when we had a chance to upload Pat's photos onto my computer, did we see what had not been visible to us at the time: an inexplicable misty area above a table near the doorway. Apparently our instincts had been correct: we hadn't been quite alone up there after all!

If you visit the Club 13, be sure to ask the bartender about any recent ghostly activity. And do go upstairs to the pool room. Perhaps you'll see a wisp of mist where there should be none, or hear footsteps crossing the floor when no one else is present.

The Mining City is rich in ghostly lore, and you may want to visit the Vu Villa Bar or, during the summer months, the Dumas Brothel and the World Museum of Mining. If that's not enough excitement, try one of the award-winning tours offered by Old Butte Historical Adventures. Many of the sites they will take you to are reputed to be haunted. Don't forget your camera!

THE ORPHAN GIRL GHOST

THE WORLD MUSEUM OF MINING
155 Museum Way
Butte, Montana 59703
Telephone: 406-723-7211
Webpage: www.miningmuseum.org

Ghostly Activity Level: Low

HISTORY: The World Museum of Mining was founded in 1963 on the site of the "Orphan Girl," a 2700-foot-deep mine that produced silver and zinc ore from 1875 to 1956. On exhibit are many rare artifacts and historic photographs from Butte's old mining days. A few yards from the museum stands a reproduction of an 1890s mining town called Hell Roarin' Gulch. Some of the 50-plus historic buildings were brought in from other mining sites, while the rest were built from salvaged materials.

PHENOMENA: The apparition of a man in a yellow slicker has reportedly been seen near one of the buildings in Hell Roarin' Gulch. Voices have been heard from empty buildings and cameras have malfunctioned in and near the Orphan Girl Mine. A visitor sitting in a car was startled when the car was rocked back and forth by an unseen force. A professional photographer's cameras all malfunctioned when she attempted to take photos of the mine's head frame (also called "gallows" or "gallus" frames), used to hoist men and ore from the depths.

Places where tragic events have occurred are often reputed to be haunted, and Butte has certainly suffered more than its share of tragedies since mining began in the 1870s. Mining is an inherently dangerous occupation, and those who escaped being crushed in cave-ins or mangled in industrial accidents often died from the toxic dust and fumes that were byproducts of mining.

Although the Orphan Girl was regarded as a "nice mine" in which to work because of its cooler temperatures, a search of newspaper archives revealed five fatalities and many injuries over the years. Two of the five fatalities resulted from falls, a third from a "ground slip," and the remaining two from miners being caught by descending cages.

Large collections of artifacts may also contribute to a haunting, and the buildings that make up Hell Roarin' Gulch are filled with artifacts dating back to the early days of mining. According to many museum curators and antiques dealers, artifacts that were routinely used or prized by a previous owner may sometimes come with embedded energies. Over the years staff and visitors have had a number of eerie encounters at the World Museum of Mining.

I first visited the museum several years ago and spoke with a young woman at the counter who told me that she had experienced some odd phenomena on the property. Part of her duties involved walking through the various exhibit buildings at closing time to make certain that no visitors were left behind. On several occasions she had heard men's voices coming from one of the buildings and went inside, expecting to find tourists. Each time the building was empty. The sense of being watched by invisible presences was strong, however, and she would hurriedly check the building and then leave.

"The hair on the back of my neck just stood up," she told me, "because I just *knew* that I was being watched by someone I couldn't see."

Recently the apparition of a man in a yellow slicker has been reported near the old Chinese apothecary in Hell Roarin' Gulch. I have not been able to substantiate this story, but if true, perhaps he's the spirit who interfered with a Butte photographer's attempts to photograph the Orphan Girl's head frame a few years ago.

Although the photographer told several friends and colleagues of her encounters at the time they occurred, she prefers to remain anonymous, so I will call her "Mary."

One autumn evening in 2004, Mary went up to the Orphan Girl mine to do some photography. "I needed to take some video and pictures of the lighting of the Orphan Girl for a DVD on Butte that I was putting together," she told me. "I had three cameras with me. One was a video camera; the second was a Kodak EZ Share, and the third just a little tiny camera I happened to have with me. I had checked the batteries before I started out and everything was ready to go.

"When I got up there, I tucked myself in a little corner of a building where I had a great angle. It was right across the way from the Orphan Girl. I turned on the video camera, and it just shut itself off. I tried to turn it on again, and it wouldn't turn on. I looked at the screen and there were green lines running across it. I took the battery off and put it back on, thinking that would work, but the camera still wouldn't turn on. Next I tried to turn on the Kodak, but it wouldn't turn on either. Then I tried the little camera, and it too wouldn't turn on. I knew that they worked, because I checked everything before I left home, so I didn't get any pictures for my project. When I got home, I tried all the cameras again, and they all worked perfectly. Just to be sure, I even took a picture inside the house. So whatever it was up there, it wouldn't even let those cameras turn on. Oddly enough, I never felt anything. I just couldn't get any pictures up there.

"I went up to the mine again one evening after Thanksgiving in 2004. It was a mild winter and there wasn't any snow anywhere, so I had decided to take some more pictures of the head frame for my DVD. I parked right by the entrance to the museum. It was flat ground, no snow, no ice. I had my mom with me for company. She's blind and has been since she was sixteen years old. I said to her, 'I'm just going to be here videotaping. I'm not going far. You'll be fine.'

"I videotaped a bit of Butte first and then I turned and started videotaping the gallus frame of the Orphan Girl. As I was holding the camera, I saw something odd out of the corner of my eye: my little Honda Civic appeared to be rocking gently from side to side. I thought, *"Is the car moving? No, it's my imagination. I'm not going to let my mind run away with me."* I started filming again, and once more I saw the car moving out of the corner of my eye. The car was definitely shaking. I ran to the car. I could see my mom's hand reaching for the handle. As soon as I opened the door, my mom said, 'Were you moving the car?' I told her I hadn't been, and she said, 'The car was moving, it was actually moving!'

"I know it was," I told her. "Thank God it wasn't my imagination! I didn't want to think I was imagining it."

"No," she said, "I was looking for the door handle to get out, because I was going to roll out of the car rather than roll down the hill." She thought that maybe the brakes had failed and the car was slipping down the hill.

"We're out of here," I said, and we left. I dropped her off at her house and then I went home. When I walked into the house, my boxer started growling and the hair on his neck just stood up. He's the nicest dog ever, but he got down on all fours and started growling and sniffing at my feet. I decided I wasn't staying and tried to put the leash on him but he wouldn't even come near me. Finally I got the leash on him and put him in the back of the car. He usually just lies down, but this time he was jumping all over the car seat but not coming near me. I had called to let my mom know we were coming, so when I got to her house I just opened the car door and he tore up to the front door and ran into one of the bedrooms. Every time he came out he started sniffing at my feet again. It probably took a day and a half before he'd even get close to me.

"I've only been back up to the mine once, one night in the fall of 2008. My son was driving, and my mom, my daughter and my sister were with us. I'd told them about our experience up there in 2004, and they wanted to see if the ghosts would do anything to me this time. We were all laughing, and I said, 'Nah, nothing's going to happen to us again.'

"My daughter, my sister and I got out of the car and walked up along the fence, while my son and my mom stayed in the car. It was a nice night, really quiet, and there were no other cars there. We'd been walking around for about five minutes when I said 'Stop! Don't you hear those bells ringing?'

"My sister and my daughter just laughed. They couldn't hear any bells. We walked back to the car, and as we got in, my son said, "Gram says she hears bells ringing." We weren't close enough to the car for her to hear me say that I'd heard bells ringing. They sounded like church bells. Only my mom and I heard them, no one else.

"Nothing bad happened to any of us after these experiences, but I haven't been back up there since."

The World Museum of Mining is a fascinating place to visit, but unless you're the adventurous type, you may not want to try taking photos of the Orphan Girl head frame after dark! And while you're in Butte, don't forget to visit the Dumas Brothel, which is open during the summer. Owner Rudy Giesick can show you some very eerie photos taken in the brothel. If you're up to an hour's walk, try one of the tours offered by Old Butte Historical Tours. You'll be visiting several haunted sites, so be sure to take your camera along. You may be lucky enough to capture orbs or even a misty figure on your camera.

THE LIVELY GHOST OF "PTOMAINE JOE"

ROCKY KNOB LODGE
6665 Highway 93 South
Conner, Montana 59827
Telephone: 406-821-3520
Webpage: www.rockyknoblodge.com

Ghostly Activity Level: Moderate

HISTORY: Rocky Knob, at the southern end of the Bitterroot Valley, began as Joe's Ranch in 1945. The Lodge itself was constructed around 1947 by Jessie B. "Joe" White, who gained the nickname "Ptomaine Joe" for her somewhat questionable cooking. Joe's talents lay elsewhere, however. The Lodge became notorious as a gambling parlor and there were rumors that the construction workers had been paid with certain "favors." Ptomaine Joe was forced to sell the Lodge in 1950 but she is still fondly remembered by old-timers in the Bitterroot Valley.

PHENOMENA: The spirit of "Ptomaine Joe" has been seen on the catwalk where "her girls" paraded themselves in the evening. A man in a plaid shirt has been seen sitting at the bar. Whenever he is asked what he'd like to drink, he disappears. The ghost of a young boy who died tragically in the game of Russian roulette is thought to be responsible for knives flying around the kitchen. On winter nights, the ghostly sound of coins dropping into the metal tray of a slot machine has reputedly been heard. The aroma of vanilla-scented pipe tobacco has been noted late at night in a room near the office both before and since the smoking ban took effect.

It seemed as if we'd been traveling for hours since we'd left Hamilton heading to the south on Highway 93. Granted, the narrow, twisting road had to be driven carefully, but there was still no indication that we were nearing Rocky Knob Lodge, even though we had been told it was only a "few miles" south of Conner. I'm one of those unfortunate people who can get lost despite MapQuest and a GPS, so I'd brought my friend Frank along as navigator. When he assured me that we were "nearly there," I gave a sigh of relief.

My interest in Rocky Knob Lodge had been caught by an article in the *Ravalli Republican* of November 28, 2007, about the lodge's colorful owner, Jessie "Ptomaine Joe" White—and her alleged ghost.

According to reporter Stacie Duce, who wrote the article entitled "Sixty Rocky Knob Years," after Jessie White bought the property, she paid the builders of the lodge with *"food, drink, and 'favors' from her female staff. As legend has it, when the large log lodge opened on New Year's Eve, 1947, the builders were still in debt to her.*

"Ptomaine Joe was famous for her hospitality, colorful language and fried chicken. She poured drinks, served food and let customers leave what they owed in a coffee can on the bar counter. After dinner she often sat in the dining room...with weary or wobbly customers reciting cowboy poetry and telling legendary stories."

In 1950, however, Ptomaine Joe's liquor license was taken away from her, and when slot machines became illegal, revenue declined to the point where she was forced to sell the lodge for much less than it had been appraised for only months earlier.

Ptomaine Joe never returned to her beloved lodge in life. But has she returned after death? Frank and I hoped to find out.

We swung around yet another curve in the road and suddenly there it was: a large log lodge on the right side of the road with a small motel behind it. The lodge looked peaceful enough now, dreaming in the mild autumn sunlight, but it had been lively enough in its glory days. Now, the lodge offers rustic accommodations to tourists, fishermen, hunters, and others who come to enjoy the resources of the beautiful Bitterroot Valley.

There were a couple of customers at the bar when we walked in, so we spent some time looking around, admiring the beautiful wooden paneling, massive pillars that reminded me of the great lodges up at Glacier National Park, and a large stone fireplace with white stones that still spell "Joe's Ranch." Judging from old photos on the wall, the lodge still looks very much as it did in Joe's day.

Manager Edna Utter wasn't available at the moment, so we ordered Rocky Knob cheeseburgers and seated ourselves at one of the huge thick plank tables with marks of the axe still visible on the sides. According to the waitress who brought us our lunch, the lodge is famous for its hickory-smoked ribs and Ptomaine Joe's famous fried chicken, made from her very own recipe, which has been passed down from owner to owner. It sounded delicious, and we promised to come back for dinner sometime.

Utter came out to greet us soon afterward. She has worked at the busy lodge for three years but has been associated with it much longer. "My sister's father-in-law owned it at one time," she explained, "and I had seen pictures from when they were here. The current owners have owned it for twenty years now." She currently supervises fifteen employees and four bartenders.

The south end of the building was the original bar, she told us, and the current bar was the last section to be added on. The center portion of the building has always been a dining room. The piano is original and according to legend had been played by Joe herself. The balcony above the dining room used to be a catwalk where Joe's ladies could survey potential clients.

"Have you ever had paranormal experiences here yourself?" I asked.

"I saw Ptomaine Joe up on the balcony one night after hours," she replied matter-of-factly, "and both the housekeeper and I have heard footsteps running back and forth upstairs. We were the only ones here."

Other staff and at least one guest have also encountered the lodge's ghostly residents. According to former employee Tara, "Sterling, Harold and I saw a woman pass from the dining room into the bar and disappear about six feet into the room by the poker machines. Just previous to that Dannette, Harold and I had been sitting in the bar and we all smelled a musky perfume. To Dannette and me it was quite faint, and nothing that either of us would wear, but to Harold it was very strong and he had felt dizzy. He said it smelled like 'Seduction' or 'Poison.'

Utter added, "One of the bartenders would see a guy sitting at the bar at closing time. He looked solid and wore a plaid shirt. When she went to serve him, no one was there. He resembles a man in one of the historic photographs, a group photo of men who were here in PJ's day, so we think he was Joe's boyfriend. We don't know who he was."

According to Utter, the male ghost had appeared just the previous night. One of the bartenders had been sitting at the bar doing the dinner count when he saw a shadowy figure walk past him and disappear.

Jen, who doubles as a waitress and a bartender, has also seen the man in the flannel shirt. "He wears a cowboy hat," she stated. "I've seen him two times." She has also had unnerving experiences in the upstairs hallway that leads to the office.

"After the dining room closed one evening, I walked upstairs to drop off money bags and turn the music off. I felt hands on my shoulders at the end of the hall. Another night I went upstairs after closing and as I passed the third room, I caught a glimpse of a little boy sitting by the window. I saw him right down to the color of his hair."

The son of another employee also does not like to go upstairs. "He has been involved with the Rocky Knob since he was four years old," his mother said. "He's now twelve, and when he goes upstairs, you will hear him say, 'Okay guys, I'm coming up, please be nice.' Then you will hear him run to the office and run all the way back downstairs. He has seen the guy in the plaid shirt and says he feels a woman in the dining room."

I asked Utter if she'd had any problems with computers or other electrical equipment. Cameras, tape recorders, televisions and alarms often malfunction in haunted buildings, possibly because ghosts are thought to draw energy from them.

Utter smiled. "The first year I was here, we put the Christmas tree up in the dining room and plugged it in. None of the lights worked. I walked into the kitchen to do something and when I came back the lights were on. I said, 'Oh, right!'One time, my calculator had half a roll of paper run through it by itself. And sometimes the television switches channels by itself. We've called the electrician and there's nothing wrong."

Employees have occasionally felt cool breezes as if someone is walking past, but nobody is there. The rest rooms in the dining room have also been the scene of unexplained incidents. Even though the faucets are checked at closing, water is sometimes found running when the lodge opens in the morning.

Utter led us into the kitchen. "One of our cooks had a blood clot about ten minutes after she got here," she told us. "She passed away in the kitchen in March, 2008. Her presence is here too." The cook may have been responsible for an incident another employee told me about later.

"I was in the kitchen playing with a co-worker's little boy," she said. "He came running toward me with his arms open. When he got close, the knob on the stove flew off and landed between myself and this four-year-old boy. He stopped in his tracks and we both just looked at each other. He seemed a little unsure, so I picked him up and told him everything was okay."

We followed Utter through the kitchen and up a flight of narrow stairs to the rooms used by Joe's girls. The catwalk over the dining room had been blocked off, but Utter removed some panels so we could get some photos "Things get more active in hunting season, because Joe likes the fellows. We had some hunters from NY stay upstairs once," she said. "We didn't tell them anything about the legend, nothing. The next day we asked them how their night was. They said, 'Fine, but there was this warm feeling, a presence in there.'

"What they didn't know was that two boys, sons of one of the owners, once lived in that same bedroom. The boys played Russian roulette with a gun, and one of them died. If that little boy doesn't like you and you're in the kitchen, the knives will come off the wall. They did to my husband and to one cook I had here. The boy absolutely didn't like them, because every day the knives would fly off the wall, right down in front of them."

She opened the door to one of the rooms, and we followed her inside. "This is the room the hunters were in, and where the little boy shot himself."

We looked around. The room was definitely rustic, and was used mostly in the autumn by hunting guides. Strangely enough, it did feel warm and somehow occupied, although no one besides the three of us was visible. I had been taping Utter's comments as we toured the building and hoped that I might pick up a ghostly voice in the little boy's room, but there was nothing unusual on the tape when I played it back that evening.

Next she showed us her office, a well-lit corner room with large windows. "Sometimes when I'm working here," she said, gesturing toward her desk and computer, "I feel like there's someone watching me."

I agreed. The moment I'd stepped into the office I'd sensed a female presence. "I can't say for sure that this is Joe," I cautioned, "but whoever she is, she's a happy person, someone who looks forward, not one to dwell on past sorrows."

Utter nodded. "I think Joe's pleased that we're fixing things up," she said, and she's probably right. According to K.J. McDonald, who helped negotiate the sale of the property, the lodge meant everything to Ptomaine Joe. In an oddly prophetic statement, he wrote: "...she built the bar, the annex and the lodge, and *she has tried to put herself into the place, she feels it is a part of her she is leaving.*" (emphasis added)

Ptomaine Joe, it seems, really has returned to the lodge that meant so much to her.

Rocky Knob Lodge is only thirty miles or so south of Hamilton on Highway 93 South. The road offers spectacular views of the mountains at each twist and turn. Why not drop in some weekend to enjoy a great burger, or sample Ptomaine Joe's famous chicken dinner or hickory smoked ribs? And if you're a sportsman, bring your fly rod—there's good fishing just across the road.

KLONDIKE LADIES

KLONDIKE BAR & RESTAURANT
33 East Bannack Street
Dillon, Montana
Telephone: 406-683-2141

Ghostly Activity Level: Moderate

HISTORY: The Klondike Bar was built in 1887 as the Fair Hotel. It is still a handsome building with distinctive decorative cornices. Framed and mounted on the wall hangs the original liquor license. The Klondike's upper floor is reputed to have once been used as a brothel.

PHENOMENA: The bar is rumored to be haunted by the ghost of a prostitute who died in the basement as the result of a self-induced abortion. Spectral black shadows have also been seen, and objects have been moved in the kitchen.

On a chilly December day in 2007 I drove to Dillon for a book signing at The Book Store. The store was full of people waiting to share their stories with me, and it quickly became apparent that Dillon had to be one of the most haunted towns in Montana.

I returned the following September to follow up some of the leads I'd gotten from the earlier trip. Among the stories were those of a possible haunting at the Klondike Bar and the old railroad depot, now the home of the Beaverhead County Historical Society.

The afternoon was unseasonably hot, so Frank and I dropped into the Klondike Bar and Restaurant to cool off and, if the opportunity offered, to ask about the rumored ghost. The bar was busy, with a lot of good-natured banter between regulars and staff. We seated ourselves at the end with cold drinks and looked around a bit. After a while business slacked off and I introduced myself to Jeanette Hatch, better known as "J.J.," who filled the roles of bartender and manager.

Hatch readily acknowledged that the building was haunted by a ghost thought to be that of a former prostitute, and perhaps by other spirits as well.

"I've been working here going on six years," she said while deftly serving a customer who had just arrived. "There've been reports of things happening."

She nodded toward at a wall behind us."Before we remodeled, that wall used to be wood slats with a space between each slat. Once, I was working in here at night, closing the bar, and I saw a shadow through the slats. I was doing paperwork at the time, and I stopped and went through the door and looked around, and nobody was there. I thought, 'Well, I'm just tired,' so I came back and was finishing up the paperwork and I saw it again. I waited for it to come back, but it never did. It was two in the morning, so I went downstairs to make sure that nobody had gone down to use the rest room or what have you, and there was nobody in the building. Whatever it was cast a shadow on the side of the building. There was no clothing you could make out, just a shadow. It scared me.

"The manager who was here before used to open up the kitchen at seven in the morning. One morning she and the waitress saw a bowl of pancake batter slide across the table. She grabbed it and put it back, and pretty soon it did it again. She grabbed it in mid-stream and put it back. The third time it went sailing across the kitchen and slammed against the wall. It scared her to death."

"What about the brothel?" I asked. Hotels that were used as brothels, as many old hotels were up to recent times, are often rumored to be haunted. Prostitution wasn't an easy life, no matter how it's been glamorized. "Working girls" lived with the ever-present fear of violence and sudden death. Old newspapers are full of reports of women who were murdered by their customers, died of botched abortions or committed suicide when their days of usefulness were over.

"There have been reports that there was a brothel upstairs," Hatch said. "One story is that a man fell in love with one of the women. Supposedly she was upstairs doing her job, and he came into town and killed her and the man she was with. There've been reports of people seeing her downstairs floating around in the galley in a white gown. Sometimes you feel the hair on the back of your neck crawl, or feel like you're being watched downstairs. I don't scare easy, but when I go downstairs to the storage, it's like there's someone in there with you. Heavy air, if you known what I mean."

I did indeed know what she meant. Whenever I enter a place with that "feel" to it, I know there's a good chance of a haunting.

After serving another customer, Hatch resumed: "We've had the security alarms go off at night and the cops have come down, but they don't find anything. One waitress did see a man standing in the doorway of the restaurant one night. He had western clothing and a cowboy hat on. Then he just wasn't there any more."

There was another witness too: Sharon Lewis, whom I had interviewed at another reputedly haunted bar. She told me a slightly different story about the prostitute who haunts the Klondike.

"A young girl committed suicide in the basement," Lewis said. "She worked in the brothel upstairs and she got pregnant from some big wig in town. She went downstairs to give herself an abortion, and that's where she died. I worked there at the Klondike, and when I was in the kitchen one night a water pitcher came flying at me off the ice machine. That was half a room away from me.

"There was a shelf above the dishes where they kept the French bread, and one day all of a sudden the French bread just torpedoed at the cook. Waitresses would put a dishrag down and it would come up missing. Sometimes they would never find it. Then the former manager went downstairs one night to her office, and when she came back up her eyes were *this* big. She wouldn't tell us what she saw down there, but it scared the heck out of her. She moved her office up from the basement.

"One night her mother was tending bar, and I was sitting visiting with her. There was nobody in there but the two of us. All of a sudden she grabbed my arm and said to me, 'Kid, don't leave.' She had just seen a pair of boots walk behind me and go down the stairs.

"When I was working there, the lady who owned the place told me there were two extra rooms downstairs. I thought I'd go down there some evening when I had to work. So one night I went down there and looked at one of the rooms. Then I decided to go back to the wine-cellar, where the lady had committed suicide, but I found that I couldn't take a step to go back there. There wasn't anything holding me, but I couldn't go back there. It scared me, and I turned around and ran upstairs.

"I was telling everybody I couldn't go past the brick wall of the wine cellar, and they laughed at me, and I said, 'If you think it's funny, you go down there and try it.' My daughter came in later on that evening and she laughed at me too. I said, 'We're going to go downstairs.' I took her downstairs and the same thing happened to her. She said, 'Mom, let's get out of here!' A couple nights later, I went back down there. That time I walked to the wine cellar and nothing bothered me."

Arthur Adams has owned the Klondike Bar for four years. The ghost stories were well known at the time he bought the building, and the previous manager claimed to have had a lot of experiences there. Adams began his tenure by renovating the basement, cleaning it up, ripping out old pipes and removing the out-dated heating and cooling system. Although the lights in the basement sometimes turn themselves on or off, he's never seen anything unusual down there. "Some of my girls don't like to go down there at night, though," he acknowledged.

The brothel on the second floor is still awaiting renovation. "It needs a lot of work," Adams said. "It's all torn apart, not even livable. You can tell where the rooms were, though. People have been up there taking care of the heating but nothing odd has happened. It's mostly in the basement or the casino." What he finds most difficult to explain is why the machines in the casino occasionally print out tickets when no one is playing them. "At night," he told me, "you just *know* somebody's in there. I just yell aloud, 'If you're going to play with the machines, put money in them!'"

Much of the early history of Dillon has been documented, but the death of a prostitute would have merited only a line or two in the local newspaper, if anything at all. Perhaps someday a researcher will run across a mention of such an event, or the murder of a prostitute and her john by an enraged lover, on newspaper microfilm. Until then we'll have to assume that, as with so many legends, there's probably at least a grain of truth to the stories.

Dillon is the county seat of Beaverhead County. It is a trading center for an area rich in agriculture, lumbering and mining. The town is also home to the University of Montana–Western, with its own ghostly legends. Why not make Dillon your headquarters for a blue-ribbon fishing vacation, or to visit nearby ghost towns? And at the end of a long day, you might drop into the Klondike Bar for a cold brew. Just don't be surprised if the conversation turns to ghosts as closing time approaches. For Dillon's spirits, you see, that's when the partying begins.

THE LADY ON THE DANCE FLOOR

METLEN HOTEL & SALOON
5 South Railroad Avenue
Dillon, Montana 59725
Telephone: 406-683-2335
Webpage: http://metlenhotel.net

Ghostly Activity Level: Moderate

HISTORY: The Hotel Metlen was built in 1897. It is a large three-story brick structure with third-floor dormers set into a mansard roof and topped by a Victorian tower. The Metlen was designed to be a first-class railroad hotel, and it served the community well for decades. As this book goes to press, new owners are renovating the Metlen, planning to offer bed-and-breakfast accommodations.

PHENOMENA: Hotel guests and staff have reported the figure of a lady in a white dress who floats across the dance floor. A local paranormal research group caught a mysterious moving figure on video camera late one night. They also picked up a woman's voice on audiotape asking, "Will anyone dance with me?" Alarms go off frequently at night for no reason, and doors are sometimes found open after they have been locked at closing time. A bartender who glanced into the mirror in the women's bathroom caught a glimpse of a woman in an old-fashioned white dress standing behind her.

The long shadows of the nearby mountains were creeping toward the town of Dillon when Frank and I arrived for a book signing. It was about four P.M. on a chilly December day but already lights were beginning to appear in windows. As we drove past the old depot toward our motel, I noticed a huge building across the railroad tracks, its imposing roofline stark against the darkening sky. It was my first glimpse of the Metlen Hotel, long rumored to be haunted.

Many historic hotels and inns claim to have permanent residents, guests who never checked out—or who "checked out" a long, long time ago. Among the hotels are the Pollard in Red Lodge with its "Charlie," the Fort Peck Hotel and its Depression-era workman, the Dude Rancher in Billings with "Annabel," and Lewistown's Yogo Inn, home to "Bob."

Reporter Maryanne Davis Silve, in an article called "Ghost Stories at the Metlen" *(Montana Standard,* November 5, 2001), wrote that doors often slammed by themselves, a jukebox played songs that weren't listed, and staff had even caught brief glimpses of a lady in an old-fashioned white dress. The most startling experience, however, happened to a young woman who had taken a Ouija board up to the old tower, where a suicide had reputedly once occurred. She and her friends opened the windows to air out the stuffy room, then lit candles and grouped themselves around the Ouija board, waiting for something to happen. The pointer began to move very quickly and spelled out, "Get out!" Simultaneously all the candles went out and the open windows slammed shut. The women hurriedly left.

Like so many other great railroad hotels of its era, the Metlen, once a showplace of the community, lost business as rail travel ended and auto travel took its place. The hotel's condition gradually deteriorated, and it became home to low-income renters. I spoke with owner Sandy Iverson, who inherited the hotel from her mother seventeen years ago and has a powerful appreciation for the historic building and its importance to the community.

"Old buildings just get better with time," Iverson told me. "Not because the bricks get older, but because of all the people who lived there, drank there, met their mates there, married there, or died there. I quit renting out rooms in 2000 when the price of heat made it impossible to heat the place. I mostly rented out to poor folks, drifters, people who had lost their way. My mother bought it in 1978. It was on a spiral downward. She put a new roof on it, worked on the heating and opened it up for renting. I couldn't just leave it when she died."

Although Iverson hasn't seen a ghost in the Metlen, she did see one when she was fourteen. "It forever changed the way that I would approach the rest of my life," she said. "You don't sit and wonder after that, you *know* there's something on the other side."

Her brother did see the Metlen's ghost, according to Iverson. "It was in the '80s, and he was doing night duty. He saw a lady in a white dress come out of the wall where the stage is now and float across the dance floor and right through the back wall where the mirrors are. There used to be a door there that went to the old kitchen area. She wore a white gown, floating away from her hips, and she glided maybe a foot and a half, two feet above the floor. My brother's not a joker, so when he told me that I knew he'd seen something. Other night men also saw it."

The haunting can be traced back at least to the 1980s, when Iverson's brother saw the ghost. Others have encountered her too. Sharon Lewis, who works in a haunted restaurant in Dillon, told me that her son "lived on the top floor of the hotel in the '80s. He saw a woman come down the stairs with a candle in her hand, and all the lights went out." And Iverson learned of yet another incident from a former guest.

"It was around 2002 or 2003," she said. "I was upstairs working on a room, building a new office, and I heard people coming up the stairs. I had put no-trespassing signs out there, so I stepped outside and here's a whole family, grandparents, parents, their brother and a young boy about seven. Somebody had already gone down the hall, I could hear footsteps.

"The seven-year-old boy said, 'We're sorry, my uncle has told us about the ghost he saw in his room, and we were coming through Montana and we wanted to come here and see if we could see the ghost.' So here comes the uncle, the fellow who had gone down the hallway. 'It was me,' he said. 'I stayed here in the '80s, just passing through. I checked in late at night, and it was the last room at the end of the hallway on the right, room 19. I was awfully tired, so I went straight to bed. I woke up about an hour later, and here was a lady in a white dress floating from the corner of the room right around my bed. She disappeared through the wall. She had no feet. I saw it, and I can't un-see it.'

"It was right over the same place she's seen on the dance floor below. Both my brother and this gentleman described a woman in a white dress with no feet. So I said, 'Let me get my keys,' and I showed them the room.'"

"Is there any historical basis for a haunting?" I asked Iverson.

"According to my mother, a student or artist supposedly committed suicide in the Metlen. And before I quit renting rooms, I had seven or eight deaths in the hotel."

So far I've been unable to track down newspaper accounts of a suicide in the Metlen, but it's certainly possible that one occurred, given the long history of the building.

There have been other witnesses to odd goings-on at the hotel. A Dillon resident told me that she'd been in the bar late one night when she and the rest of her party all heard heavy footsteps from upstairs. The bartender went up to check, as the upper floors were off limits to the public. No one was there. Another woman told me that when she toured the Metlen with her high school class a few years ago, they were allowed to go up to the tower where the suicide is reputed to have occurred. "The windows were shut," she said. "But when I turned around again, they were all open. We were listening to our tour leader at the time, but I didn't hear any noise from the windows."

Claire, one of the Metlen's bartenders, has worked eight months at the hotel. "Two or three times I'd hear a girl talking and thought I'd locked someone inside," she said. "I'd go out in the hallway and there's never anyone there, so I'd check both bathrooms and no one's in there either. It's just this girl talking. I can't understand what she says, it's muffled. It sounds like a younger girl, not a child or an old lady, but an adult. All my experiences have been fine," she went on. "I think they're nice ghosts. My friend actually saw the ghost a week ago. It was a pretty quiet night, probably ten or twelve people in here, so she went to the bathroom. While she was washing her hands she looked up and there was this girl, this woman, in a white dress behind her, reflected in the mirror. She said something like 'Oh, hi!' and turned around and the woman was gone. She came back out and said, 'I just saw the ghost.'

"One night I was closing with one of the other bartenders,' Claire continued, "and he went upstairs to make sure no one was there. There's a picture of a covered wagon on the right, and he said he saw the covered wagon move to the left. Now he's freaked and won't go upstairs. There's a certain point upstairs about halfway along one of the hallways where I've felt light-headed. It didn't go away until I started back down the stairs. One of the customers heard a male voice say, 'Get off my floor.' There might be more than one ghost, maybe a janitor. There've been times when we've locked the door to Sandy's mother's apartment and when it's time to close, the door is standing open. It's kind of creepy at night when you're by yourself."

Iverson gave us a tour of the hotel's ground floor, including the front bar, the dance floor where the ghost has been seen, her mother's apartment, now used for storage, and the ornate second bar room, open in the evening. Its ornate back bar was built around 1900 when there was a resurgence of mining in Bannack. After the gold rush faded in 1917, the bar was brought to Dillon. And that's where Brad Marquez, founders of DOPS, Dillon's Only Paranormal Society, took a very strange photo. "The ghost busters took photos of the back bar," Iverson confirmed. "The stools were all up when they took the photo, but the mirror didn't reflect the stools."

Frank and I quickly took several photos, hoping for similar results, but our photos looked perfectly normal. No orbs, no mists, nothing unusual at all. I'd arranged to meet Brad Marquez at the book signing that evening, so I could find out more about his experiences at the Metlen.

Although Marquez has had a number of paranormal experiences, he considers himself a skeptic and looks for scientific reasons to explain phenomena. He and his team have investigated the Metlen three times. "Our first day investigating the Metlen was back in July," he told me. "We were newbies and it was our first job but we came out with great success. We were all sitting down at the front bar and I left my digital voice recorder about twenty feet away on the dance floor. When I played it back, there was a man's voice saying 'Get out of the bar.'

"About three A.M. we were up on the third floor, which is off limits to the public, and we started smelling cigarette or maybe cigar smoke very heavily. We didn't hear anything at the time, but my digital recorder picked up a loud sigh. The second time we went to the Metlen was in August or September. We were joined by Idaho Spirit Seekers. They came out with one photo with two possible apparitions in the back bar, a woman in a bonnet and a man wearing a cowboy hat. That's the only piece of evidence they caught. DOPS didn't catch anything that time.

"The third time we had a little more equipment, video recorders, digital voice recorders, EMF detectors, thermometers. We actually got video evidence of a woman coming off the stage onto the dance floor, floating at a steady pace toward the front bar and then dissipating. She's not completely visible. The only things you can see are ripples in her dress, hands down by her thighs where a woman would lift up her dress to walk, a little bit of her face and a little bit of her hair. We also got EVPs (electronic voice phenomena) that say, 'They don't know that we're dead.'

I asked whether they had gone up to the old tower, scene of the reputed suicide.

"We investigated it three times," Marquez replied, "and got nothing but dust orbs. No EMF, temperatures changes, or EVP. My wife was on a tour up there once and saw one of the windows slide up by itself, though," he added. "I didn't feel any hostility toward us at all. There was no negative energy."

He's also interviewed the employees. "One of them feels like she's being watched at times. Another one said he'd never experienced anything, but while we were going upstairs after an investigation to slide the keys under Sandy's door, he happened to look in the mirror. Nobody was there. When he looked again, there was a man in a cowboy hat looking at him."

Next time you're in Dillon, why not plan to spend a night at this newly-renovated historic hotel with its two saloons? You can ask the bartenders about the ghosts. And don't forget to visit the bathrooms. Perhaps you will glimpse someone standing just behind you—a lady in an old-fashioned white gown. If so, consider yourself fortunate—you've just met the White Lady of the Metlen Hotel.

LASTING IMPRESSIONS

LASTING IMPRESSIONS BED AND BREAKFAST
214 N. 13th Avenue
Forsyth, Montana 59327
Telephone: 406-346-7067
Webpage: www.lastingimpressionsmontana.com

Ghostly Activity Level: Low

HISTORY: This elegant two-story home with its octagonal tower was built by Louis Wahl for Joshua and Grace McCuistion in 1914. Mrs. McCuistion had visited the Far East and reportedly chose the flaring rooflines to remind her of the architecture she saw on her travels. She is said to have examined each board used in construction and sent back those that didn't meet her standards. The house was sold to Whit and Elsie Carolan in 1928. They also traveled widely, visiting Italy, Japan, England and Puerto Rico before they eventually divorced. Elsie Carolan lived in the house for forty-six years, taking in boarders and teaching piano to students. In 1974 she finally sold the house. It passed through several more hands before Carol Klinker purchased it in 1997 and became only the seventh owner of the house. In 2003, Klinker opened her house as a bed-and-breakfast inn.

PHENOMENA: A large black dog has been seen lying at the top of the stairs. A tall, thin shadowy figure has been seen several times, and owner Carol Klinker saw a phantom lady reflected in a security monitor. A security system sometimes reacts as if someone is passing through a doorway although no one is visible. Guests sleeping in the McCuistion Room at the top of the house were awakened by the spirit of a woman who stood beside the bed watching them.

It's said that spirits sometimes linger in homes they once loved. If so, it's not surprising that former owners of this warm, comfortable, and welcoming bed and breakfast inn may occasionally drop by to see how things are going—even decades after their deaths.

Most of the witnesses to the phenomena have been the current owner, her family and friends, but two guests who were staying in the McCuistion Room at the very top of the house also had a ghostly encounter during their stay.

"A guest once asked me if I had ever thought that my place might be haunted," Carol Klinker told me as we sat in her comfortable living room one evening with bowls of popcorn. "I replied, 'Why do you ask?' The guest explained that she had been awakened in the middle of the night and felt a presence in the room. She woke her husband and he could feel it as well. They both felt it was the spirit of a woman who stood next to the bed, just watching them.

"Was that the first time you suspected that you might have a house ghost?" I asked.

"Well, before I opened the bed-and-breakfast in 2003," she replied, "I had a photography studio in my house. The strobe lights used to flash on and off and wouldn't stop. I just brushed it off. But one night I got up to go across the hall to the bathroom. I was still sleeping upstairs at the time. I looked over at the top of the stairs and there was this big black dog that was lying there. I jumped and looked again, I thought that maybe the door had been left open and a neighbor's dog had come in. It turned its head and looked at me and poof, it was gone. I've never seen it again, but I think my granddaughter may have when she came to visit one time. It was two or three years ago. She's eleven now. I was in my office working. She was standing sideways in the doorway talking to me when she happened to look down the hallway and said, 'Is that—oh no, you don't have any animals.' I wish I'd asked her what she saw but I didn't, because it looked like it bothered her.

"Another time when I was upstairs, I heard footsteps loud enough that I was sure someone was coming up the stairs, even with the carpeting. It scared me, because I knew I was alone in the house. I was almost afraid to peek out, but I never heard it again.

"My grandson was here last summer, and he ended up with an ear infection. He had a pretty high fever, which could account for what happened. Alex wanted to sleep with me, so we put a blow-up mattress on the floor beside me. For some reason he wanted his head at the foot of my bed and his feet up by the head end of my bed. He'd wake up often, asking for a glass of ice water, and I'd get him that. Afterward I would lie down again. I could hear whispers so I crawled to the foot of my bed and put my head down to see if he was making that noise I kept listening, but I couldn't make out any words. Pretty soon Alex said very clearly, 'I can't understand you!' and then I didn't hear anything more. I wondered if he was talking to someone or if it was just the fever, but it was more than one voice, like a conversation between at least one man and one woman. The next day I asked him who he was talking to in the middle of the night, but he didn't remember talking to anyone.

"One afternoon I was taking a break, sitting in my recliner, covered with a blanket and watching TV. All of a sudden it felt like someone took the end of the blanket and jerked it down. I could actually see my foot go down. I thought it was something under my chair, but nothing was there. It hasn't happened again.

"Another time I came into the living room and could see something dark on the floor. I knew I had picked up the room so I turned on the light and found this little figurine on the floor. It's a small fairy figure and it normally hangs above the fireplace mantel from a string attached to a metal loop in its back. At first I thought the string broke, but it was still hanging above the fireplace, still tied. And there's no opening in the metal loop where the string could come out."

Klinker walked over to a spot about two feet in front of the fireplace. "That's where it landed," she said. "If it had fallen, it would have dropped straight down. It couldn't have landed that far out."

"I've heard of things like that happening," I told Klinker, and recounted what hostess Sylvia Little had told me about a large picture that had inexplicably fallen from its hook in her room at the Fort Peck Hotel (see *Haunted Montana* Volume 1 for the story). Little expected to find the screws had pulled out of the drywall or the wire on the back of the picture had broken, but the screws were still firmly in the drywall, the wire was intact and the picture was not damaged. There doesn't seem to be a normal explanation for either incident.

"Things seem to happen when I'm sitting in my chair watching television," Klinker went on. "Once I saw a form that was solid and black. I couldn't make out any details. I thought someone had come in my house, but no one had. Another time I was watching television, and I could see the doorway and window of the room behind me reflected in the TV. As I was looking at it, I could see a person crossing the room behind me. It looked like a black shadow that was very tall. It took up most of the doorway." I looked at the doorway. It had to have been at least seven feet high.

"Do you know if any of the previous owners were unusually tall?" I asked. Klinker thought for a moment. "It's said that Josh McCuistion was very tall," she replied.

Oddly enough, while she was talking to me I thought I saw something round and dark momentarily obscure the light fixture in the hallway. It appeared to be about the size of a softball and was near the ceiling. Since we had just been talking about a similar occurrence in that hallway, I had to dismiss it as the power of suggestion, but I'm reasonably sure that the light had been blocked out for a moment.

"One night I saw a woman standing in the living room. I was in my office working at my computer, and I glanced over at the security monitor that was sitting next to it. I could see the reflection of the living room in the monitor and saw a lady standing beside the window that faces the courthouse. She wore a light-colored dress with a wide waistband and puffed sleeves, more in the McCuistion era than the Carolan era. She was standing with her hands behind her back. Her hair was up on top of her head and I could see the profile of her face. She had a long nose and looked very serious. It was like she was standing watch. Maybe she was Mrs. McCuisition and she was making sure that I was doing the renovations to her liking!"

Ghosts are notoriously resistant to change, and owners of haunted properties have told me that activity seems to increase during periods of renovation. Grace McCuistion, who examined every piece of lumber before she allowed it to be used in the construction of her house, would almost certainly want to observe the renovations.

"Oddly enough," Klinker continued, "before I opened the bed and breakfast I hired Andre Philbrick to draw a pencil sketch of the house so I could use it in my advertising. She told me that when she had finished she stepped back to take a look at it and realized that she had drawn a lady standing in the front window. Thinking I wouldn't be pleased with it, she took her out. It was the same window where I saw the lady.

"My son was quite concerned about safety when I first opened the bed and breakfast, so I had a security system put in with a motion detector on the door into the kitchen. It would go off if the door opened. You'd hear 'ding-ding' if someone walked through. It would go off several times a day even though the door was open and no one was in sight."

Apparently the motion detector was reacting to something not visible to the human eye. I wondered whether it might be residual energy, tracing a path that former owners had taken hundreds of times in their lives. Another incident witnessed by Klinker suggests an intelligent entity rather than residual energy.

"I was given an old Edison Standard Phonograph a few years ago and finally found parts to repair it. In order to make it play you have to wind it up, flip a switch and pull out a pin to drop the needle down on the cylinder. My mother and I had just finished having breakfast on Mother's Day, 2001. I went into my office to get some work done before church and Mom went upstairs to rest. All of a sudden I heard a strange sound and thought my mother was doing something so I got up and went to investigate. The noise was coming from the dining room, where the phonograph is. I walked over and it played the whole cylinder and quit. It was 1900s band music. I stood there saying to myself, "It is really playing by itself!" I went upstairs to ask Mom if she if she had wound it up or messed with it at all and she hadn't.

"My boss came to lunch one day, and she said, 'The weirdest thing just happened. It felt like a feather or something was pulled through my mouth.' No one else was there."

Frank and I had been given the Lloyd Room for the night, a beautiful room with antique furnishings, a sitting area, and large windows overlooking the park across the street. The room is named for David Lloyd, a former owner who is a well-respected author of historical fiction. When Klinker showed us the bathroom, just across the hall from the Lloyd Room, I couldn't help peeking into a neighboring room with a gorgeous bedspread. This was the Carolan Room, named for another former owner, the world-traveling piano teacher Elsie Carolan. I stepped inside to look around. The room had a warm, friendly feel to it. It also felt *occupied.*

"Do you feel anything there?" Klinker asked from the doorway.

"I sense a woman here," I replied slowly, groping for words to describe the feminine influence I felt in the room. "She seems kind and content. She's short and rather plump. Not fat, but rounded. A little partridge of a woman. I don't know if it's just residual energy or an actual spirit, but there's something."

Klinker nodded. She too had felt a woman's energies at times in the room, perhaps those of one of the two women who were closely associated with the house: Grace McCuistion, who invested such energy into the building of her house, and Elsie Carolan, who lived there for forty-six years. Possibly photos, if any exist, will give help us identify the spirit of the woman who has left an impression in that room.

We had left the hallway light on in case either of us needed to get up during the night, and whenever I woke I would look at the gap between the bottom of the closed door and the floor to see if the ghostly black dog might be standing just outside. The house was silent, however, and we woke after a peaceful night just in time to see the sun clear the ridge to the east.

We had a delicious breakfast of Strawberry Cheesecake Pancakes with fresh strawberries next morning and parted with promises to return soon. Perhaps I'll ask for the McCuistion Room at the top of the house, just to see if the ghostly lady of the manor will pay me a visit. Or maybe I'll be lucky enough to catch a glimpse of the phantom black dog at the top of the stairs. Even if the ghosts don't put in an appearance, Carol Klinker's gourmet breakfasts and the chance to enjoy a night in a historic home are well worth the drive to Forsyth.

THE GHOSTLY COWBOY

IRON HORSE SALOON & CASINO
905 Main
Forsyth, Montana 59327
Telephone: 406-346-7463

Ghostly Activity Level: High

HISTORY: Forsyth was founded in 1882 when the Northern Pacific Railroad platted the town as a layover stop for its crews. Local rancher and businessman Thomas Alexander built the American Hotel in 1896. The hotel was later renamed the Alexander Hotel and served as a community center and Greyhound bus stop for decades. The hotel has stood empty for about 30 years, but the bar and restaurant on the main floor are both busy places. In the 1930s the hotel's bar was named the "Joseph" in honor of Nez Perce leader Chief Joseph, whom Thomas Alexander had known during his scouting days with General Howard back in 1877. The name has been changed twice since then, first to "Tom's," and then, in 2007, to the Iron Horse Saloon and Casino.

PHENOMENA: Heavy footsteps have been heard upstairs, although the upper floors are vacant. The ghost of an unknown cowboy wearing chaps and hat has occasionally been seen leaning on one end of the bar, and another ghost, a man wearing a baseball cap, has been seen at the other end of the bar. A third ghost, this one described as a tall thin man wearing a white dress shirt and bolo tie, was also seen floating in the casino. Early one morning, two employees heard pounding coming from the door to the basement. Thinking someone had been locked in the basement, they phoned the owner. When he arrived and opened the door, no one was there.

I learned of a possible haunting at the Joseph Bar in Forsyth during a Halloween television interview in 2008. One of the television crew had worked at the old bar for a few months and recalled an unusual experience she'd had there early one morning while "swamping" (mopping) the floors. Although she'd heard stories about a ghost in the bar, she'd never worried about being alone in the building. Something seemed different that morning, however, and she found herself glancing around uneasily. Suddenly the atmosphere seemed to change, and she looked up to see a cowboy "with chaps and everything" leaning against a doorpost watching her. He looked hazy, and the doorpost was visible through him. Shaken, she dropped the mop and hurriedly left. When she described the ghost later to other employees, they told her that he'd been seen on other occasions, usually leaning on the bar. Despite their assurances that the ghost seemed to be merely curious, the young woman left to find another, and preferably un-haunted, place to work.

Dick Smith, who has owned the bar since 2002, remembered the young woman and confirmed the story of the phantom cowboy. "A bartender used to see an old cowboy at the end of the bar all the time," he told me when I stopped by to interview him. "In the old days, they'd put their feet up and lean on the bar. Could be the same cowboy the swamper saw. I've never seen him, but several people have seen him at that end of the bar. He just shows up. I don't know who he is."

The ghostly cowboy may have even been caught once on camera. According to Smith, an employee took a photo on her cell phone that showed "a kind of aura of an old guy standing at the bar. There's a different ghost at the other end of the bar," Smith continued. "This one wears a baseball cap. They call him ol' Ernie Post. Ernie used to do a lot of the plumbing here. Ernie put in the plumbing and the heating system. He died when he was about ninety percent through with the job, although he didn't die here. He did a lot of nice work here and at the bank building He's only been gone about thirteen years.

"Bev, my casino manager, sometimes hears footsteps going back and forth across the ceiling. The first time it happened she called me and said, 'You need to get down here, there's some kids playing upstairs. Sure enough, you could hear footsteps, but not running, just clonk, clonk, clonk. I snuck upstairs with my flashlight and there was nobody there. Another time Rita and I were in here one morning about five and we saw a shadow that went all along the wall. I thought, 'Who the hell is back there?' so I went back and the kitchen was locked and nobody was in the bathroom. It was definitely a man walking. I thought someone was going to the men's room."

Bev has had a number of other eerie experiences in the bar. "I've managed the casino since 2001," she stated. "I come in at five in the morning and empty the machines. I used to do it in the back room, and sometimes I would hear what sounded like someone shuffling their feet across the dance floor. Your hair would stand up, it was so scary. Finally you'd get the nerve to come out and peek around the corner. There was nobody. It kept happening, so I would just stand and listen until it was quiet. One day Rita was here cleaning and I heard her screaming 'Bev, come quick!' We came over to the door that goes to the basement and somebody was pounding on it. It was 5:30 in the morning but I got Dick on the phone and said, 'Dick, get here now!' I was so scared. As soon as I hung up the phone, the clock fell off the wall behind us. We were just freaked out. When we opened the door we found nothing, absolutely nothing.

"A lot of times when I empty machines I can feel something behind me. Sometimes it touches my shoulder. Everything that happens is on the original side of the building. We had a machine in that corner, and every time I emptied it in the morning I could smell a man's aftershave. It was a very nice smell. I'd ask the girls if anyone played that machine the night before, but nobody ever had. It was very, very fresh. When I was here by myself I could hear footsteps upstairs. It definitely increases in the fall and winter. Our alarm system has gone off a few times and we don't know what's caused it."

Shirley works nights in the casino, and she too has had heard footsteps upstairs. "They were heavy male footsteps," she said. "I called Dick." But the most startling encounter, and one that may give as clue to the identity of at least one of the ghosts, happened one night when Shirley was behind the bar. "I looked down at the end of the bar and here was this figure floating. He appeared to be tall and thin, and he had on a white dress shirt and a bolo tie. He just floated. He didn't look solid. I couldn't really make out his features. When I described what he looked like, people said, 'You've just described Tom Alexander.' I had no idea what he looked like."

Thomas Alexander, the original owner of the hotel, died in May of 1918 when he was struck by a bolt of lightning while climbing over a pasture fence. Legend has it that the haunting began shortly after he died, and Larry Waymire, who is related to Tom Alexander, confirmed that the hotel was regarded as haunted when he was growing up in the 1940s. "When I was a kid and the hotel was going," he told me, "people would come down and say they heard stuff."

Alexander's granddaughter Janet McDonald owned the bar from 1958 to 1995. She sold the bar to Jim Kuckler. "This was a gathering place," Kuckler emphasized. "When people came to town, if they had to go to the bank or the doctor, they'd say, 'We'll meet at the Joseph.' Lots of deals were made in this building. It's been a drug store, a soda fountain, a bowling alley, a bar, a hotel. The Greyhound bus used to stop here."

Kuckler hadn't owned the bar for very long before he began to notice noises he couldn't logically explain. "When I was here by myself with no juke box on, cleaning, you'd hear something. Sometimes things would be misplaced. I had the same bartenders for nine years, and they'd say, 'Tom was in again last night.'

"Tom Alexander was the first homesteader. He persuaded the

railroad to build to Forsyth. He gave them the land. I changed the name of the bar from the Joseph to Tom's Lounge at the suggestion of Janet McDonald. After I sold it to Richard Smith in 2002, he changed it again, to the Iron Horse Saloon."

A small room now used to store cases of beer may be haunted by a female spirit. "We've experienced temperature differences in the beer room," Kuckler told me. "We'll have the heat just blasting in there in the winter and it'll be just cold as the dickens. Janet lived in the beer room for two years. That lady could drink with the best of 'em. She'd put her wig on, didn't matter if it was sideways or not."

"It's supposed to be haunted by a woman who's really angry," Dick Smith added. "Thomas Alexander lost his first wife and remarried. The second wife was always angry because her husband was gone all the time and she was always dissatisfied with the way she was treated. That's my guess as to who it is."

A ghostly woman in a dress even showed up in a photo taken at a birthday party a few years ago, according to both Larry Waymire and Jim Kuckler. No one knows whether the woman was Janet McDonald or Tom Alexander's second wife, but the photo was seen at the time by many witnesses.

Poltergeist activity has also occurred, most notably when current owner Dick Smith and his wife Alecia were moving Dick out of his old office. They had left their daughter Stevie sitting at Dick's desk while they stepped out for a few minutes. "A couple of minutes later she came running into the bar," Alecia said, "and told us that all the thumbtacks and the pens that were sitting on the desk suddenly whirled around and flew all over. When we went back to the office, they were scattered all around. In our minds there was no way she could have picked them up and scattered them like that. It frightened her enough so she wouldn't stay.

"Dick had been doing some work on his computer, and all of a sudden a bunch of gibberish came across the screen. We thought that the keyboard was stuck, but it wasn't, so he got out of his program and closed it. The gibberish started coming over the screen again. We unplugged the keyboard and the mouse and the hard drive but it just kept coming across the screen. Dick said, 'There's someone in there and he wants to talk to us,' so we started asking questions and it would answer us. We'd say, 'Oh, this is bullshit!' and it would reply, 'No bullshit!' We printed it off so we'd have a hard copy.

"We leased the kitchen to Deb of Big Sky Café last fall and Deb has had several experiences. Right behind the toasters is a container where she puts stuff, and one day the container moved to the other side. She thought it might have slid on water, but nope, the counter was completely dry. Sometimes things fall off the can rack, and a couple of times someone has knocked at the back door. We opened it instantly but no one was there. The radio sometimes goes off and then comes back on."

At this point, I suggested, "Maybe there were guests who died in the hotel." When I replayed the audiotape, a whispery voice answered, "Yeah."

Dick's daughter Jena has waitressed and cooked for three years, and has had her own experiences in the kitchen. "We have can racks in the back room, and we put our twelve-packs on top of them. Once we heard a big noise. Pop cans had flown out of the box, right off the can rack, spraying everywhere. We have a dumb waiter that goes from the basement to the top floor, and sometimes we'll be doing dishes and the dumb waiter will open. Those are heavy doors and they don't just open by themselves. Above our plate warmer," she continued, "we have our spice rack, and sometimes we'll find three or four spices sitting on the counter. And once in a while, at the end of the night when all the customers have gone, we'll be sitting eating and we'll hear a crash from the back. We'll find our Tupperware has been tossed around. Or we'll find a twelve-pack on the floor. It's crashed hard enough so the pop explodes and is spraying all over."

"There's a tiny lip on our shelves," Dick added, "and there's no way a twelve pack can fall over by itself."

Just two days earlier, Jena went on, chef Deb heard someone scream while working in the kitchen, so she opened the side door to check the alley. It was about 3:30 in the morning. No one was in the alley. Then the swamper from the bar walked into the kitchen and asked if someone had screamed. She had heard the woman scream too.

There seems little doubt that the historic Alexander Hotel/Joseph/Iron Horse Saloon is haunted. Credible eyewitness reports can be traced back many years. The questions still to be answered, perhaps by a future paranormal investigation, are *why* and *by whom*. Ghosts are thought to haunt for various reasons, including unexpected death and unfinished business. If true, we can venture a guess at the identity of at least some of the hotel's several ghosts: Thomas Alexander, who probably left unfinished business behind when he died unexpectedly in 1918; "ol' Ernie Post" who could often be found at the bar in life and may still be worrying about the work he left undone, and Janet McDonald, who owned the bar for almost forty years and may still drop in from time to time just to keep an eye on the place she loved. As for the ghostly cowboy who sometimes props up one end of the bar, no one knows who he was or why he returns. Is he the man whose heavy footsteps have been heard crossing the floor upstairs or pounding on the basement door? What about the phantom youngsters who have been heard running down the corridors? As former owner Jim Kuckler pointed out, the Joseph was a gathering place for the entire community, and tens of thousands of people must have made their way through its doors for well over a century. We'll probably never discover the identity of some of the ghosts.

Interestingly, my digital recorder captured two unknown voices while I was interviewing the staff and owners of the Iron Horse Saloon. One was a female voice that called faintly, "HellOOoo!" Dick Smith suggested that she could be Janet McDonald, who was known to greet people in that manner. The other voice was male. It said clearly and distinctly, "Jiggers." A "jigger" is a shot glass large enough to hold a single swallow of whiskey. "Oh, jiggers!" was also a common exclamation many years ago.

If the voice belongs to the ghostly cowboy who has been seen bellying up to the bar, perhaps all he wants is another drink. Make it a whiskey, please!

Downtown Forsyth still echoes to the whistles of approaching trains, just as it has for over a century. It's a pretty town, nestled along the banks of the Yellowstone River, and offers visitors the opportunity to camp, fish, go boating or hunt for prized moss agates. In season, hunters can seek game birds, antelope or deer. Why not drop in to the Iron Horse Saloon for a cold drink on a hot summer's day? The staff would be happy to share their ghostly experiences with you. If you catch a glimpse of a cowboy who props a booted foot up at the end of the bar before vanishing, consider yourself lucky. You've just met one of the ghosts of the historic Iron Horse Saloon. And if you'd like a great steak, stop in at the beautifully renovated Joseph Café, with an entrance on the side street.

GHOSTS IN THE STACKS

CHOUTEAU COUNTY LIBRARY
1578 Main Street
Fort Benton, Montana 59442
Telephone: 406-622-5222

Ghostly Activity Level: Moderate

HISTORY: The Chouteau County Library is a Carnegie library, one of hundreds funded by grants from the wealthy industrialist and philanthropist Andrew Carnegie in the early 1900s. The building was constructed around 1913-14 and a new addition, carefully designed to match the original, was built in 1992. The Chouteau County Library was the first county library in the state.

PHENOMENA: Ghostly activity has occurred in both sections of the library. Staff members have heard what sounds like invisible pages turning or someone bustling around the stacks when no one can be seen. A paranormal research group from Great Falls experienced a wide variety of phenomena when they investigated the haunting: cold spots, voices captured on tape, unexplained rapping noises, and objects that moved apparently by themselves.

During my thirty-four year career as a librarian, I heard many stories of haunted libraries. Some of the spirits are apparently dedicated library staff members who "checked out" a long, long time ago, or former patrons who enjoyed reading newspapers or doing crossword puzzles at their local library. Occasionally, a haunting may be related to events that occurred long ago on site. When I worked in the science department at the main branch of the Minneapolis Public Library, staff had many odd encounters in the sub-sub-basement. Books mysteriously toppled off shelving, temperatures would drop suddenly and as quickly recover, and several employees saw a booted male figure in a blue Civil War uniform. Oddly enough, he was visible only from the waist down. We finally discovered that the library had been built on the former site of a Civil War recruiting and training camp. The main library has since been demolished, and I can only hope that the spirit of the Union soldier has finally been released from duty.

The Green River Library in Wyoming is another example. The library was built on the site of a former cemetery. Apparently not all the bodies were removed before library construction began, and the spirits of those left behind are thought to be responsible for some of the well-documented disturbances inside.

When Michelle Heberle of M.A.P.S (the Montana Association for Paranormal Studies) told me that the Chouteau County Library in Fort Benton had been built on the former site of Native American campgrounds and that paranormal activity had been reported by staff, I wondered whether this might be a situation similar to that of the Green River Library. At the invitation of Library Director Jill Munson, I drove to Fort Benton in August 2009.

The library is a handsome sand-colored brick building, its rooms open and inviting. I was greeted by Library Director Jill Munson and her assistant librarian Debbie Wellman.

"I didn't know anything about a haunting until I worked my first night," Munson told me. "I felt like there was somebody over in the adult fiction section but there was no one there. When I mentioned it to the library director the next morning, she said, 'Oh yes, it always sounds like there's someone there. I've even gotten up from the circulation desk and gone over to the stacks because it sound like someone's going through the books or walking through the stacks.' And that's exactly what it sounded like to me,"

Munson continued. "I wasn't scared, it was just interesting. You really notice it more in the fall and winter when we're open evenings.

"A patron was on the computer one evening, and our library clerk was sitting here behind the desk. The patron looked up from the computer and asked, 'Are we the only two in here?'

"The clerk replied, 'Well, yes.' And the patron said, 'What is that sound back among the stacks? I know I heard something." They had both heard what sounded like footsteps or a book being put on the shelf.

"'Well, that's our spirit,' the clerk said. 'It's nothing to be afraid of, but that's what you're hearing.'

"Oddly enough," Munson said, "I've never felt anything strange in the old side, just the new side. I have a theory about that. There were Indian encampments all around the fort in the old days, and the Native Americans were not allowed in the fort after dark. They had to return to their camps at sunset. I think some of them were buried here. No bones were found when the new addition was built, just old bottles and such, but it's a possibility.

"When M.A.P.S came to investigate, they played some Native American music in the basement. It was night, and we had closed the curtains, so it was perfectly dark inside. They'd set up cameras that covered the room, and they came running up to tell me 'You've got to see this!' The cameras had captured unexplained lights flashing to the beat of the music. As soon as they shut the music off, the pulsating lights stopped. Then they played modern music, and there was no reaction at all."

Michele Heberle of M.A.P.S confirmed that her team had experienced unusual phenomena during their investigation of the library. They had brought along a Flir thermal imaging camera that detects temperature fluctuations and left the case on a chair in the Carnegie Room downstairs. Minutes into the investigation, the case slid off the chair. It was picked up and set back on the chair. Again it fell off and was replaced. An hour later, it fell off a third time. "We got a photo of a good-sized orb by this chair," Heberle stated. "Jill told us later that she had left a similar case on that chair all day and it never moved."

She also confirmed that they had gotten a reaction to the powwow music they had played in the children's room. "The thermal camera caught what looks like a figure dancing in time with the music. Then we played modern music, and it stopped. When I mentioned how authentic and beautiful the powwow music was, the recorder picked up a very faint 'Thank you'."

During the investigation, Heberle felt something touch her left shoulder. "It felt icy hot, and spread down my arm and up my head. I called Chris to bring the thermal camera over and my body temperature was about nine degrees hotter in these areas." When the team asked questions aloud, they heard knocking sounds in response. Some of the answers seemed to indicate the presence of a Native American spirit, perhaps someone who once camped on the site.

There may be a second spirit in the building as well. When Jill Munson unlocked the door of a small study room in the basement, I sensed an odd atmosphere in the room. It felt as though we had intruded on someone who had quickly gotten up from the table and retreated to a far corner. My impression was confirmed when Munson explained what had happened to her in that room one day. She had been doing paperwork at the table, door closed for privacy, when the room had suddenly turned icy cold. Although she opened the door to allow warm air into the room, it remained abnormally cold and she had finally gone back upstairs.

I had been taping the interview, and when I played the tape back the next day, I found that it had captured a whispery voice in the small room. Unfortunately, the words could not be made out. Next, we had gone to the Carnegie Room, where bound volumes of newspapers and magazines are stored. This was also the room where Michelle Heberle's camera case had repeatedly fallen from one of the old wooden chairs. I carefully ran my hand over the chair seat and found that it actually sloped backward, so it would have been almost impossible for the case to have fallen by itself from that chair.

While we were in the Carnegie Room, Munson mentioned that children liked to look through old newspapers to see what things cost many years ago, particularly cars and houses. At that point on the tape, the whispery voice broke in once more, but again the words were unintelligible.

We returned upstairs, and as I prepared to leave, we compared professional opinions on how busy modern libraries have become. "I've never had time to read a book at the library," Munson acknowledged with a laugh. Once again, our unseen listener interjected a comment, and this time the words were perfectly clear: "I read one." The voice sounded elderly and spoke unaccented English. If I had to put a gender to it, I would lean toward male, although that's just a guess.

So who roams the stacks of the Chouteau County Library? According to the evidence collected by the Montana Association for Paranormal Studies, one of the spirits seems to be that of a Native American. Another may be the spirit of an older person who loved to read. In either case, there's nothing to worry about. According to Jill Munson, "It's a good feeling, a playful feeling, nothing fearful at all."

Fort Benton is a historic river town that has been called the "Birthplace of Montana." Next time you're in the area, why not stop at the Grand Union Hotel for dinner or even an overnight stay in one of its haunted rooms? And do visit the Chouteau County Library. If you hear a rustling in the fiction stacks or hear a book topple over and no one's there, you may just have encountered one of the friendly spirits of Montana's oldest county library.

HOOFBEATS ON THE STAIRS

GRAND UNION HOTEL
Fort Benton, Montana 59442
Telephone: 406-622-1882
Website: www.grandunionhotel.com

Ghostly Activity Level: Moderate

HISTORY: Founded as an American Fur Company trading post in 1847, Fort Benton is known as the "birthplace of Montana." During the 1860s its location at the head of navigation on the Missouri River attracted thousands of miners on route to the new gold fields of Virginia City and Bannack. Saloons, brothels and hotels quickly sprang up along the muddy bank of the Missouri to supply the needs of the miners. Fort Benton soon gained a reputation as a violent and dangerous town. The Civil War was raging at the time and no soldiers could be spared for law enforcement on the frontier. Historian John Lepley writes in his Birthplace of Montana: A History of Fort Benton that over a ten-year period an average of three men per month were killed on a block that became known as the "bloodiest block in the west." Today, Fort Benton is peaceful, its once dangerous streets attracting tourists from all over the world, eager to explore a town with such a colorful history.

PHENOMENA: Footsteps have been heard in the upstairs corridor of a former hotel, the Choteau House. Doors open and close by themselves and objects have been mysteriously moved around. The phantoms of a woman and two small children have been seen crossing a church yard and residents of a house on the "hoodoo block" report hearing the sound of footsteps on the stairs. Guests at a historic hotel have seen blue lights darting across their room during the night, and housekeeping staff report that freshly-made beds are sometimes stripped by an invisible prankster. A paranormal investigative team recorded a variety of phenomena.

Fort Benton has just about everything: a picturesque location on the winding Missouri River, a magnificent historic hotel, a monument to a devoted dog whose lonely vigil captured hearts all over the world, a partially-restored fortified trading post, an unsolved mystery surrounding the disappearance in 1867 of acting governor Thomas Francis Meagher from a steamboat docked at the levee, and a violent past. The oldest part of town has also been designated a National Historic Landmark District.

I'd never heard of a haunting at Fort Benton, but with all that going for the town, there just *had* to be a phantom or two lurking in old buildings along Front Street or drifting along the levee at twilight. My query to the Fort Benton *River Press* brought a prompt response from ghost researcher Mary Doerk, and at her invitation I drove to Fort Benton with Frank and Sue on a mild October day to meet Mary and several other ladies who had each encountered something uncanny in the area.

Mary Doerk had arranged for us to visit the Choteau House, a former hotel just down the street from what used to be called "the bloodiest block in the west." The hotel was built as the Thwing House in 1868 by T.C. Power. When the gold rush ended around 1870, the hotel quartered military officers, who were rumored to smuggle ladies of the night up to their rooms. In 1879 the building was bought by Jere Sullivan, who changed its name to the Choteau House. With the passage of years the hotel could no longer attract enough guests to remain profitable. Eventually the building was abandoned. It stood vacant and slowly deteriorating until Sharalee Smith and her brother

Sherwin Smith bought it. They hope eventually to restore the building.

The hotel isn't quite as empty as it appears to be, however, because both Smith and her brother Sherwin have encountered the ghost of a woman they call "Belle" in the abandoned building.

"The hotel had been absolutely trashed," Sharalee told me. "The former owners had taken out all the furniture and piled mattresses in one room, and there was paper up to the ceilings in other rooms. We got a big dumpster and started shoveling things out of the original two-story section of the hotel. We'd leave the doors open so air could circulate through all the rooms and whenever we'd go back, the door of one room on the second floor would be shut. We finally started leaving it closed, and when we'd go back it would be open. That's when we really started to wonder what was going on.

"One day I moved most of the papers next to the door so next time I came I could take it out to the dumpster. When I came back the next weekend it was all back against the wall."

Her brother, Sherwin Smith, said, "I have heard Belle three times. Each time I was working on the second floor at the east end of the original part of the Choteau House. I would hear someone walking up the stairs from the front entrance and down the hall to the room, and then I would hear the door open and close.

"Every time this happened I thought it was Sharalee coming up to see what I was doing. I would call out but no one ever answered me. And when I stepped out into the hallway to see if it was Sharalee, no one was there. I think the ghost goes into the third room down the hall on the south side of the building. If we close the door to that room, the next time we go up the door will be open. If we leave the door open, the next time we go up it will be closed. The door to that room latches very securely so it can't pop open by itself."

Sharalee and her brother have no idea who the ghost may have been, but it seems more active when Sherwin is around, so they assume she was probably one of the "good time girls" who, according to local legend, offered all the comforts of home to lonely soldiers in the 1870s. They plan to disturb Belle's room as little as possible, for after such a lively career, Belle probably enjoys her privacy.

On the way back to the café where we had left our cars we visited the "hoodoo block," once the site of the log jail, a gallows, and a well. The gallows was where a shady character named Billy Hensel, who had persuaded the townsfolk to set him up as marshal, was hanged by a vigilance committee after he had been implicated in a number of robberies. That was just the beginning of a number of unfortunate events. The jail burned down not long afterward, killing three soldiers who had been locked up for drunkenness, and the bodies of several Indians who had been shot by townspeople were dumped down the well, which quickly became known as the Well of Death. It was eventually filled in and no one seems to know exactly where it was located.

One would assume that such a violent history would leave an unpleasant atmosphere, and indeed those who built on the "hoodoo block" in later years seemed to have nothing but bad luck. Homeowners died suddenly and buildings burned down or were blown down in storms. The bad luck has apparently run its course, but echoes from Fort Benton's past still reverberate in the area. Connie Jenkins, who owns one of the older homes on the block, told me that the entire family has heard footsteps going up the stairs to the second floor although no one is visible. Her son once saw the ghost of a woman in an old-fashioned long dress on the second floor. No one knows who she was.

We decided to stroll along the levee to look at the historic Baker House, where acting governor Thomas Francis Meagher dined not long before he mysteriously disappeared from the steamboat G. A. Thompson, which was moored at the levee across the street. Meagher was unwell and had gone to his cabin to rest, but about eleven o'clock that night a watchman heard a splash and a cry. Despite an extensive search, Meagher's body was never found. Meagher was known to be a heavy drinker, and there is considerable debate about whether he simply fell overboard or was pushed, perhaps by political enemies.

Does the ghost of General Thomas Francis Meagher haunt the

scene of his untimely death? Apparently he does not. There have been no reports of anyone encountering Meagher's ghost in the 140 years since his drowning. Nor has anyone reported the ghost of Fort Benton's famous sheepdog, Shep, whose master's body was sent back east to relatives after he died in 1936. For several years afterward Shep met every train, waiting patiently for his master to return. On a cold January day in 1942 the aging dog slipped and fell beneath a train, a sad end to a story that made headlines all over the world. Let's hope that he and his beloved master were joyfully reunited in the afterlife.

By the time we had taken several photos of Shep's monument in River Park, the shadows were beginning to lengthen. It was time for us to check in at the Grand Union Hotel, built in 1882 and now on the National Register of Historic Places.

We headed back to the hotel, outlined against the afterglow in the western sky. The autumn evening was cool and crisp, and as we strolled through River Park toward the hotel I thought the park had an uncanny resemblance to a Norman Rockwell scene, with its old-fashioned street lamps, huge cottonwood trees and heaps of fallen leaves. About halfway along the levee I paused, enjoying the heady scent of the river and wondering if this was the spot where Meagher had disappeared so long ago. As I gazed musingly at the black water, I saw ripples spread across the surface of the water a few yards from the bank. I knew that they were caused by fish coming to the surface to feed, but in the twilight I had the uncomfortable thought that a drowning man, groping toward the surface, would also create ripples like that.

I had heard a vague story about a cowhand who had tried to ride his horse up the hotel's main staircase long ago and been shot by the night manager. Supposedly the clatter of ghostly hoofs could sometimes be heard on the stairs, although as often happens I was unable to find eyewitnesses. Just in case there was something to the tale, I had booked a comfortable suite at the top of the main staircase.

We all slept peacefully that night at the Grand Union Hotel. Was the story of the cowboy who tried to ride his horse up the stairs a myth after all? Perhaps not; historian John Lepley has an undated article which states that the night manager at the Grand Union Hotel "took exception to a cowhand who insisted on riding his horse upstairs to his bedroom" in order to win a bar bet. Fourteen .44 caliber bullets supposedly struck the luckless cowhand, and there are still rumored to be bullet holes concealed in the walls near the staircase."

Not long afterward I received an e-mail from a woman who had worked as a housekeeper at the Grand Union. A number of eerie things had happened to her there. "I worked as a housekeeper there for several years during summer," she told me. "One day I was working with the head housekeeper and we were making up the beds in a room with two double beds. We finished making the bed nearest the door and then moved on to make the next bed in the room. We finished our work and turned around to leave the room and discovered the comforter and pillows had been flipped back on the first bed we had made. We are both absolutely sure that we had finished making the bed. It wasn't a creepy feeling, more like a funny ghost was pulling a gag on us.

"Also, one day I was working at the front desk at the hotel when I got a call from the kitchen. The chefs were talking with a food supplier on the phone. The supplier had driven by the hotel moments before and wanted to know what was going on at the Grand Union. He told the chefs that he could see people through the windows dressed in old costumes. He insisted that a man in costume was watching him from the window above the kitchen. I quickly ran upstairs to check the room but there was no one there. The supplier was insistent that a man 'in a war uniform' was looking out the window."

A pair of women guests also had an unusual experience one night, again in one of the second floor rooms. They told a waitress at a café the next morning that they had been awake all night, watching beautiful blue lights dance around their room. Neither woman felt the slightest fear, just a sense of awe.

In May 2008 owner Cheryl Gagnon invited the M.A.P.S, the

Montana Association of Paranormal Studies, to investigate the haunting at the hotel. M.A.P.S was founded by Michelle Heberle of Great Falls. She and her group had previously investigated a number of reputedly haunted locations in Great Falls.

Heberle and her team of eight brought infrared video cameras, a thermal imaging camera, tape recorders, EMF readers, and temperature probes. During the night several of the team had unusual experiences in the rest rooms, including the door's opening by itself, footsteps, an EMF meter going off and the urinal flushing by itself. No one was there.

The most astonishing occurrence happened in the saloon later that night. While changing batteries in one of the camcorders, a team member laid a flashlight down on the table.

"We asked the spirit to move the flashlight," Michelle Heberle said, "and the flashlight started moving. It rolled about halfway around the table, stopped in front of Chris for a few seconds then rolled all the way back to Kenny and sat there. Then it rolled to me, sat there for a while, and rolled around the table again. We called Heath down and after a while it started again. We decided to leave and as we were walking out of the room the tape recorder picked up a voice that said, 'I'm curious, I want to go with you.' We tried to manipulate the flashlight in the morning to see if we could replicate its actions but all it would do was roll off the table."

The team also took a number of photos of the outside of the hotel. One of them showed what appeared to be a figure at the women's parlor window on the second floor. Another showed what looked like a man in a long coat looking out of the window in Room 306.

In August 2009 I returned to the Grand Union with my friend Frank. This time we booked Room 202. A guest who had stayed there with his wife, a beautiful blond, had reported being pushed out of bed by an apparently jealous ghost! And the previous night, two sisters who had shared the room told owner Cheryl Gagnon that they had been kept up most of the night by men's voices, apparently coming from within their room. No one was visible.

Another guest who had stayed in that room saw a tall man wearing an old-fashioned frock coat and a stovepipe hat walk in even though the door was locked. He sat down on the sofa and stared at the television before vanishing. The guest, who was already in bed, felt no fear but was definitely annoyed that someone had walked into a room for which she had paid.

We had hopes that something would happen during the night, but the man in the top hat did not drop by for a visit. When we checked out, we mentioned the story to the desk clerk. Much to our delight, she was able to suggest a possible identity: her several-times great-uncle Charles Rowe! Mr. Rowe came to Fort Benton in the 1870s and opened the Overland Hotel. Later, he became manager of the Grand Union Hotel and lived there with his second wife and their four children from 1891 to 1899. Their apartment on the second floor probably included Room 202. Rowe died in 1902. He would, of course, have worn a top hat in the 1870s. Perhaps he returns briefly for a nostalgic visit to a place where he and his family were happy for so many years. If so, he must be pleased that this wonderful old hotel has been so lovingly restored by its owners, Jim and Cheryl Gagnon.

Be sure to stroll across the old bridge when you visit Fort Benton. You may startle a herd of mule deer in the bottoms on the far side or hear phantom footsteps that have been reported from time to time. Choteau House is not open to the public, but if you pause to look up at the second floor window that has a shade halfway lowered, perhaps you'll see the ghostly form of Belle smiling back at you. And if you enjoy historic hotels, do plan to stay or at least have dinner at the magnificent Grand Union Hotel. Maybe you'll be lucky enough to hear the clatter of hoofs on the main staircase.

LITTLE MARY

KRANZ FLOWERS AND GIFTS
1305 3rd Avenue South
Great Falls, Montana 59405
Telephone: 406-761-4141

Ghostly Activity Level: Moderate

HISTORY: In 1891, German immigrant Mathias Kranz established the Montana Floral Exchange where he and his family grew salad greens and vegetables for the commercial market. Crates of vegetables were shipped out by stagecoaches that made special stops at the business. Kranz, who learned his trade working for the landscape department of Imperial Germany, built the first hothouse in Great Falls and eventually had over 40,000 square feet under glass. The business was owned and run by the Kranz family from 1891 to 1992, when it was sold by Mathias' grandson Dale Kranz to current owners Doug and Rose Forbes.

PHENOMENA: A ninety-year-old player piano occasionally plays a couple of notes even when it's not turned on. A child's voice was heard during a paranormal investigation although no child was present. Strange shadows have been photographed in the attic above Charles Kranz's workshop. An unknown male voice was caught on audiotape in the basement where the floral design room was once located. EMF meters have detected unexplained fluctuating electromagnetic fields in the main greenhouse.

In my younger days, I spent several years working for florists, so when Michelle Heberle, co-founder of the Montana Association for Paranormal Studies, told me that M.A.P.S had done an investigation at an historic floral business in Great Falls, I was naturally interested. Not only does Kranz Flowers have ties to two of Great Falls' prominent businessmen, Mathias Kranz and his son Charles, but for fourteen years an elaborate Halloween "haunted house" was held on the premises to raise money for charity.

Ironically, Rose Forbes, co-owner of Kranz Flowers, and her employees had long suspected that the business really was haunted. Certain areas felt oddly uncomfortable to them at times, dark shadowy figures were glimpsed moving in an attic, and the beautiful antique player piano player occasionally played a few notes although it was not turned on. Curious to find out if one of the Kranzes might be keeping a spectral eye on the business, Forbes contacted the Montana Association for Paranormal Studies, and on August 12, 2008, a team of nine people led by Michelle Heberle held an investigation at the historic business.

The team set up cameras and other equipment to cover the office, storerooms, boiler room, floral design area, greenhouses, the break room upstairs, and the basement. Heberle then decided to try a new technique that uses music of different eras in the hope of attracting spirits.

Since Mathias Kranz was German, she began with a recording of Bach that she thought might appeal to him. "The Bach CD played fine," she said. After a few minutes, she switched to hardcore rock from the television show *Charmed*. "We asked if the spirit liked the music," she said. "As soon as we did, the music shut off and we could not get it to play again. We also got extreme electromagnetic field readings of between 7 and 10 in the area around the CD player and the temperature jumped back and forth between 84 and 90 degrees.

"In the back storeroom and tool area, our photos showed some strange shadows. Charles Kranz had his workshop there, and that's where Rose and her workers say they sometimes feel uncomfortable. Then we went upstairs to the rooms where the caretaker used to live. At the top of the stairs, I felt terrible chest pains. Rose then told me that the caretaker died of a heart attack up there.

While in the basement, two of our teams heard a child's voice. There was no child present. My group heard someone say "help" in approximately the same area. When Rose went out in the main green house, she heard what sounded like an old time wooden screen door closing.

"We also got pictures of what looks like a head poking up from behind the planter near the piano that we were told plays by itself every once in a while. And we got video of three very bright lights or orbs that appear to be about dessert-plate size."

After reading Heberle's report, I asked her to set up a meeting with the owners of Kranz Flowers, and on a hot August afternoon Michelle, her husband Chris, my friend Frank and I met with Rose Forbe's daughter Crystal. We were given a tour of the extensive property, including the main greenhouse, workshop, the former floral design room in the basement plus the groundskeeper's living quarters upstairs. Both the basement and the upper floor had been elaborately staged for Kranz's much-anticipated Halloween haunted house. In 2008 this popular event attracted almost 18,000 people and raised thousands of dollars for charity.

We had agreed that it might be worth trying to communicate in German with Mathias Kranz, if it were indeed he who haunted the place, so I dredged up what I could recall from my college German courses.

"Who are you?" I asked in various locations. "Why are you here?" We listened intently, but there was no reply. Then, since Heberle's team had reported hearing a child's voice during the previous investigation, I asked, "How old are you?" Again, we heard nothing, but hoped that our tape and digital recorders had captured a ghostly reply.

Meanwhile, Michelle had picked up high electromagnetic field readings near some benches that had just been installed in the main greenhouse. We checked nearby outlets but they did not appear to be the source. Paranormal activity often picks up during construction or demolition, perhaps because spirits seem to dislike change, so I asked in German, "Is anyone here with us today?" Immediately I felt a strong tingling sensation at the top of my head, as if I were standing in a strong electromagnetic field. At the same time, Michelle's EMF meter spiked.

"It seems to like you," she commented. We followed Crystal back to Charles Kranz's old workshop, and the tingling feeling followed us all the way.

The workshop area had a heavy atmosphere. "You get the feeling you're not welcome here," Crystal told us. "Charlie spent nineteen hours a day back here. He built the greenhouse benches by hand. He was always building something. He's not happy with us being back here." She glanced around uneasily. "I won't come back here at night."

On a sudden impulse, I spoke aloud to the presumed spirit of Charles Kranz, apologizing for the intrusion into his private space and promising that we wouldn't be there for long. The oppressive atmosphere seemed to lighten, although that may have been my imagination. Or perhaps the spirit of Charles Kranz had been mollified by my apology.

Mathias Kranz and his wife had four children, two of whom died in infancy. One of them, Mary, is thought to be the little girl whose voice was heard during the investigation by M.A.P.S. Now, standing in the workshop, we all felt the air temperature drop. At first we attributed it to air currents flowing down a nearby ramp, but then the EMF meter began to react to something. Michelle Heberle decided to repeat an experiment she had done during the investigation and invited "Mary" to show us that she could count.

"What comes after five, Mary?" Heberle coaxed. The EMF meter edged up to six, then seven, eight and nine. When Heberle asked the spirit to count backward, the EMF meter hesitantly dropped. It was as though we were watching a very young child struggling to recall numbers.

Next, we followed Crystal down narrow stairs to the basement, which had already been set up for the annual "haunted house." The room where Charles' flower designers had worked was cramped, with no windows, and smelled faintly musty.

"This is where Charlie made them design flowers," Crystal told us. "Most of our employees won't come down here anymore."

I looked around, imaging what it must have been like to work down there day after day, and said faintly, "Oh my."

When I played the audiotape back the next day, it was obvious that we had not been alone in the basement. At the point where I had said, "Oh my," a light male voice commented, "Yes, this is where they..." The rest of his words could not be made out. The voice had no German accent, so presumably was not that of Mathias Kranz. Could Charles Kranz, relieved that we were no longer in his private workshop and curious about us, have followed us down to his old floral design room? M.A.P.S hopes to investigate the basement again in the future, so perhaps they'll be able to find out.

Kranz Floral has recently been sold and the Halloween "Haunted House" is no longer being held at this location. You might drop into the Lobby Bar instead. Perhaps you'll see their ghostly "lady in red" reflected in the bar mirror. Or you could have supper at the popular Tracy's Restaurant downtown, where the late owner, Mr. Tracy, still makes an occasional appearance wearing his favorite blue sweater.s

THE COWBOY IN THE WINDOW

LOBBY BAR
518 Central Avenue
Great Falls, Montana 59401
Telephone: 406-453-1727

Ghostly Activity Level: High

HISTORY: The Davenport Hotel was built in 1914 by J.G. Anthony. During Prohibition it is rumored to have become a speakeasy and brothel. On November 17, 1925, a fire destroyed part of the hotel. Although the newspapers reported that the fire started on the roof and caused little damage, legend has it that several of the "working girls" died in the flames. Charred wood is still visible near a stairway on the second floor. In 1937 the hotel became home to the famous Jockey Club and its jazz musicians. Longtime residents of Great Falls recall visiting a brothel on the upper floor as recently as the 1960s and '70s. The upper floors are currently vacant but the Lobby Bar takes up most of the main floor.

PHENOMENA: The sound of booted footsteps has been heard on the second floor where the figure of a man in a red plaid shirt and cowboy hat is often seen looking down from a window. The scent of a delicate perfume is associated with the ghost of a woman in a pink 1930s gown, and an elderly lady in a red hat has been encountered in one of the bathrooms. At times the odor of smoke or wood ash has been noted on the second floor. The screams of a number of women were captured on audiotape by a member of the Montana Association of Paranormal Studies. Security cameras have caught bottles of liquor jumping out of the cabinet.

The Lobby Bar offers everything a hopeful paranormal investigator could ask for: a lively history, a dash of mystery and plenty of ghosts. Erected just before World War I as the upscale Davenport Hotel, the bar attracts unconfirmed rumors of a connection with Prohibition-era bootleggers . More substantial is the story of a suspicious fire in 1925 that may have killed a number of prostitutes who had rooms on the second floor. The hotel probably reached the height of its fame in the 1940s when a nightspot called the Jockey Club attracted patrons from far and near to enjoy hot jazz music. Eventually, as happens with most aging downtown hotels, business dropped off and the upper floors were divided into low-rent apartments. Now the building stands forlorn and empty except for the Lobby Bar and the ghosts of its lively past.

Paranormal activity has been observed on all floors including the basement, but since only the bar and the casino are open these days, most of the reports come from those areas.

On October 22, 2007, an article entitled "Ghosts in Lobby Bar building? Many say yes!" was published in the *Great Falls Tribune*. Reporter Richard Eke interviewed several employees about their eerie experiences in the bar. Among the phenomena they had sensed were the sound of booted footsteps in an empty corridor; the scent of a delightful perfume in the vacant lobby, and apparitions of a man in a white baseball cap, an elderly lady in the bathroom, a man wearing a pinstriped suit and fedora who is thought to be a an early owner, and a man in a cowboy hat who stands looking out from an upstairs window.

All this sounded simply too good to pass up, so I contacted Michelle Heberle of M.A.P.S, the Montana Association of Paranormal Studies. Michelle and her team had spent months investigating the old building and they invited me to join them on an investigation.

Among the pieces of equipment that MAPS brought along

that evening was a thermal camera, capable of providing visual evidence of temperature changes. Warm temperatures registered as red on the screen, while colder temperatures registered as blue. I'd never seen one in use and looked forward to whatever it might reveal.

Our investigation began in the basement and then moved to the upper floors. The hotel's grand staircase with its skylights and beautiful woods was still impressive, although the rooms that must once have echoed to the tap-tap of ladies' high-buttoned shoes were now dusty and choked with broken furniture. Heberle pointed out a room in which her team had seen a chandelier swinging by itself. After it came to a stop, they tried to reproduce its movement by jumping up and down on the floor above, but couldn't make the chandelier swing again. They also saw the shadow of a hangman's noose move rapidly across the wall in the same room. Both phenomena were caught on videotape.

In another room, half-burned floor beams from the fire in 1925 were still visible. I touched one of the exposed beams, and for just a few seconds I caught the stench of charred wood before it faded away. Psychic odors are among the most commonly reported phenomena in haunted places, although not everyone in a group will notice them. The chilling screams of several women had been recorded in the same room during a previous investigation, supporting the so-far unsubstantiated story that a number of prostitutes had died in the fire.

Heberle then led the group to a room at the end of the corridor where EMF meters sometimes indicated electromagnetic activity. As we entered, four of us heard what seemed to be a child's whimper. Back out in the hallway, Heberle, team member Wendy and I compared notes on what we had heard. Suddenly the temperature seemed to plummet, although our thermometers did not register the drop. At that moment Wendy said that she felt someone touching her hair. I backed off a few steps and took two Polaroid photos of the two women. The first photo showed an inexplicable fog enveloping Wendy's head. The second photo looked normal.

The cold seemed to move off down the hallway, so another

team member scanned the hallway with the thermal imaging camera. *The camera clearly showed a human figure in the hallway. No one was visible to the eye.*

By then we were all getting chilled and tired, so we went downstairs to the lounge to unwind. Alan Watts, a swamper, or custodian, had just come on duty, and readily agreed to tell me about his experiences in the building. Watts has worked at the Lobby Bar for seven years, and has no doubt the building is haunted. As he put it, "I've seen 'em, heard 'em, smelled 'em, and had one of 'em touch me."

Watts believes there are several ghosts: two former Lobby Bar patrons named George; the ghost of a man in a 1930's fedora and dark blue suit who is thought to be a Mr. Peterson, owner of the Jockey Club and the Lobby Café & Bar in the late 1930's; a cowboy with a black hat and red-and-black plaid shirt, an old woman wearing a red hat who has been seen in the ladies rest room, and another older woman wearing a beaded 1930s dress who leaves behind a delightful fragrance.

"We've seen George Mullen here at Christmas when this place is busy," Watts told me. "He'll be right in the middle of the crowd. He wears a white baseball cap. Then the other George, George Washington, he likes to watch cowboy movies. Sometimes he messes with the bar stools.

"Mr. Peterson—the first time I saw him I was sitting here reading a book and drinking coffee. I and the bartender were the only ones here. I looked up and saw him clear as hell in the mirror. I said to the bartender Celeste, 'Who the hell was that?' and she said, 'Probably one of our ghosts.' He was dressed like you see in one of those old movies, a dark blue pin-striped suit and a fedora. When I turned around, he was gone. He looked real solid, just like a real person, just staring into the mirror about halfway down the bar by the cash register.

"There's an old cowboy up on the third floor at the east window. The only time I've ever seen him has been around two or three in the afternoon. First time I saw him, I came in and asked if there's anyone upstairs. They said no, so I grabbed a baseball bat and flashlight and went up. I couldn't see any footprints in the dust, but I looked in all the rooms and there wasn't anybody up there. He wears a red and black shirt, check or plaid, a black cowboy hat, large rectangular belt with a cowboy buckle. He looked like he was in his late fifties or early sixties, a lean cowboy look. He shows up every couple of months. The third floor used to have low-rent apartments. Maybe the cowboy died up there and doesn't know he's dead.

"One night Lisa was tending bar, and we were clear down at the other end, standing there talking, when we heard a thud. We were the only two people in the building. I looked back and saw one of the wine bottles had come out of its rack and was lying there on the bar counter. It couldn't have slid out of that rack by itself. Then three Saturday nights in a row I went to grab the dust pan and little broom from under the far sink and found a bottle of Jack Daniels sitting there. Nobody would admit to putting it there. On the fourth Saturday night I found a bottle of O'Doule's sitting there, and then it quit. Maybe the ghost didn't like the non-alcoholic stuff.

"Another night I saw a chunky older woman standing in the doorway in a real light blue dress with beading on it, mid-'30s–style blue hat. Then she just walked away. Twice I've smelled the nicest perfume in the hallway. I've even asked her what her brand of perfume was, because it was really nice, but she never answered.

"Another time I was cleaning the bathroom and I heard water running in the sink. I checked both stools, no water running. I was sitting right at the faucet and could hear it running. I ran my hand under it, no water, and then it just quit."

Nothing was visible to Watts on that occasion, but the ghost of an elderly lady wearing a red hat had been previously seen washing her hands in that very bathroom. She was later identified by another patron as a Mrs. Schroeder, a retired teacher from Fort Benton who often visited the Lobby Bar and was renowned for her hats. Perhaps the sound of water running was an echo from the past.

"At closing time," Watts continued, "we check all the doors

and make sure nobody's hiding. I've been here at night alone and heard someone walking down the hall upstairs wearing cowboy boots. First time I grabbed a key and went upstairs and there were no footprints down that hallway. A couple times I've been down the basement 'bout 2:30, 3 A.M. and the lights went off. It made me madder than hell, so I made my way up and found the light switch at the top's been turned off, the circuit breaker had been turned off, and I could smell Old Spice. Same thing happened to another cleaner. It might be the guy who owned this when it was All Sports. His storage area was in the basement, and he wore Old Spice. He might be the one who turned the lights off."

I asked Watts, who has a degree in computer engineering, whether he had an explanation for the haunting at the Lobby Bar. "The ghosts might be in a different dimension," he offered, "and bump into ours once in a while." But whatever the explanation, he isn't afraid of them. "They're harmless," he said as I thanked him and prepared to leave. "They don't hurt anything. In fact, to me they're kind of entertaining."

Paranormal activity continues: on Halloween night, 2008, M.A.P.S. held a ghost hunt at the Lobby Bar to help raise funds to restore the building. Hundreds of people toured the upper floors, usually off limits to the public, and several of them reported being touched or grabbed by an invisible presence. An inexplicable dark shadow also appeared in many photos. And in January 2009, when Michelle Heberle and two others were standing in a room on the third floor, they heard what sounded like a door opening. When they went out into the hallway, they saw that the door leading onto the fire escape was open.

"The cold air outside looked like an eerie movie effect coming through the opening," Heberle recalls. "A few seconds later it quit, probably because the temperature in the corridor had dropped to the same temperature as the outside air. There were no footprints in the fresh snow on the fire escape. The door was only open about three inches so no one went out. When we told Al, he said 'You are kidding me! Those doors are sealed!'"

The Lobby Bar truly deserves a "high" Ghostly Activity Rating. Paranormal activity occurs randomly but fairly frequently on all floors. Although the bar is the only floor open to the public except by special arrangement, you have a good chance of experiencing something eerie here. Bring your camera and tape recorder! And you may want to contact M.A.P.S. at www.montanaparanormal.com to find out about future tours of the building.

THE PERSNICKETY GHOST

NAPOLITANI'S RISTORANTE
315 South 3rd Street
Hamilton, Montana 59840
Telephone: 406-375-2307

Ghostly Activity Level: Moderate

HISTORY: The two-story house was built in 1909 by Grace E. Johnson, who served as Ravalli County Treasurer from 1916 until the 1930s. She lived there until her death in 1956. The house was then purchased by Mona Thompson, a former schoolteacher who died June 11, 1977. The historic home was purchased by Lynne and Mike Morris in 2002. It has been renovated and is now a fine Italian restaurant.

PHENOMENA: Objects have been moved, limping footsteps have been heard crossing the upstairs rooms, and the odor of freshly-popped corn has been noted at times even though no one has made popcorn. The present owners have caught glimpses of the ghost, thought to be Mona Thompson, several times. The strong odor of cigarette smoke has at times been noticed indoors, although the building is a "smoke free" environment.

I first became aware of a haunting at the Napolitani when I discovered an article by Stacie Duce in the *Ravalli Republic* published on Oct. 31, 2007. According to the article, the ghost is

Mona Thompson, a former owner of the historic house. Although Thompson was active in many community groups, those who knew her recalled that she had a reputation as a "persnickety" housekeeper who never allowed visitors inside and always cooked in a cottage behind the house because she didn't want cooking odors in the main house. Not surprisingly, this strong-willed and house-proud spirit did not take kindly at first to a busy restaurant on the main floor of her former home. Current owner Lynne Morris described the ghost's reaction succinctly: *"She was not pleased."*

Lynne and Mike Morris realized they were sharing the house with someone they couldn't see shortly after they closed the deal.

"We heard someone upstairs," Lynne Morris was quoted as saying, *"and my husband ran up the front staircase and my daughter ran up the back steps... We completely expected to catch a thief. There was no one there. Although it was cold inside, they could smell popcorn. My husband was always skeptical of ghosts, but it made a believer of him."*

Morris went on to state the ghost's displeasure with the remodeling was displayed in various ways. One morning Morris's daughter Ericka, the restaurant's chef, came in to find that all her cookbooks had been knocked off the shelves, and the newest cookbook had somehow been stuffed into the bowl of her bread mixer. When she was really annoyed, Mona would hit ladles in the kitchen or cause the pans to swing as she flitted past. Occasionally Lynne or Ericka would catch a glimpse of her, usually looking like a "wisp of fog" in the library where she had been married.

Lynne Morris told the reporter that the ghostly activity quieted down once the remodeling was completed. She said she still heard Mona's footsteps upstairs at times, but felt that Mona was pleased that the house and the grounds were once more in pristine condition.

My friend Pat and I both enjoy Italian cuisine, so when we pulled into Hamilton in early September we immediately made reservations at the Napolitani. We'd driven from Glacier Park that morning and were really looking forward to a tasty dinner in pleasant surroundings. Perhaps we might even catch a glimpse of what Ericka had described in the newspaper article as a "wisp of fog" in the library!

The two-story white house sits in a pleasantly tree-lined neighborhood, surrounded by a white picket fence and rose gardens. The flowers seemed to glow in the soft light of evening as we walked up to the house, and I could make out two women sitting in wicker chairs on the porch, quietly talking. They introduced themselves as chef Ericka and a friend. The usually bustling restaurant had emptied out as locals headed for the Friday night high school football game, so the staff had taken a few minutes' break while waiting for us to arrive. Pat and I would have the entire restaurant, its staff, and its ghosts, all to ourselves for the rest of the evening!

We were greeted inside by Jeff Olson, who is the restaurant's host and also a cousin of the owners. I noticed that Pat seemed distracted and kept looking up the staircase before Olson led us to a brightly-painted room with large windows overlooking the street. The house felt warm and comfortable, more like a family home than a restaurant, an impression strengthened by the family photographs displayed on the walls and on mantles above the fireplaces. As he handed us menus, Olson told us that although he has yet to see or hear Mona, he had felt her presence a couple of times.

"When we had a laundry upstairs," he admitted, "at times the hair just stood up at the back of my neck." He thought it added a unique aspect to the house and couldn't imagine it being unpleasant or scary in any way for the diners.

Olson told us that occasionally someone who is psychically sensitive comes to visit. One young woman who had been aware of spirits all her life promptly began to describe a woman whom she "saw" standing at the foot of the stairs. The description matched that of Mona Thompson.

"She also said that the woman's husband was standing at the end of the fireplace," Olson continued. "She said Mona was happy that Lynne and Mike had bought the place. Mona liked Ericka too, but felt that the restaurant was open too late in the evening, when she should be resting. We're open only at night, and it kind of bothers her."

According to the young lady, Mona also appeared very concerned about her house.

"Mona was not very social," Olson said. "She didn't like children, and everything had to be 'just so' in her home. She even made her husband stay in the carriage house because she didn't want him messing up her house. She was very attached or bonded to her home. Mona's probably comfortable with me because I'm always cleaning and taking care of her house."

I wavered between ordering the wood-fired pizza or Ericka's special lasagna before deciding in favor of the lasagna. As soon as our meals had been served, Ericka hung the "Closed" sign on the restaurant's door and she and Jeff seated themselves at the next table and began to tell us about their experiences with Mona's ghost.

"Mom always talks to Mona," Ericka said. "Right from the beginning she told her 'We're not going to hurt you, we're not going to hurt your building. We're here to be with you.' Sometimes we hear footsteps from upstairs. They are very distinctive, limping footsteps. Mom thinks Mona must have hurt her foot somehow. But that's not all we've heard. One day Mom was scraping wallpaper in the stairwell and she could hear music like from the *Titanic* days coming from upstairs. There wasn't a radio on anywhere. Mom sang along with it. She feels really close to Mona. We all try to acknowledge her and show her respect, and she's been very nice to us."

Ericka gestured around the room where we sat, with its fireplace, beautiful woodwork and long windows. "This was the library at one time," she said. "This whole wall was full of books. Mona got married in here. This is where she and her husband would dance. When I see her in here, I see her dancing. She'd look like wisps of cigarette smoke. I used to do a lot of the ringing up at night. I'd ring up the tickets and I'd look up and see her go by. When she gets mad, she'll go by and hit the ladles in the kitchen, or she'll swing the pots and pans."

"My daughter Isabella loves to take a nap on the staircase," Ericka said. "In the summer, it's the coolest spot in the house. One day I had two people come, and the lady looked up the staircase and said, 'Hi, Mona, how are you? How do you like Ericka?' She said Mona replied, "I like Ericka and I love her daughter, I help her with everything.'"

Pat had been listening intently, and I saw her nod as if the association of the staircase with Mona had confirmed her own impressions when we first arrived. She told me later that she had strongly sensed a female presence surveying us from the landing and was pleased to know that others had also sensed Mona on or at the foot of the stairs.

Mona wasn't always so welcoming to children, even though she had four of her own. Ericka said that one of Mona's granddaughters came to visit one day and told her that she used to play with one of the boys down the street. He picked a rose from Mona's garden to give to his mother on his parents' anniversary, and Mona forbade him to walk on the sidewalk after that!

Apparently Mona isn't the only ghost who haunts the property. Her husband Lloyd, who wasn't allowed to smoke in the house, has been seen in the carriage house.

"I looked toward the carriage house one day," Ericka said, "and I saw a man with a bald head sitting at a table. We all went running out there but of course no one was there."

"Did he react to you at all?" I asked curiously, a forkful of Ericka's excellent lasagna momentarily forgotten. Some ghosts are intelligent entities that react to the observer, while others are considered residual energies, and do not react to living persons.

"He saw me," Ericka said with certainty. "He followed me with his eyes. Mona made her husband stay in the carriage house. She didn't want him smoking in the house or messing it up. One day, though, the smell of cigarette smoke was so strong inside the house that it was in my face while I was trying to cook. This is a smoke-free building."

I had to smother a grin at the thought of Lloyd Thompson, who was not permitted to smoke in the house during his lifetime, now gently teasing his wife by filling the house with the forbidden odor of tobacco smoke!

Mona was left a widow when her husband died twelve days after a brutal beating by a man he had hired to cut firewood at his ranch near Hamilton. The *Helena Daily Independent* of November 24, 1934, described him as a *"famous hunter, widely known in Montana as a predatory animal hunter for the Biological Survey. His death came shortly before he had been scheduled to leave for Tibet, where he hoped to capture Chinese bears for American zoos."* He was only 41.

Unfinished business is said to be one of the reasons spirits linger, and Lloyd Thompson certainly had plenty of business yet to finish before his unexpected death. Perhaps that's why he has been seen and sensed, standing beside the fireplace in the room where he and Mona had been married.

Much later, Pat and I settled back with a sigh of contentment over coffee. Ericka had definitely inherited, along with her recipes, her great-grandmother's talent for cooking! Now it was time to return to our hotel. We made our farewells, with promises to return, and left.

Halfway down the walk, I couldn't resist turning and gazing up at the darkened second floor windows. I saw no one, but nodded politely anyway, just in case Mona Thompson was standing there watching. Courtesy is always appreciated, especially with a woman known to be "persnickety" during her lifetime—and her afterlife as well.

If you enjoy wonderful Italian food, why not make reservations at Napolitani's Ristorante the next time you visit Hamilton? And you may want to stop in at the Ravalli County Museum, formerly the courthouse, just across the street. It's rumored to be haunted.

THE FLIRTACIOUS COWBOY

WINDBAG SALOON & EATERY
19 South Last Chance Gulch
Helena, Montana 59601
Telephone: 406-443-9669

Ghostly Activity Level: Low

HISTORY: This historic building dates back to 1882. It was once connected to the old St. Louis Hotel on Jackson Street and is still known as the St. Louis Block. Over the years the colorful Italianate-style building has reputedly housed a boot store, bank, a vaudeville house, a motion picture theater, a bowling alley, several bars and a furniture store. Upstairs were the apartments known as "Dorothy's Rooms," home to Helena's last madam, "Big Dorothy" Baker, until she died on May 14, 1973. The Windbag Saloon was established in 1978 and currently occupies the main floor. The stone walls and tin ceilings are original.

PHENOMENA: Doors sometimes open by themselves, the stereo changes stations by itself, lights turn on by themselves, and staff members occasionally see "something" pass by. The apparition of a smiling cowboy was seen by a female guest.

The Windbag Saloon is located on Helena's famous Last Chance Gulch just across from a historic street car. Known for its tasty food, the Windbag is a clean, smokeless bar and restaurant that is usually crowded with locals and tourists. The Windbag's name comes from a jocular reference to the "hot air" from legislative doings on Capitol Hill, and it's still the haunt of politicians—and perhaps "Big Dorothy" herself—to this day.

Frank and I dropped in at the Windbag on a warm summer afternoon for a cold soft drink and to take advantage of a lull in business to question the bartender about the Windbag's rumored ghosts.

The bartender had worked at the Windbag for only a short time, so he asked one of the cooks to come out to talk with us instead. I'll just call him "Cook," since he preferred to remain anonymous. Cook told us he had worked at the Windbag for eighteen years and believed the place probably was haunted.

"I always come in through the same door when I come in the morning," he said. "Anyway, I was looking at the paper at the end of the bar with my back to the door. I'm the only one in here. All of a sudden that middle door opens up and closes and there was nobody there. The front door was locked.

"I've had the channel changed on the stereo too," Cook continued. "One day the stereo went out, so I came out here to see what was going on with it. It had been turned off. When I turned it back on, the channel was changed to classical music and the volume was turned all the way up. I've had the ghost turn on lights that weren't on. Mostly it happens when you're in here by yourself. Sometimes you'll see things go by from the corner of your eye but nothing's there.

"A while ago we had a lady who was sitting in the dining room with her husband. She was facing one way and her husband the other way. She said she saw a cowboy dressed up with bandanna and chaps, and he tipped his hat at her. He just kept staring at her. She told her husband, 'That guy keeps staring at me.' He turned around and looked, and there was nobody there. She could see him, but her husband couldn't."

The bartender had been listening while Cook spoke, and now he volunteered one of his own experiences. "We lock the door in the restaurant side at closing so you can get out but not in again. Employees leave by that door. There are rows of extra chairs nearby. Well, one night I grabbed the till, put it in the safe, locked the safe, punched out, walked back here and a chair was placed against the door. There was a kid in the kitchen, but he'd have had to sprint down and back and I'd have seen him when I punched out."

The cowboy isn't the only spirit to linger in these surroundings. According to ladies who work on the upper floor, once home to "Big Dorothy" Baker, ghostly voices are sometimes heard. They are thought to be the voices of the "working girls" that lived in Big Dorothy's Rooms.

According to a file at the Montana Historical Society Library, Dorothy Baker was born Dorothy Putnam in 1916. Her photo in a 1933 Great Falls High School yearbook has a handwritten notation: "Don't tell" that is signed, "Dorothy." Her activities immediately after graduation are unknown, but eventually she went to work for Helena madam Ida Levy under the name Dorothy Baker. She died in a Great Falls hospital at the age of 57, possibly of complications from diabetes, although one report mentions a brain hemorrhage. Dorothy, who gained the nickname "Big Dorothy" for her bulk, was well respected during her lifetime. City Commissioner Ed Loranz was outraged when Dorothy's establishment was raided and closed down. "She's always been a fine woman. She was always doing something for somebody. She'd lend you money. She'd tip the police off to drug pushers."

Dorothy was described as a short, round, grandmotherly woman with a pleasant face, very polite and genial. She occasionally bought rounds for customers of some of Helena's livelier bars, and was always treated with utmost respect. By the time she died in 1973, she was a Helena icon.

Her place was described by police as "plush." According to an article on May 14, 1973 in the *Rocky Mountain News*, the house had five sitting rooms and seven beds. "One of the rooms is about 18 foot by 18 foot, red carpet on the floor, king-size bed with red velvet covers, and red wallpaper on the walls. Another room is a nice blue. The whole place is like that. And it is constructed so that when one customer came in he'd never know anybody else was there."

Does Dorothy's spirit occasionally return to the building where she spent so many years? Lance M. Foster, founder of Helena's walking ghost tours and host of the Yahoo group paranormal montana, held an investigation with a friend at the Windbag one night in May of 2008 to find out. Here's his account:

"The night was long," Foster began. "People kept coming in and the bar stayed open until almost midnight although it usually closes at ten. We talked to the staff, and everyone seemed to believe the place was haunted. They don't like to use the rest rooms, and the women will often use the men's rest room because they feel more uneasy in the women's room. One morning a man heard a furious loud knocking at the back door and went over and opened it, but no one was there. They also don't like to go downstairs, and some refused to.

"When the saloon finally closed, it was just the two of us in the darkened bar. The night cleaning crew were mostly in the back kitchen but occasionally came out to talk with us. They have had a lot of experiences and don't like to leave the lit areas to go into the main bar area. They said if you sit at the bar and look in the mirror behind the bar, you will often see movement behind you.

"We went downstairs and took photos but nothing showed up. There had been reports of mysterious winds from the staff but we located some old pipes set in the walls that allowed for a cross breeze so we figured that was the cause. The tales of chains and shackles were only urban myth. There are two separate basements, one under the restaurant and one under the bar. Both are eerie and old, with remnants of décor, flooring, and electrical elements and evidence of water damage. There are entrances to the old tunnels under the mall, but they had mostly collapsed, although there were some spaces between the rubble and you could sometimes hear sounds of water dripping or small movements, perhaps rodents, in the dark.

"Dorothy's photo hangs on the back wall of the bar, along with newspaper clippings telling her tragic story. I talked to Dorothy, hoping for some kind of response that could later be heard as EVP (electronic voice phenomena) on the tape. I commiserated with her unfortunate situation, an aging lady evicted from her home by the moralistic crusaders of the 1970s. Both of us heard a sudden bump on the floor in the main bar. We didn't pick anything up on the tape recorder, although you could hear us say 'What was that?' We did get a few odd EMF (electromagnetic field) fluctuations, one of which seemed to move as we were using the meter.

"While I was sitting at the table behind the bar, I saw the silhouette of someone walking outside about five feet from the front door. It was about 2 A.M. and raining. The person walked very slowly and carefully north, as if they were old or drunk. I walked over to the front door and looked out on the mall, but didn't see anyone out there.

"We did not investigate the upper rooms where Dorothy actually lived, as they are rented separately by other businesses. However, I was told by several people that they had heard soft music and female laughter up there, and the scent of perfume could be detected sometimes. Supposedly there is one bathroom that remains just as she left it, decorated in her individualistic and colorful style

"When my family came to Helena in 1966, we were looking for a place to live. My mom called a place called "Dorothy's Rooms," thinking that it was a boarding house. Dorothy told her, "Oh, honey, this ain't the kind of place you want your family staying at." Everyone I talked to had nothing but nice things to say about her and how it was a real tragedy that Helena officials in 1973 decided there was no place for the likes of Dorothy in the bright new future they envisioned for downtown Helena. It seems Dorothy might have had the last laugh though, because the Windbag is really the only consistently lively place in that downtown block."

The Windbag is always busy in the evenings, so if you'd like to try your luck at spotting a ghost, you may want to drop by for lunch. If your female companion suddenly leans forward to tell you about a man in full cowboy rig who is watching her with a twinkle in his eye, turn

quickly. You might just catch a glimpse of the phantom that hasn't lost his taste for flirtation even though he's been dead for many years. And who knows—you may even catch the fleeting scent of a lovely perfume and know that, in some other time or dimension, "Big Dorothy" Baker is home again.

SOMEONE'S IN THE KITCHEN!

YOGO INN
211 East Main
Lewistown, Montana 59457
Telephone: 406-535-8721
Webpage: www.yogoinn.com

Ghostly Activity Level: Moderate

HISTORY: The opening of the new Milwaukee Train Depot in 1910 raised community hopes that the Lewistown route would eventually become a main line. After World War II, however, passenger traffic began to decline and in 1956 the line ceased operation. The depot stood empty for several years and would probably have been demolished if it hadn't been for two hotel fires in the 1950s that left Lewistown with a shortage of rentable rooms. A new hotel was definitely needed, and it was decided to incorporate the historic depot, with its beautiful beamed ceilings, into the new building. Named after the world-famous Yogo sapphires mined nearby, the Yogo Inn opened in 1962 with 120 rooms, several conference rooms, an enclosed courtyard and an indoor pool. The depot's waiting room, the former crew quarters and the original kitchen were renovated and are still in use today.

PHENOMENA: Several employees of the Yogo Inn have witnessed pots flying off shelves in the kitchen, and a housemaid making up rooms in the historic crew quarters saw a woman wearing a long, old-fashioned dress in the corridor near the now-vanished stairway that once led down to the waiting room. Telephones sometimes ring repeatedly with no one on the other end, and a night auditor working at the front desk witnessed the heavy key drawer open by itself with a loud jangling noise.

Several years ago, a former employee of the Yogo Inn approached me after one of my Halloween talks and told me that she had witnessed "things flying around the kitchen" at the inn. I added the story to my files but it wasn't until August 2009 that my friend Frank and I were able to get to Lewistown, where we checked into the Yogo for a two-night stay. Sure enough, one of the Yogo's brochures mentioned a ghost: *Searching for something mysterious? How about a stay in one of our former conductor rooms where "Bob," one of our "unexplained guests," might visit you. He is known to frequent the old depot or walk through the kitchen turning water on or tossing pots and pans around. You might try your luck at getting a photograph of "Bob."*

That afternoon I interviewed several staff members who had encountered "Bob." Craig, the head cook, has worked for the Yogo Inn for five years. He hadn't known about the ghost until he started seeing movement out of the corner of his eye. When he looked around, no one was ever there. He's also seen pots fall off the racks. "One time we had high school kids working with us, and one was prepping," he stated. "I happened to look over and a pot fell off, landed on his head and shattered the plate he was working on. Everyone assumes that it's the spirit of Bob, a former kitchen manager who died after falling down the stairs to the basement about thirteen years ago."

Craig's girlfriend also had an experience while working in the kitchen. A loud male voice said something behind her, although she couldn't quite catch what he said. Startled, she turned around to see who it was, but nobody was there. The only other worker in the kitchen at the time was busy and hadn't spoken at all. Whatever the unseen speaker said didn't sound like a name or a word, just a loud noise like an "Urghh!" Was it Bob, playing pranks again?

Anita has worked for the Yogo for ten years, starting as dishwasher. She's now the morning cook. "Bob'll throw stuff on you or throw pots and pans around," she told me. "You wouldn't even be near the racks where the pots and pans are and all of a sudden something would fall right off the racks onto the floor. One night I had to swamp the place after everyone was gone. There were funny noises and the back screen door would slam by itself." She, too, has seen someone go by from the corner of her eye. As usual, there is never anyone visible.

"When I was a dishwasher, other people told me Bob liked to throw things and make things fall. Now, we just holler, 'All right Bob, we know you're around!'"

Ann Marie, Rooms Division Manager, has worked almost six years at the inn. "I used to work audit, which was graveyard shift, and I used to hear a bang in the kitchen. I'd go back there and find a pot on the floor, or the side of the grill would be on the floor. It would happen periodically but mostly around Christmas. I never saw anything, though."

Given the long history of the depot, Bob may not be the only spirit at the Yogo Inn. Ann Marie told me about a sighting a few years ago. "We had a housekeeper who had seen a woman's figure in the hall above the old waiting room. She was cleaning the rooms up there and was just entering a room when she felt something odd and looked back down the hall toward the old stairway that used to lead down to the waiting room. She saw a woman wearing a long dress, turn of the century. The ghost disappeared almost instantly so she couldn't make out more detail, but it left a faint lilac scent behind."

Delicate floral scents, especially rose and lilac, were very popular in the early 1900s, and long skirts were still being worn by older women into the 1920s.

Raelyn, front desk supervisor, has worked for two years at the Yogo, usually on the 3 to 11 P.M. shift. "This last December the pipes above the dining room broke so we had to close it down for a few days. There was no wall between the dining room and the front desk then, so I could see all the way to the windows. I was working by myself. The lights were turned off in the dining room, but I could have sworn I saw somebody walking back and forth in front of the windows. It looked like a shadowy man. I couldn't make out any details.

"Other things happened too," she continued. "Sometimes the phones would ring and there wouldn't be anyone there. It would do that all through the night, day after day, usually from an outside line but once in a while from an inside line.

"Something odd happened while our night auditor Geramy was working. He said he'll be standing here and all of a sudden the key drawer will open. It's kind of a creepy sound, especially at 4 A.M. when nobody's here." She unlocked the drawer to show me what it sounded like. It opened with a loud metallic jangle that would definitely be startling in the quiet of the night. "He hears the noise, turns around and sees it's open. He's a steady sort of guy and doesn't get spooked easily, but he says it really gets him."

Ron the bartender was the next to be interviewed. He's worked three years as head bartender and hadn't heard any tales about a ghost before he started work. Soon, however, he began to notice odd noises late at night, usually around closing time.

"One night I had all the lights off and was ready to shut down, when I heard somebody knocking on one of the walls. I had that door locked, but I opened it, and nobody was there. A few minutes later, just as I was getting ready to leave the room, it happened again. Nobody was there. I thought somebody must be playing a joke, so the next day I asked the maintenance manager about it. 'I hear funny noises. Could it be the pipes or something?'

"He said, 'Oh no, it's probably Bob.' And I said, 'Bob? Does Bob work late?' And he said, 'No, Bob died.'

"The weirdest thing was when it sounded like someone was walking across the ceiling, probably six or seven steps. It was about 2:30 in the morning. There's probably not enough room to walk up there because the owner raised the ceiling. The only people who have keys are the maintenance guys.

"It doesn't really freak me out, but you wonder sometimes

what's really going on. It's normally late at night, when you're by yourself and the closest person would be the night auditor at the front desk, but they're normally pretty quiet.

"Aside from that, bottles fall right off the shelf. I've heard stuff in the back too. I've worked bars before, late at night, and never had anything happen. It's not all the time, maybe five to ten incidents in the three years I've worked here, more in the fall and winter.

"A female bartender went out to grab somebody's food order about 9:30 one night, just before the kitchen closed, and when she came back a glass shelf had come down. It was shattered and all the bottles on it broke. The shelf had been there for almost three years and wasn't overloaded. It only had six or seven bottles on it."

Another eyewitness to Bob's pranks is Mary, who started as night chef ten years ago and is now the Yogo Inn's auditor. She had her first encounter with Bob soon after being hired. "It was my second day on the job," she told me. "I was in the kitchen and I saw the plastic ice scoop sail right past me and bounce off the wall about twenty-five feet away. It didn't arc, it wasn't thrown, it moved like someone was carrying it. No one was there."

Like Craig and Anita, Mary also caught a glimpse of shadows from the corner of her eye. She also heard a loud male voice when only women were in the kitchen. "It was a scoffing sound, like 'Aghhh!' Things happen mostly when there's something going on that Bob doesn't agree with. If you talk to him, acknowledge him, it'll stop."

"There's definitely something," she continued. "I heard that Bob was the night chef and that he had a heart attack and fell down the stairs to the basement where canned goods were stored. It could have been way back when the Depot was operating though."

I told her that Frank and I had encountered something odd when we checked into Room 304 near the indoor pool. After dropping off our luggage, we walked over to the restaurant for supper. When we returned to the room later, the entryway was full of the scent of 1950s face powder. No one who grew up in the '50s would mistake that scent for anything else, like a cleaning solution. We went out again later, and when we returned, the scent was still there, but much fainter. It was gone in the morning and never came back.

Mary had never heard of anyone reporting a phantom scent in that area, but she herself had often noticed the odor of a chicken coop near the guest laundry. An elderly man she met on an excursion on the Charlie Russell Chew Choo told her that his parents used to live in a small house where the 300 wing is now. His father worked for the railroad and his mother raised chickens.

So how many spirits call the Yogo Inn home? Well, apparently there's a lady in 1900s clothing who appeared in the corridor above the old waiting room; the woman who wears 1950s face powder, and "Bob," who plays pranks in the kitchen. Is Bob also the shadowy male figure who was seen in the restaurant, or teases the night clerks by pulling out the key drawer and causing the phones to ring? And what unseen presence occasionally walks across the ceiling of the bar and raps on the door at closing?

Perhaps you'll find out, if you spend at night or two at the Yogo Inn. Bring your camera and tape recorder. Who knows, Bob may pay you a visit!

The Yogo Inn is well-known for comfort and excellent food. Just don't order a "full stack" of pancakes for breakfast unless you're very, very hungry, or willing to share—they're "Montana sized," as big as dinner plates! And if you happen to stroll uptown, stop in at the historic Bon Ton for an old-fashioned chocolate malt or a bowl of raspberry ice cream. You can even stick your finger in a carefully preserved bullet hole in a front window. It's thought to date from a gunfight in 1883.

THE DISGRUNTLED DISPATCHER

LIVINGSTON DEPOT
200 West Park Street
Livingston, Montana 59047
Telephone: 406-222-2300
Website: www.livingstonmuseums.org/depot

Ghostly Activity Level: Moderate

HISTORY: In 1882 the Northern Pacific Railroad decided to build a large repair facility halfway between St. Paul, Minnesota, and Seattle. Tourists arrived on four trains each day, and businesses quickly sprang up to meet their needs. The Northern Pacific Railroad Depot was built in 1902, in the elaborate Italianate style and featuring a curving colonnade. This depot was the first rail gateway to Yellowstone National Park. Passenger traffic ended in 1979, and the building was donated to the City of Livingston in 1985. After restoration, it reopened as a museum with exhibits highlighting railroad and local history, managed by the Livingston Depot Foundation. It is open to the public from Memorial Day to Labor Day, and for special events during the winter.

PHENOMENA: Ghosts stories about the Depot were circulating as far back as the 1950s, according to railroad workers. More recently, the figure of a man with a "buzz" haircut brushed past the museum director on the stairs. Heavy footsteps have been heard from the third floor when the building is empty. A railroad telegraph sometimes operates by itself although it is no longer connected. Staff members have frequently discovered that the model railroad set has mysteriously been turned around and is running the opposite direction when they arrive in the morning. The most prominent ghost is thought to be that of a former railroad dispatcher named "Harold," who is still remembered by old-time railroaders. Stall doors in the women's rest room have been known to slam by themselves.

Anyone who is active in genealogy is aware of the inexplicable "coincidences" that occur while researching one's ancestry: books falling open to an entry about a particular person, chatting up someone in the grocery store only to find they are distant relatives, and so on. I've learned not to be surprised when "coincidences" happen on ghost-story collecting trips either.

I'd heard rumors about a haunting at the Livingston Depot years ago, but somehow never managed to make it to Livingston to interview staff during the summer months when the depot was open to the public. The depot closes for the season each year on Labor Day, so when my friend Pat Cody and I rolled off the interstate at Livingston two days after Labor Day I assumed that I was too late again. Once more, "coincidence," if there is such a thing, took a hand.

We had just planned to grab a quick lunch and head out again, but we noticed a door ajar at the depot and peeked inside. Several people were hard at work dismantling exhibits, and the museum director, Diana Seider, happened to be one of them. I introduced myself and Pat and explained my project. Despite a hectic schedule, Seider graciously agreed to tell us about some of the paranormal activity at the depot.

"I've been here for fourteen years," she told us. "I've had experiences here myself and so have several staff members. We've been told by old railroaders that our ghost is named Harold, and that he was a dispatcher a long time ago. My sense was that it may have been in the 1930s or 1940s. Apparently he was fired and kept coming to work anyway, so we call him the

Disgruntled Dispatcher. He's more of a trickster, playing jokes on everyone."

"Do you think there really was a dispatcher named Harold?" I asked. Many times a tale evolves to explain a genuine haunting, but has no basis in historical fact.

"Oh, yes," Seider replied with certainty. "There are some railroad employees who actually knew Harold, so he was an actual person. I don't know why, but apparently he keeps coming back to make his presence known."

"You mentioned that you've had odd experiences here yourself," I said. "What stands out the most?"

"Well, I had an encounter with someone in the stairwell once when I was coming down. This figure just kind of brushed by me. He looked like an accountant. He wore a white shirt, a skinny black tie and a "buzz" haircut. We had a whole row of accountants' offices here. He just went past me on the stairs.

"This year," she continued, "we've had more episodes of electrical issues than we've ever had. This summer it's been the telegraph. It just starts going by itself. What's odd is the person who set the whole system up for us died this summer. It all started after he died. He always took care of it every year for us.

"During another museum season, something would happen to our model train layout almost every day. We would come in and it would be turned around and going the other way. That used to drive one of my maintenance staffers up the wall because things would be changed.

"And we have electrical things that work some days and not work other days, and when they're checked they're perfectly fine.

"There was one time I was closing the museum. It was already set up for the summer season. My young daughter and I were the only ones in the whole building. We locked everything and were standing right here by the entrance, ready to leave. Suddenly we heard footsteps clomping across the ceiling. It sounded like someone with real heavy boots. Our collection storage and our offices are up there, but we had already secured the building from the top down as we always do, and there was nobody else here."

I thanked Seider and left, making a mental note to check newspaper archives to see whether I could locate any articles about a dispatcher named Harold.

Not long afterward, I was contacted by Sharon Raines. Her father worked for the railroad in Livingston from 1954 to 1963 before he was promoted and rotated out. She recalled hearing several ghost stories from her dad and his coworkers.

"Dad was working in the baggage room one day when he saw a man in a gray suit walk past the door on the track side, look in and keep going. Passengers were always told to get their baggage from the street side, because if a train came by fast and they weren't right up against the wall, they could be sucked underneath. He went out to warn the man and there was nobody there.

"Once in a while if Dad had to work weekends and Mom needed to go shopping, I'd stay with Dad in the baggage room. He'd put me to work sweeping the baggage cars or make me sit in the office behind the door because I wasn't supposed to be there. If he had to go upstairs for some reason, I'd have to go with him. He'd leave me in the outer foyer of the bookkeeping office, and I'd hear the steps creak all the time whether people would be coming up or not. It sounded like someone was coming up the stairs. After they stopped passenger service, sometimes my brother and I would play "human checkers" on the black and white tile floor of the passenger depot. Once in a while I'd see people walking by, but if I turned to get a better look, there was no one there.

"According to some of the guys, there was a ghost steam engine that came in at night. They'd hear it whistle and let off steam but there was no train on the track. There was a haunting at the shops too. There was a hydroxide pit where they cleaned the motors, and sometimes someone would fall in. There was a new guy, and they told him that when the pit was open he wasn't to go up on the walkway, because if he fell in, nobody could save him. Of course he fell in and was killed. For a couple of years afterward, the guys in the shops would see him on the walkway looking down at him. When they tried to get a better look, he'd be gone."

Is the Livingston Depot haunted? Many emotional departures and arrivals have taken place at railroad depots, particularly during wartime, and it wouldn't be surprising if the walls have absorbed some of that energy. The interference with the model train layout and the telegraph, however, points toward an intelligent entity, as does the forceful slamming of the stall door in the women's rest room witnessed by a former employee. Perhaps it's Harold, still unwilling to admit he was fired from his dispatching job long ago.

Livingston has long been a gateway to Yellowstone Park. and tourists enjoy visiting the restored depot during the summer. If you drop by, check out the ladies rest room. Who knows, maybe the heavy door will slam for you! And if you're in search of a refreshingly cool drink on a hot summer's day, why not try one of the local bars? Several of them are rumored to be haunted, and you may feel a chill that cannot be brushed off as air conditioning.

SHADOWS ON THE STAIRS

ELKS LODGE #537
619 Pleasant Street
Miles City, Montana 59301
Telephone: 406-234-3234

Ghostly Activity Level: High

HISTORY: Miles City owes its existence to the establishment of nearby Fort Keogh in the late 1870s. During the 1880s and 1890s, soldiers and cowboys up from Texas filled "Milestown's" notorious saloons, gambling halls and brothels with rowdy crowds. By the early 1900s, the great cattle drives were over and the infantry had been withdrawn from Fort Keogh. Homesteaders began to settle nearby, and the area prospered in the years leading up to World War I. Milestown, by then known as Miles City, became a center for trade and agriculture. Fraternal organizations built handsome lodges that offered their members comfortable places to meet. The four-story Elks Lodge was constructed in 1914. The building includes a basement meeting room, a main floor clubroom and bar, a second floor with a ballroom and a third floor with small rooms for guests. During Prohibition, it is said that illegal liquor, gambling and other entertainments were available on the upper floor, and a suicide supposedly occurred there in 1936. According to a spurious legend, Bonnie and Clyde sat in the speakeasy playing cards one night.

PHENOMENA: Footsteps and a dark shadow have been reported on the stairs. The ghost of a man wearing a green jacket has been seen at least twice. A female ghost wearing a long flowing dress occasionally glides across the Fireside Room. Tongs once flew off the back bar by themselves. A member who stayed in one of the apartments found a chair had mysteriously moved to the far side of the room when he returned late one night, although his apartment had been locked all day. Unexplained cold spots and "walls of energy" have been noted. A skeptic once felt invisible fingers brush through her hair.

Rumors have swirled about a haunting at the Elks Lodge for decades. Robin Gerber, the late historian and collector of Miles City ghost stories, was intrigued by the rumors and conducted a short investigation at the lodge in 2007. Although her digital recorder did not capture ghostly voices or EVP (electronic voice phenomena) she did photograph an orb, thought to be a form of spirit energy.

"When I walked into one room," Gerber told me, "my stomach did a twist and I took several photos. When I reviewed them, I discovered an orb. What was most unusual about the orb was that there was only one. If dust had been raised in the area there should have been several orbs. The orb didn't appear on any other pictures. I was totally shocked when this came out on the digital picture."

I contacted the Elks and was assured by lodge secretary and former Exalted Ruler Rita Sayre that the building was indeed supposed to be haunted, although she herself had never had an experience. The ghost stories had been around for decades but were treated as jokes by many members. When Shawn Armstrong became the club manager in 2004, however, he quickly discovered that the stories were not fabrications.

"You can trace the stories back at least to the 1970s," the former Leading Knight and Exalted Ruler told me. "There were several club managers before me who were terrified to be in the building. I was here daily, seven days a week for several years. At first I didn't notice much, just the occasional odd noise that I wrote off as an old building settling. Then one day I was busy in the club, wiping tables or something, and I noticed movement out of the corner of my eye. It was a female figure, gliding across the Fireside Room. It wore long, flowing, old-fashioned clothing and didn't seem to touch the floor. It wasn't in color, just shades of gray. I thought my eyes were playing tricks on me."

Armstrong saw the female apparition several times after that, always crossing the Fireside Room in the direction of the club room. In the early days, members' wives and female visitors were allowed only in the ladies' lounge, next to the Fireside Room which was a library at the time. There they would be able to chat, read, and have drinks. Since the apparition never reacts to onlookers and always follows the same pathway, it may be what is called "residual" energy rather than an actual spirit.

Another female ghost (or perhaps the same one) appeared in the rest room of the women's lounge during preparations for a wedding. "The girls were using the rest room to dress," Armstrong said. "I was in the club, and I heard them run out screaming. They had been standing in front of the mirrors putting makeup on, and a white misty entity formed next to them. They came charging out to the Fireside Room, some of them still in their slips."

Armstrong's young son Tommy had a conversation with one of the Lodge's ghosts about three years ago. The incident happened in the balcony of the ballroom when Tommy was only four years old. The ballroom is huge, with a balcony at the back and a stage that once held a 50-piece band at the front.

I took a few photos while Armstrong walked upstairs to the balcony. "That's where it happened," he said, pointing to his left. "Two high school girls came in one evening. They had heard there was a balcony and wanted to practice projecting their voices from the balcony. I asked Tommy to take them up there. I had never shared any of the ghost stories with him because of his age. About twenty minutes later the girls came back down to the club room where we were playing pool. They'd been standing on the balcony singing and Tommy had wandered over to a corner of the balcony.

He had his back turned to the girls and was looking up, talking to someone.

"They asked him what he was doing, and he turned to them and said, 'I'm talking to Mr. Jenkins.' When they came down, and told me about it, I asked Tommy what went on upstairs. He said, 'Nothing.' I asked him if he was having a conversation with someone other than the girls, and he gave a big sigh and said, 'It was a ghost, Dad. Mr. Jenkins was a ghost. He wears a green jacket.' That has been the officers' attire for this particular lodge for many years. It's like a sports jacket."

After listening to Armstrong's account, I turned to Tommy, who is now seven years old, and asked if he recalled the incident. Tommy nodded. Could he recall more details? Tommy thought for a moment, and said in a soft voice that the ghost had brown hair and was "kind of see-through." He didn't recall what the ghost had said to him, but wouldn't be afraid to see him again since he seemed to be a nice man.

The ghost in the green jacket has been seen at least once more. "An older man came in about 5 P.M. on a New Year's Eve to ask about the party," Armstrong said, "then he wanted to use the rest room. When he came out, I saw him just standing in the foyer staring at the doors, so I went over and asked him if he was okay. He said, 'Somebody just went through those doors and up the stairs.' I thought he meant it was just somebody who'd come in off the street. The old gentleman got kind of agitated and said, 'You don't understand. I just came out of the bathroom and this individual went *through* the doors and up the stairs. He was an older man and he had a green jacket on.'"

So who is the ghost with the green jacket? According to Armstrong, the ghost was always referred to as Mr. Bohling, who was a member of the Lodge from 1908 to 1978. Henry Bohling worked as a caretaker and was also the Lodge's secretary for fifty years. For part of that time he lived in an apartment upstairs. He is said to have "ruled the Lodge with an iron fist." Tommy Armstrong's encounter with a "Mr. Jenkins" brought up another possibility.

"A couple of us decided to look at the Wall of Memory, which honors members who were in good standing when they passed away," Armstrong said. "Somebody goes, 'Oh my God—there's a Jenkins here!' and chills just went up and down me. Ray Jenkins was a member from 1935 to 1970. Now where's a kid going to come up with the name Jenkins? And he called him Mister Jenkins. Somebody who grew up in the old days would probably have introduced himself as Mister, not like today."

Odd things continued to happen, often in front of many witnesses. "While I was working the bar," Armstrong continued, "you would hear a light knock at the door behind the bar that leads to the basement. It happened many times and there are dozens of witnesses. It was always two raps and all of a sudden the door would swing wide open."

At least one odd photo taken in the Lodge reputedly showed a ghostly figure. The Lodge used to have a full-bodied elk mount in a corner of the Fireside Room. It was transferred to the state capitol in Helena many years ago. "When the Lodge members were getting the elk ready to transport up to Helena," Armstrong said, "someone took a last photo of it. The photo was in black and white, and in back of the elk was a transparent image of an individual." The photo hasn't been seen in years, but several of the members recall seeing it at the time.

The grand staircase seems to be a focus of much of the activity. Not surprising, perhaps, considering the tens of thousands of people who must have gone up and down the stairs in nearly a century. "One man was coming up the first flight of stairs," Armstrong said, "and suddenly he stopped and seemed to be watching something. He said he saw a dark shadow going up the next flight. 'It definitely wasn't my shadow.' He had a real white look to him when he told me that.

"One Halloween night, four of us decided to come up here after closing. We locked all the entry doors so no one could get in. There were four of us, two girls and two guys. One of the girls lit some candles and we sat around holding hands while she asked questions. Nothing happened, so we went upstairs and sat in the ballroom with the lights out. After a while we went up in the balcony and hung over the railing, talking. All of a sudden, we hear people coming up the stairs. I've always discounted creaks as just an old building settling but these were footsteps. We could hear people talking, men and women, a gay, party-type conversation, excited and happy. I thought there was someone in the building, so we came down from the balcony and there was nobody on the stairs.

"Another time when we were sitting in the ballroom we could hear shuffling. People were getting a little scared, so I suggested that we go down to the club. On the way down, it became very apparent that we were being followed. Fellow member Larry Jellison was about two steps behind me. The others had already made it to the bottom of the steps. I could hear *boom boom boom boom boom* like someone was stalking down the stairs behind us. It sounded aggressive, so I turned. Larry had his back to me, already in a defensive stance, so I know he heard it too. The ones at the bottom were standing there with their mouths open.

"There were two more *booms* and then it ended on the landing above us. We couldn't see anything but it felt like it was standing on the landing looming over us, telling us *"I want you out of here and I want you out of here* NOW!*"* I had never felt threatened or anxious in this building until that moment.

"One Halloween an educational after-school program for students held a Halloween dance and haunted house party in the Fireside Room here. They set up tables with centerpieces all around the room, and framed a heavy piece of stone to look like a tombstone. Just before they opened the doors that night, the tombstone suddenly slammed down to the floor so hard that it broke. It had been up in that position for over a week.

"The next day the lady who organized the haunted house came in at 7:30 A.M. to start cleaning up. She was alone in the building. No one else was due to show up for an hour, so she decided to take down the centerpieces and tablecloths, and started with a table in the corner near the door. She had worked her way about halfway around the room, then something startled her and she turned around. On the first table was a glass half-filled with water. The water was still shimmering in the glass. I kept the glass behind the bar for a long time. We called it Henry Bohling's glass, because his secretary's office had been right next to the table. It was an old, wide-mouth glass.

"One evening we were sitting in the club room with candles lit asking questions. There was a jar on the back bar with bottled franks or pickled eggs or whatever. A set of tongs was resting on top of the jar. I was behind the bar and everyone was looking in this direction when the tongs came up off of the jar. They came up in an arching fashion and struck the bar and broke three or four glasses that I had washed and set aside to dry. We tried to recreate it by hitting the tongs but there's really no explanation for it.

"A skeptic came to visit one day. She'd heard the stories and told me that ghosts didn't exist and I was full of bull. I gave her a tour of the building. When we got upstairs where the old speakeasy is alleged to have been, her eyes got really wide and she just froze there with a really startled look on her face. She said someone just ran their hands through her hair. I was about fifteen feet from her. She beat me down the stairs."

Former Elks member John Jackson also experienced odd phenomena when he lived upstairs in a small apartment from 1995 to 1996. "I was the groundskeeper and also worked as a bartender at the time," he recalled. "When I moved in, everyone kept telling me ghost stories. I didn't buy it. I lived there for perhaps a month without anything happening, and then I began to hear big band music in the ballroom. They used to have a lot of big band music, a lot of dancing in the old days. The music always started around 3 A.M. and their favorite tune was "Begin the Beguine." Nobody believed me. There would also be occasional knocks on my door."

I mentally pictured myself in that third floor apartment late at night, knowing I was the only person in the building, and repressed a shiver. "Did you ever answer the door?" I asked Jackson.

"Yes, I would open it, and nobody would be there. The knocking stopped the instant I opened the door. There's just no way somebody could have jumped back that fast. I thought it was somebody playing a joke. I would run into the balcony of the ballroom or I'd try the door of the other room next door.

"The knocks never followed a pattern like the big band music. It went on for about a month. I know I was the only one in the building. I would lock up and check the whole building.

Sometimes you'd hear footsteps following you on the stairs. You'd get to the top and stop and the footsteps wouldn't stop.

"The knocks also happened in the bar, on the door that goes from the bar down to the basement. The bartender used to open the door and nobody would be there. It used to drive her crazy. There's no way to get downstairs unless you had a key to get in.

"There was supposed be have been a suicide in the apartment I lived in. An older member told me at the time that someone had sat down in the bathtub and killed himself with a .38 caliber revolver. I installed a shower in there. It had just been a bathtub before so I had to spend quite a bit of time in the storage room next to my room to put the plumbing through. That's the room where Robin Gerber got the photo of the orb. It's just a storage room but I would swear it's always at least five degrees colder in that room than anywhere else.

"Nothing ever happened inside my apartment except for a chair moving a couple of times. The time that really freaked me out was one time when I went out to get a pack of cigarettes about 3 A.M. I locked the door when I went out, and unlocked and re-locked the door when I came in. I had chairs in my apartment set up in a certain way so I could sit at a card table and eat, and one of my chairs had been moved to the other side of the room.

"Sometimes a month or more would go by before anything more happened. Once in a while, the door that goes into the balcony wouldn't open. You could turn the handle and the latch would move, but you couldn't open the door. Ten or fifteen minutes later, the door would open easily. And there have been instances where people have been brushed on the stairway, almost to the point of being knocked over. If anyone does an investigation there, they need to be very careful on the stairway.

"I always treated the ghosts with respect, and I felt a real sense of peace up there, almost as if the ghosts were watching over me."

Elks meetings and social functions traditionally end at 11 P.M.

when the Exalted Ruler recites the moving "11 O'Clock Toast." This tribute to absent members includes the tolling of a bell eleven times and the following poignant lines:

It is the golden hour of recollection,
the homecoming of those who wander,
the mystic roll call of those who will come no more.
Living or dead, an Elk is never forgotten, never forsaken.

The Elks Lodge is open to the public for weddings, parties and other functions. If you are a guest of a member, you may be privileged to offer this beautiful toast yourself. Just don't be surprised if the room feels briefly more crowded as members who walked those halls long ago answer the "roll call of those who will come no more."

Next time you're in Miles City, why not spend the night at the historic Olive Hotel? Ask for Room 250—if you dare! Club 519 offers excellent dinners, and if you're lucky, maybe a visit from one of its spectral residents. And don't miss the Montana Bar, with its famous collection of mounted longhorn steer heads. Not all the spirits there are the 80-proof kind. If the Elks Lodge is open, drop in for a nightcap. Maybe you'll hear two ghostly raps on the basement door—before it opens by itself.

CAMPUS GHOSTS

UNIVERSITY OF MONTANA
Brantly Hall
Between Connell Avenue and Daly Avenue
Missoula, Montana 59812

Ghostly Activity Level: Moderate

HISTORY: Brantly Hall, originally called North Hall, was built in 1922 as a dormitory. It has been an administrative office building since the mid-1980s.

PHENOMENA: According to legend, a female student killed herself in 1929 when her father lost his money in the stock market crash. The ghost of a dog, thought to have belonged to her, has been seen in the building. Custodians have heard the sound of loud hand-clapping when alone in the building, and an eerie "sense of presence" has been noted on the second and third floors and in the basement. Staff members working late at night sometimes hear doors opening and closing when no one else is present. A female voice was heard calling when the building was dark and locked, and a staff member saw feet wearing old-fashioned shoes beneath the partition of one of the toilet stalls.

Nearly every campus, from elementary schools to sprawling universities, has its ghost stories. Some of the stories are terrifying, others poignant. A few may even cause a chuckle or two, like the experience of a long-time friend of mine at Eastern Montana College, now Montana State University–Billings. Late one night she returned to her dorm room in Petro Hall, exhausted and worried about a difficult music final early the next morning. As she lay in bed too tired to sleep, a "glowing green figure" glided through the wall of her room. "Oh please," she groaned, "go away! I have a final in four hours. I need to get some sleep! Go away!" The figure disappeared through the wall between her room and the room next door. Moments later she heard a loud scream from that room. When she encountered her neighbor the next day, the neighbor told her breathlessly about the ghost she'd seen emerge from her wall. My friend confessed years later that she had never gotten up the courage to tell her neighbor that she had unintentionally sent a ghost to her room that night.

Many campus ghost stories involve murder or asuicide. Some tales may be loosely based on historical fact, but most cannot be traced back to an actual event. It's been suggested that such tales are a psychological mechanism that helps students process the symbolic "death" of adolescence and make the sometimes difficult transition to adult life. Not surprisingly, one of the stories at the University of Montana's Brantly Hall does involve a suicide.

According to Debra Munn's *Montana Ghost Stories* (Riverbend Publishing, 2007), Brantly Hall was rumored to be haunted at least as far as the 1970s, when it was still a dorm. The ghost is supposed to be a female student who committed suicide in 1929 when her father lost his money in the stock market crash. Although no records of a suicide have been found, there have been many credible eyewitness accounts of a presence in the building.

The old dorm stood vacant from 1987 to 1989, when it was converted to an office building. Bill Johnston, Director of Alumni Relations, was unaware of the ghost stories when his organization moved into the building in 1989. On a hot summer's day in July, 1990, he had an odd experience that he still cannot logically explain.

"I had a former student lounge as my office," he told me. "It had a fireplace and a long meeting table plus my desk. I was sitting at the end of the table with the door closed, all the windows shut and the blinds pulled to keep as much heat out as possible. The table had solid panels on either end rather than legs. My feet were up against the solid panel when I had the sensation that cold air was swirling around my feet. Then it moved up my legs, around my body to my torso, my chest and up past my head. It wasn't something blowing on me, it was spiraling around me. I thought, *"That's odd."* It wasn't a breeze. Once it moved up past my knees, my feet were no longer cold. After it passed my head, it was gone. I thought, *'That's really strange, it's July, everything's closed up and I'm sitting against a solid panel.'* I decided to call it a day and go home.

"I'm probably more of a skeptic than a believer. People here have reported doors slamming, dogs barking, and voices, but we have interconnected buildings with tile walls and linoleum floors, and it's surprising how sound travels. I've always dismissed those incidents as being explainable. I'm sure there's an explanation for what I experienced too, but I don't know what it would be. It definitely wasn't a breeze. There's no air conditioning in the building, and the flume in the fireplace has been closed for years.

"I do recall feeling a sense of presence at the time. I work here in the evenings a lot, and sometimes you feel there's something with you or behind you. It doesn't happen very often, but one day when my wife picked me up I told her, 'I'm glad to leave the building, because it felt like something was with me all day.'"

An article by Josh Mahan in the *Missoulian* on October 31, 2000, quoted Andrea Balazs, a work-study student who encountered something eerie in Brantley Hall. Balazs had gone down to the basement and she happened to glance at a door as she passed by. Reflected in the opaque glass of the door was a figure behind her. She looked around and saw no one. When she looked at the glass again the figure was still visible. Frightened, she ran back upstairs.

The same student also saw the German shepherd dog that is said to haunt Brantley. At the time, she was unaware of the ghost stories and assumed that the dog which ran up to her was a real dog. *"I leaned down to pet it and totally missed, which was strange because it was right next to me,"* the student told the reporter. *"I turned around and it was gone."* A week later she saw the same dog, which ran up the stairs and disappeared. She asked around, and eventually learned that the dog was a ghost and that it was supposed to have belonged to the female student who had committed suicide in 1929.

Recently, Sarayl Yellowhorse, manager of the University of Montana Phonathan, encountered a female spirit when she returned to Brantly Hall late one Sunday night to drop off timecards. The building was locked and dark.

"I entered through the back door, turned on all the lights, and dropped off the timecards in the mailroom," she told me. "Then I turned the lights off and walked up the steps to the front exit. As I began to open the door, I glanced down the dark hallway and heard a woman howl *'Helloooo!'* I opened the exit door and ran down the stairs. My heart was beating fast and I couldn't stop shaking. I went to Albertsons but I was still so scared that I forgot my groceries on the lower part of the basket. When I got home, my fiancé said I should have confronted the ghost, but I didn't want to see what it looked like nor did I feel like having a conversation with a ghost. After I shared my story with a few staff members and heard their experiences, I accepted this ghost because I realize this is an old building and there will be a lot of things lingering around. To this day I leave all the lights on when I have to come back to Brantly at night."

Mary Kukowski, who works in Computer and Software Support, encountered a female ghost one afternoon, in the second floor ladies' rest room where Corbin and Brantly Hall meet.

"The door to the rest room is a heavy wooden door and it takes an effort to open it," she said. "I looked down at the floor of the stall next to me and suddenly there were feet in some really old-looking shoes. They were brown leather, somewhat pointy and almost flat. Nobody had walked in. I opened my door to go wash and there was no one in the stall next to me. There was no way for the person in the next stall to get out of there before me—and I would have heard the heavy wooden door. I was never scared or worried, just accepted the fact there was a ghost in there."

Kukowski had been a skeptic until she moved into a house that was haunted by the spirit of a little boy. "It's been in the past ten years or so that I have come to accept that there are supernatural beings amongst us, although I *will* say that it was a hard sell," she said.

I knew that several of the reputedly haunted buildings on campus had been investigated in 2005 by Tortured Souls Investigations, co-founded in 1999 by Erik Bratlien and his son Kris, so I contacted Kris to see if the evidence the group had gathered was strong enough to conclude that Brantly Hall was indeed haunted.

"We went up to room 248, which is supposed to have belonged to the girl who committed suicide," Kris told me. "Nothing much happened, and I began to think we were wasting our time. Just then we heard the floor creak like someone was walking on it and we noticed a floral smell like an old perfume. It dissipated, and nothing more happened. My sister and I decided to go down to the basement with our infrared cameras. We had no flashlights, just the cameras. When we got halfway along a passage we heard a noise behind us and turned, but nothing was there. Then we heard a door slam ahead of us. We looked through the camera but no one was there. When we got down to the end of the passage, I picked up the lock on the door and jiggled it to see if it was really locked, and the same floral smell we had noticed upstairs came back."

Bratlien has spent days going through school annuals and historical files at the Mansfield Library as well as death records at the public library and has found nothing to either prove or disprove a suicide at Brantly Hall in 1929. Although the legend may have no basis in fact, there does seem to be a well-substantiated record of paranormal sightings at Brantly Hall.

Next time you visit the beautiful campus of the University of Montana, keep an eye out for a German shepherd dog that is said to wander between Brantly Hall and nearby buildings. And if it vanishes when you lean down to pet it, consider yourself fortunate—you've just met one of the University's legendary phantoms.

TRAGEDY AT THE THEATRE

UNIVERSITY THEATRE
32 Campus Drive
Missoula, Montana 59812
Telephone: 406-243-2853
Webpage: http://www.sfa.umt.edu/sitemap.html

Ghostly Activity Level: Low

HISTORY: The University Theatre opened in 1935, part of the University of Montana's new Student Union Building that also included a bookstore and badly-needed space for relaxation and entertainment. The building was remodeled in 1997, when an impressive rotunda was added. Many famous actors have graced the stage over the years, perhaps most notably Carroll O'Connor, of "Archie Bunker" fame.

PHENOMENA: Faculty and students have reported unexplained cold breezes, the sounds of locked doors opening and closing and a ghostly figure in the auditorium. During one memorable performance of *Macbeth,* traditionally considered an "unlucky play," the cast heard screams that apparently no one in the audience heard. A "sense of presence" has also been noted at times.

Why are so many theaters haunted? One theory is that emotion given off during an intense performance can be absorbed by the building and used by spirits to produce various types of phenomena. If that's true, one could also theorize that a brand-new theater would not be haunted. That proved to be the case at a newly-opened theater I contacted a couple of years ago. The staff told me that they "had hopes" that a ghost would be attracted to their sadly un-haunted theater, and their optimism was justified. Six months later they called me back to proudly announce that they now had their very own resident spirit!

The University Theatre on the campus of the University of Montana was built in the 1930s, and ghost stories were circulating as least as far back as the early 1970s. According to Debra Munn, (*Montana Ghost Stories*, Riverbend Publishing, 2007) the haunting was attributed to a construction worker who had been killed during the construction of the building in the 1930s, although research so far cannot confirm a fatal accident at that time.

Even though the stories cannot be traced back to an historical event, plenty of eyewitnesses over the years have documented apparent paranormal activity at the University Theater. Some of the stories are unsettling.

A female student interviewed by Munn told her that that one morning she entered the theater around 5:30 A.M. to join a tour that would be leaving from the building. She was the first to arrive, and the atmosphere in the empty theater was decidedly eerie. When she heard a door open and close, she assumed some of her friends had arrived. She went to look for them, only to discover that no one had come in. She heard the doors open and close several more times over the next few minutes and even felt cold breezes as though someone had come in, but no one was ever there. Unnerved, she finally decided to wait for her group outside.

During the 1970s, children were sometimes brought by their parents to rehearsals and would watch from the balcony. On several occasions, Munn reported, the children insisted they could see a man watching from the auditorium, although the actors on stage could not see him.

A former director who was working late one night also sensed a presence, although he could see no one. The atmosphere became so oppressive that he grabbed his coat and left.

The current director, Tom Webster, has been at the University Theatre since 1997. He acknowledged that stories of ghostly activity at the theater were well known when he took the job.

"We do think there's paranormal activity here. My former technical director was sitting in his office on the third floor a few years ago with all the windows and doors closed, and all the papers on his desk started ruffling. He said the hair stood up on his neck and he got the hell out of there because there was no way that wind could have gotten in."

Shy Obrigewitch has been the theater's assistant technical director for the past three years.

"One day, I came in about four or five o'clock," he told me. "I was in the lighting booth and I looked out toward the stage. The only light was the ghost light. It's a light we leave on stage so if we come in when it's dark we don't bump into anything. There was an image that appeared about ten feet to the left of the light. It looked like a guy walking, but it was visible only from the knees up. It passed in front of the light and walked another ten to fifteen feet to the right of it and just disappeared. It was completely see-through. The image was pretty faint. I didn't have a long time to look at it, but it wasn't wearing a suit and tie, more like regular work clothes. I'd guess he was in his thirties."

"What was there before?" I asked.

"There's a stage there now, but it used to be a scene shop. There hasn't always been a stage there," Obrigewitch replied. "I wondered whether the ghost had been walking on the floor level as it had been when he was alive. Or perhaps he just didn't have the energy to fully materialize."

"Debra Munn mentioned a story that might explain the ghost you saw," I offered. "Apparently a man was killed during construction of the theater back in the 1930s. It's never been proven, but children in the 1970s reported seeing a man sitting in the auditorium watching a rehearsal although none of the adults present could see him."

"There was another accident on February 10, 1998," Tom Webster stated. "A scaffold two guys were working on tipped over and they fell forty feet to the floor. One worker was killed and another was seriously injured. I watched one guy pass away."

The man who was killed when the scaffolding collapsed in 1998 had been in his late 30s, according to newspaper reports, which matched Obrigewitch's estimate of the ghost's age. It's also possible that the figure he saw predates the scaffold accident and was the same man seen by the children in the 1970s.

"It's pretty eerie when you're in the building all by yourself," Obrigewitch said. "We do have a lot of heat pipes that make a lot of noise when they heat up or cool down. If I hear noises when I'm here alone, I don't even look up. I think he's here, but I don't think he's very active. He's not malevolent, so I'm not afraid of him. If he wants to hang out, that's okay."

Tom Webster agreed. "There are times when you're here late at night by yourself and you have the feeling you're not really alone. It's a really old building. We have friendly, Casperesque ghosts here. We just co-exist with them."

Kris Bratlien, who had investigated Brantly Hall with members of Tortured Souls Investigations, also investigated the theater. The first time nothing much happened, but the second investigation was more productive.

"We split into two teams," he said. "One group went into the Fine Arts section of the building, and the rest of us stayed in the theater. We were recording an EVP (Electronic Voice Phenomena) session on the stage, and my father was sitting four or five rows back in the auditorium, filming us with a camcorder. We asked questions, and got some bangs from behind the stage. When we got done, my dad said, 'You have to check this out. I got a shadow on my video camera.' He rewound the tape and played it. It's all in night vision, and you can see the flashes on the stage from cameras, and all of a sudden a shadow passes from the right side to the left, about three rows in front of my dad. "

Bratlien sent me the video clip, and there definitely is a large shadow that passes quickly across the screen a few rows in front of the camera. There seems to be no plausible explanation for it.

Is the theater's ghost the man who died when the scaffold

tipped in 1998, or is he the man who, according to a woman interviewed by Debra Munn, was seen by a group of children in the 1970s? Perhaps Kris Bratlien and his group will find new clues in future investigations.

Next time you attend a performance at University Theatre, spare a kind thought for the man who still walks the building many years after his death. And why not visit historic Fort Missoula while you're in the area? You may be one of the fortunate visitors to hear ghostly footsteps in the old quartermaster's house, now a museum.

THE OPERA HOUSE GHOSTS

THE OPERA HOUSE THEATRE
140 Sansome Street
Philipsburg, Montana 59858
Telephone: 406-859-0013
Website: www.operahousetheatre.com

Ghostly Activity Level: High

HISTORY: The two-story masonry McDonald Theatre was built by Angus "Red Mac" McDonald in 1891. Renamed the Granada Theatre in 1919, it became a motion picture house in the 1920s. Over the years, the building has also housed a soda pop bottling company, a bank, a livery stable and various other businesses. Tim Dringle bought the property in 1989. He and his wife Claudette have spent many years painstakingly restoring the building from basement to roof. The Opera House Theatre seats 350 people and offers professional theatre productions during the summer. It is the oldest continually operating theatre in Montana. The Philipsburg Historic District is listed on the National Register of Historic Places.

PHENOMENA: Footsteps have been heard walking up a stairway between the theatre and the adjoining actors' lodging. A face was reportedly seen in the empty lighting booth by actors, and several photos taken by various people have shown transparent figures or swirls of a misty white substance. Unexplained cold spots have also been felt at various locations.

Philipsburg is a delightful town to visit, full of colorfully-painted Victorian buildings, a genuine sapphire mine, an old-fashioned soda shop, and a haunted theatre. Oh, and did I mention a *huge* candy store? When Pat Cody and I arranged to visit the Opera House Theatre, we arrived early enough to make a fortifying stop at the fabulous Sweet Palace. Housed in a beautifully-restored Victorian building, the Sweet Palace offers over 900 kinds of candy, including 50-plus kinds of homemade fudge, imported varieties of licorice, taffy, and old fashioned candies of all kinds. We didn't leave empty-handed. Ghost hunting takes a lot of energy, after all!

The nearby Opera House Theatre was impressive, much larger than I had expected, with colorfully painted corbels and trim work at the roofline. Claudette Dringle greeted us at the door and led us into the lobby where she handed us a framed photograph.

"What do you think of this?" she asked. Claudette's husband Tim had taken the photo, which showed two friends posing in front of one of the private boxes near the stage. Although no one sensed anything unusual at the time, the resulting photo was definitely not normal. The two men were enveloped by swirling white mist and funnel-shaped vortices, believed by many researchers to be forms of ghostly energy. Pat and I agreed that this photo was one of the best examples of paranormal photography that we had ever seen.

We followed Claudette into the darkened auditorium. While she turned on the theatre lights we took photos of the interior. Or rather, Pat did. My camera, which had worked perfectly outside, simply refused to turn on. Then my tape recorder quit. I had installed brand-new batteries just that morning, and they should have lasted several hours.

We're never surprised when equipment fails to work in haunted places. One theory is that ghosts use electrical energy from cameras, tape recorders and other electrical equipment in order to materialize. That's why we always carry spare batteries—lots of spare batteries—when we visit haunted places. We hoped that the energy drain meant that something unusual was about to happen.

The most common phenomena reported in haunted places are

inexplicable odors, noises, a sense of being watched by someone unseen, cold spots, physical touches, and full or partial apparitions. Rarely does one building offer all types of phenomena. The Opera House Theatre is one of the exceptions.

"One gal swore she could smell cigar smoke," Claudette told us. "We don't allow smoking in the theatre, so I don't know if that's even possible."

I assured her that it was indeed possible, and that unexplained odors are often noted in haunted places. They can be pleasant scents, like perfume or the fragrance of baking bread, or nauseating, like the stench of rotting flesh that Pat and I had encountered near the Slaughter Pen at Gettysburg. Oddly enough, sometimes only two or three people in a group will detect the odor, even if it seems overpowering to those who can.

We followed her onto the stage. The original trap door used in vaudeville acts had been nailed shut, and a larger one built. The sets stored backstage were covered with actors' signatures, some dating back to the 1920s.

Claudette gestured toward the auditorium. "I find seats down all the time too, but I don't pay any attention to that," she said. "Apparitions seem to be more common. Jeff photographed a female figure in the back stairway, and there is another photograph where Joyce is coming out the back door, and there's someone just behind her. Down the back stairs is where the film guy got a picture that freaked him out. It was male, with a top hat. And the actors swear they saw a face up in the light room."

Claudette's husband Tim has also had experiences up in the light room while working on the film projector. Although he didn't see anything, he sensed someone standing very close to him, apparently interested in what he was doing. It was so distracting that Tim finally told it to go away so he could get his work done.

"The acoustics are great here," Claudette continued, "and when there's just my husband and I in the building, I can hear him in the basement even from our upstairs apartment. And he can hear me upstairs. The biggest thing for me has been footsteps. I've heard what I thought were people coming up the stairs to the apartment. There are all kinds of noises in an old building, but you can tell the difference. Footsteps coming up bare wood stairs are not normal creaks. That happened more than once. I used to go check, but there's never anyone there. When the construction guys were staying next door, they said they heard footsteps too. They were actually going to move."

She offered to take us next door to the Off Broadway Actors' Lodging where the construction workers had stayed, and we began walking toward the lobby. Pat followed us, a few yards behind. Suddenly I heard her say tensely, "Karen! Take a photo, *now!* My back just got very cold, and I feel someone walking behind me."

I couldn't see anything unusual, but I quickly raised my camera, hoping that it would work this time. Again, it malfunctioned. I gave Pat an apologetic shrug. Whatever she had felt behind her was surely gone by now.

We stepped outside the theatre. The actors' lodging was part of the same building but separated from the theatre by stairs leading up to the Dringles' apartment. According to Claudette, the lodging had formerly been used as a bakery, a bank, and a laundry, with the Philipsburg Commercial Club upstairs.

Maintaining a historic building takes unending work. "You have to work with the place," Claudette stated. "You can't work against it. It won't let you."

The Dringles had recently finished re-roofing the theatre. "There were seven layers of old roofing to take off," Claudette told us. "I couldn't straighten out for three weeks. Then we had to sand all the floors in the actors' lodging."

The actors' lodging provides housing for actors during the summer season. During the rest of the year, the lodging is available for rent. It consists of six bedrooms, laundry facilities, and a spacious common area consisting of kitchen, dining and lounging areas. During the renovation, Claudette had an odd experience.

"We had sanded the floors and I was just vacuuming up all the dust when I felt a tug on the hair ornament I was using to hold my hair back. I thought I had caught my hair on something, but a few minutes later it happened again. I cannot explain it."

She glanced around the open, attractive area that was the result of the renovation and added, "I do feel that our ghost likes what we're doing."

We thanked her, said our farewells and headed out to the car. My audiotape was still running, momentarily forgotten, while I unlocked the car and got in. I always check my recording equipment several times during interviews to make sure it's working, and I rewound the tape to see if it had recorded the last few minutes of conversation. It had, and more: just after we exchanged our final goodbyes with Claudette, the tape had recorded an unfamiliar female voice that said "Hellooo" in a drawn-out, stagey manner. Moments later she said "Hello" again, this time in a more normal manner. Claudette was still standing in the doorway of the actors' lodging about ten feet away and there was no one else within sight.

"My impression of the theatre," Pat said as we drove out of Philipsburg, "was that there are several spirits—you might say a *troupe* of spirits. They're still performing, still arguing, still exaggerating every-day interactions. They seem to like Claudette and her husband. The atmosphere is friendly and playful, like a group of children having an ongoing pajama party."

I thought of the stagey "hellooo" caught by my tape recorder and had to agree with Pat's impressions. While we don't know for sure how many ghosts roam the Opera House Theatre, one thing is certain—the audience at each performance is undoubtedly larger than can be seen.

Bring your camera and hiking boots if you visit Philipsburg. There are plenty of trails and opportunities for wildlife photography nearby, and you can "pan" for sapphires at a real working mine. Round off the day with a live performance at the Opera House Theatre and a great steak at the Silver Nugget Saloon. You might want to reserve a room at the Broadway Hotel, a restored Victorian hotel where the marks of miners' axes are still on the floor next to the pot-bellied stove.

SPIRITS OF THE BACK COUNTRY

Would you enjoy spending a night at a remote forest service cabin in the mountains south of Livingston? Sounds idyllic, doesn't it, with great stars blazing overhead, the quavering call of an owl in the distance, and warm light glowing through the windows of a rustic cabin. But if you need to visit the outhouse at the Mill Creek Work Cabin in the middle of the night, beware! You may be accompanied by someone—or something—not of this world.

The cabin was built by the Yellowstone Ranger District in 1927. It overlooks Mill Creek and is a rustic one-bedroom building with a wood-burning stove, electricity, and an outhouse. Forest service personnel still stay there at times, but the cabin can be rented from the Livingston Ranger District when it is not otherwise in use. In May 2008, Dee Brown of Billings and her husband Ed decided to spend three nights at the Mill Creek Cabin.

"The first night we were tired," Brown told me, "so we went to bed early. We spent the second day hiking. That evening I decided to go to the outhouse before going to bed. It was twilight when I started down the steps of the cabin. Usually my dog follows me around, but he wouldn't go out that time. I was still on the steps when I happened to notice a glowing ball of light about eight feet up in the trees. It wasn't bright and it didn't seem to move, but I had the feeling that someone was out there watching me. I stood looking at the light for a few more moments and decided I didn't really want to go out to the outhouse, so I stepped back inside the cabin and locked the door. I also turned the yard light on.

Later that night my husband got up to go out. He was surprised to find the door locked. Apparently whatever it was had gone by then, because he didn't mention seeing anything when he came back. The next day I was reading the logbook that previous campers had written in and someone had written, "Look out for the ghost in the outhouse."

A retired teacher who worked as a seasonal wilderness ranger for fourteen summers wasn't surprised to hear about Brown's experience at the Mill Creek Cabin. "Ranger X," as I will refer to him since he prefers to remain anonymous, stayed at the Mill Creek Work Cabin a number of times. Although he never saw anything strange there, he often heard odd noises that he knew from long experience were not caused by animals or wind. He felt that it was just "some of the old-time guys" coming around to see who was staying in their cabin.

Ranger X also recalled an eerie encounter on the Slough Creek–Independence Trail, which leads from the old mining town of Independence to the Slough Creek Ranger Station. According to notes in his private diary, it happened on August 4, 1966, at about 7:30 P.M. As he wrote in his diary that evening, "I was approaching the intersection of the Lake Abundance Trail when I saw a man wearing a woolen checked shirt and gray trousers tucked into knee-high black boots slowly pushing a small two-wheeled cart. The man was short in stature, maybe about 5'6" tall, with long black hair and beard. He wore a black 'old style' brim hat with a light-colored band. The cart was wooden, apparently empty, and the wheels were solid with no spokes.

"I walked toward him and called out, 'Hello!' There was no response from the subject and he just kept walking north on the trail. It struck me as strange. It seemed unlikely that the subject did not see or hear me."

Ranger X turned to get a better look at the man, but he was no longer in sight, even though there was no way he could have gotten himself and the barrow off the trail in just a few seconds.

"This was the first person I'd seen since leaving Abundance Trailhead seven miles back," the diary continues. "I turned south toward the Slough Creek Forest Service Guard Station about two miles distance. The trail just north of Frenchy's Meadow and the Duret log cabin site was now dirt. It dawned on me there were *no wheel or foot tracks.* Mine were very visible. I wondered if I had seen Frenchy's spirit? My pace quickened to the station and I am thinking about what I saw this evening as I write this for my personal diary. Since I had no personal contact this will not go in the Forest Service log. Hope I don't have a visitor tonight."

Joseph "Frenchy" Duret was a notorious poacher who often made the trip to Nye from his cabin on Frenchy's Meadow, about nine miles beyond Independence—pushing a barrow loaded with furs. In 1922, Duret was killed and partially eaten by a grizzly that had broken loose from a bear trap. He was buried near his cabin in Frenchy's Meadow.

Ranger X saw the figure for the second time in 1969. Once again the figure appeared not to notice him, and disappeared with his barrow over a small hill. The ranger followed him at a distance, and when he topped the rise, the figure was gone.

The vicinity of the former mining town of Independence, high in the Absaroka-Beartooth Wilderness Area, was the scene of another mysterious sighting by two young men several years ago. They had spent most of the day exploring the ruins of the miners' cabins, the old brothel, mine shafts and outhouses that in winter are buried under as much as eleven feet of snow. When the shadows began to lengthen late in the afternoon, they decided to leave so they wouldn't be caught on the difficult trail after dark. About halfway down, they suddenly saw a man wearing old-fashioned miner's gear crouching alongside a steep bank at the side of the road. When the man caught sight of their oncoming car he ran straight up the bank and disappeared into the woods. The two young men could hardly believe their eyes, because no living person could have climbed the bank at that speed or without scrambling for handholds. Puzzled and a little uneasy, they continued driving down the trail. About twenty minutes later, the same man reappeared, once more stooping beside a steep bank that flanked the road. The figure straightened, seemed to look right at them, ran up the nearly vertical bank and disappeared into the trees. Now really spooked and convinced that what they had just seen was not of this world, the two young men were relieved to reach the end of the narrow road.

When I contacted a rancher in the area who takes summer visitors up to the ruins of the old town, and asked him about ghost stories, he recalled vague stories of a murder in "the old days." I've found nothing about a murder in old newspaper indexes, but it's certainly possible. Or he may have died in an accident. Mining was and still is a notoriously dangerous occupation, and there was a well-documented accident in 1937 when two men were killed in an explosion at the mine.

If you feel up to a serious hike, or own a four-wheel drive, you might explore the ruins of Independence some warm summer day. Don't be surprised if you catch a glimpse of moose, elk, deer or grizzly along the trail—or the ghost of an old miner. And if you decide to attempt the long trek to Frenchy's Meadow from Independence, maybe you'll be the next one to encounter the mysterious figure pushing an old-fashioned barrow.

The back country of Montana is strewn with decaying cabins built by miners and early settlers. Ranger X had yet another encounter with the uncanny not far from Cooke City in the 1960s. He was accompanied this time by a friend, a retired airline pilot who enjoyed long hikes. It was a warm day and the two men eventually grew thirsty. Near Lulu Pass, they found an abandoned cabin and approached it, hoping to find a spring of fresh water nearby. The cabin was still sound enough to be used as emergency shelter, and they noticed that an old rocking chair in the window was gently rocking. Expecting to find other hikers resting inside, the two men looked in through the window. No one was there, and there was no breeze to move the rocking chair. Ranger X told the owner of a neighboring cabin what he'd seen, but the neighbor didn't seem surprised. He replied that he'd often seen the previous owner sitting in his old rocking chair, smoking a pipe. "If you'd blink your eyes," he told Ranger X, "he'd be gone."

Lance Foster of Helena also had an unusual encounter in an old cabin. In 1994, Foster was working on an archaeological survey for the Forest Service.

"I don't count spooky feelings," he told me. "I have to hear or see something to count it. Otherwise I would have gone nuts with all the vague forebodings and eerie shadows in some of those old mining places." The following experience is still vivid in his memory.

"It was up on the divide between the Helena and Deerlodge Forests, in the Elliston area. The weather was sunny and bright, but the old miner's cabin I was surveying was shadowed by Douglas-firs and it was too dim inside to take a photograph. Instead, I stood in the center of the small room, sketching the rough, homemade furniture made of milled lumber.

"When I began measuring the interior dimensions of the cabin, I heard the sound of boots approach from the door just a few feet away. You could hear the heel-step, heel-step, pause, heel-step as the invisible person circled around me. The footsteps sounded like someone wearing cowboy boots walking around in a very small cabin with a wooden floor. I did not feel any menace coming from the walker, just an irritation and concern and a questioning, as one might have upon coming home and discovering a stranger in your cabin in the deep woods. I suppressed an urge to leave. I needed to finish what I was doing, so as I kept measuring. As I did so, I talked to whatever was in this cabin. I said, 'I am just trying to do my job, trying to understand this place of yours. You did a nice job on your furniture. You have a nice place. I just need to finish my work and I will leave right away and you will be alone again.'

"The footsteps slowed. The atmosphere grew heavier, the silence broken only by the humming of the wasps. *Enough of this,* I thought, *I'm out of here.* Trying not to show my fear, I walked to the door and opened it, saying, 'I am sorry to have bothered you, I am going now.' And that was it. I left that place and did not look back. Whoever or whatever walked in that place was very attached to it and didn't like unannounced guests."

Foster also had an uncanny experience while exploring an abandoned mine. "After I did a site report for the Charter Oak Mine in 1995 when it became Forest Service property," he said, "I revisited the site with Mary Horstman, a mining historian for the Forest Service. We walked around the site and then went up near the lower adit. Suddenly we heard a rhythmic tap-tap-tap coming from deep inside the adit. We looked at each other. Could it be dripping water? Rock shifting? The metallic-sounding taps were very regular. Occasionally they would pause, then begin again. It sounded like a hammer or pick sampling rock, not water dripping.

"Mary saw the look on my face and said what I had been thinking: 'A tommyknocker.' Mary had been born into a mining family, and the stories of the mine spirits were something she had grown up with. We sat there for a while, listening to what sounded like someone hard at work taking samples and breaking rock. After a while the sounds ceased. When you go hiking and come across an old abandoned adit, you might hear the tap-tap-tapping coming from far, far inside. It might be the drip of water or the shifting of ancient rock. Or it might be a tommyknocker, or the ghost of a long dead miner."

Barbara Miller of Billings had a strange experience at Quake Lake, formed when a devastating 7.3-magnitude earthquake caused a massive landslide that dammed the Madison River on August 17, 1959, and created a lake 190 feet deep.

"It happened on a motorcycle trip in 1987," she told me. "We were coming up the hill, intending to stop at the visitors' center. Before we got there, I began to feel this horrible feeling of dread. Further up the hill, I had a sort of vision. I saw what looked like a big room, a hollow space inside a mountain, and inside it were all these people, at least nine, maybe a couple more. I remember seeing a blond girl, young, probably late teens, long blonde hair, holding an infant. There was a man sitting at a table made of rock. He had dark curly hair, and an older gentleman with longish hair, shoulder length, and a gray beard, and he had an old-type cane. He was hunched over. An older lady had her hair pulled back in a type of a bun, gray hair. There were maybe two or three younger kids, school age, six to eight, that I remember seeing. Those were boys. Maybe there was a younger girl, about four. That's all that's coming back at this point. When we got up to the point of the mountain, on the right was the mountain, on the left the visitors' center. I told them at the visitors' center what I had seen, thinking they would tell me I'm crazy, but they didn't seem surprised. They said other people had seen things too."

The events of that terrifying night in 1959 were recounted in a book called *The Night the Mountain Fell.* An estimated 28 people known to have been camping in the area were killed. Some were never found and are probably buried beneath the landslide. Local residents report occasionally sighting large balls of light floating several feet above the ground. They may be "earthquake lights," caused by geomagnetic forces or, as some have theorized, indicate the presence of spirits.

Still inclined to go hunting, fishing, camping, hiking, paddling or exploring in the back country? Just remember, no matter how remote the area, others have been there before you: Native Americans, explorers, trappers, miners, and pioneers on their way to a new home. You may find that some of them have never quite left.

WHERE ALL THE GHOSTS ARE FRIENDLY

KEMPTON HOTEL
204 Spring Street
Terry, Montana 59349
Telephone: 406-635-5543

Ghostly Activity Level: Low

HISTORY: The Kempton Hotel is the oldest continually operating hotel in Montana. Owners Russell and Linda Schwartz believe the original eight rooms were probably built in 1902 since the millwork is identical with that used in the 1902 construction of the Franklin Hotel in Deadwood, South Dakota. An addition with thirty-four rooms was completed around 1911. The builder's name is uncertain, although he was probably a member of the Kempton family who ranched south of Terry. Berney Kempton, an early proprietor of the hotel, was a famous rodeo champion and roughrider who toured Europe and Australia with Carver's Wild West Show. Guests have included Theodore Roosevelt, Calamity Jane and the famous historian and naturalist George Bird Grinnell.

PHENOMENA: The clink of china and the sounds of dinner being served have been heard from the old restaurant late at night. A guest reported that his doorknob rattled as if someone were trying to enter. When he opened the door, no one was there. The sound of heavy furniture being dragged across the floor has been heard from the attic. The jingle of spurs has been heard in another room. A skeptical guest came down one morning to report that "something" had grabbed his toe during the night.

I love the ambiance of historic hotels, haunted or not, so when Jim Schafer, Executive Director of Custer Country Montana, Inc., told me that the Kempton Hotel, one of Montana's oldest, was haunted, I just had to drop in for a visit.

The big white hotel is impressive, even after more than a century of exposure to eastern Montana's harsh weather. At the time of its construction it must have been spectacular. Most rooms at the Kempton Hotel had their own sink, unheard-of luxury at a time when pitchers and basins were customary. The hotel's elegant restaurant, where Mrs. Kempton served dinner to her guests every evening, featured linen napkins, tablecloths and fine crystal. Although the restaurant closed in the mid-1940s, older residents of the area recall it as a wonderful place to celebrate on special occasions.

The Kempton Hotel still offers comfortable accommodations for long-term residents and tourists who wish to explore the nearby Terry Badlands Wilderness Area. In season, the hotel plays host to hunters from all over the region. Owner Russell Schwartz has spent years gradually renovating the hotel while retaining as much as possible of the original décor. Even Mrs. Kempton's favorite floral wallpaper has been carefully preserved in two of the rooms.

My friend Frank and I arrived at the hotel early one January afternoon. No one was at the registration desk, so we looked around the small but cozy lobby with its comfortable furniture and paintings of cowboys on the walls. A minute or so later a young lady came in and introduced herself as Beth. I explained my project, and was delighted to learn that Beth had read my first book, *Haunted Montana*.

Beth began to develop an interest in paranormal research after a visit to Alcatraz at San Francisco. The old prison, now a museum, is considered to be one of the most haunted properties in the country. During her visit, she had placed a hand on one of the horizontal bars of a cell. Something she could not see put a cold hand over hers. Beth has also had an experience or two in the five years she has worked at the Kempton Hotel.

"One time a guest in Room 18 heard his doorknob rattle," she recalled. "No one was there when he opened the door, but he heard footsteps run down the corridor. I was coming around the corner at the time and whoever it was would have had to go right past me. I saw no one, and I didn't hear any footsteps.

"Another guest took photos one night in the old dining area and got orbs and vague figures. That's where people have heard the sounds of dinner being served when no one is there.

"Then there are rooms in the back part of the hotel where there is a lot of static electricity. When I'm making the beds I get shocked a lot. Mrs. Kempton did the wallpaper herself. She cut out all the flowers and pasted them on the wall. That may be one of the reasons why the hotel is haunted."

Beth is probably correct, since the upstairs bedrooms retain much of the original 1900s décor. Paranormal researchers theorize that energy can be absorbed by the fabric of buildings or their furnishings. If conditions are right, anyone who happens to be in the room might be able to sense those energies.

At that point, Russell's sister Peggy arrived. I asked her whether she had ever sensed anything odd at the hotel.

"My sister and my cousin feel a presence," Peggy replied, "and my sister thought she saw someone one time. I hear lots of things here late at night, people walking up and down the hallways. One night I heard huge thumps and bumps like furniture being moved. I wondered why anyone would be moving their furniture at night. It was like a big dresser being dragged across the floor. It was weird. I asked the people in that room why they were rearranging furniture at night, and they said they hadn't been. I don't believe in ghosts and I've never seen a ghost, but I definitely heard someone moving furniture, and it was *big* furniture."

"Do you remember what room it was?" I asked her.

"It was right above my room," she replied. "It would have been Room 18."

"That's the same room where the doorknob rattled," Beth stated. She offered to show me around upstairs, and I followed her up the wide staircase. She pointed out Room 18. I tried the doorknob, and it did not jiggle. Even if vibrations from a heavy coal train or a passing semi-trucks could have caused the rattling, that would not explain the retreating footsteps heard by the occupant of the room—and which Beth, who had just come around the corner and had a clear view of the empty corridor, had not heard.

I took a couple of photos down the hall, and then followed Beth to one of the rooms where she felt an unusually high level of static electricity. The moment I stepped inside the room, the hair on my arms stood up. If I'd had an EMF meter along, I'm sure it would have registered a high electromagnetic field.

I wondered whether there were high-powered transmission lines near the hotel. Strong electromagnetic fields are found in many places that are reputed to be haunted and are thought by many researchers to provide some of the energy needed for various phenomena.

Beth pointed out the early 1900s floral wallpaper that had been one of Mrs. Kempton's favorite patterns, and then led me to the attic staircase.

"I won't go upstairs. It makes me feel paranoid," she explained. "Maybe it's the lighting." The lighting looked normal to me, but I decided that my arthritic knee might not make it up the steep stairs. I made a mental note to ask Russell about the attic. If a level-headed young woman like Beth felt uneasy up there, perhaps there was a reason.

As it turned out, there was a very good reason. When I caught up with Schwartz later, he told me about the tragic deaths that had occurred in the attic during the deadly Spanish influenza pandemic of 1918-1919. Montana was among the hardest-hit states, with most of the deaths in Prairie County occurring late in the epidemic, during the winter of 1919-1920.

"During the epidemic, the attic was used to house the overflow of patients from the hospitals," he explained. "My grandmother, who started working for Mrs. Kempton at a very young age, said that they put cots in the attic for the patients. My uncles felt that the ghosts in the hotel were those who died during that terrible time. Maybe some of the sounds people hear of furniture being dragged across the floor actually come from the attic, not the rooms on the second floor."

By the end of the 1930s, the hotel was already regarded as haunted. At least one local resident, now in his late 80s, recalls hearing the stories when he was a young cowboy working to repair a damaged wall between rooms 20 and 22. "During the Depression," Schwartz said, "whenever there was an overflow of guests, they were put up on cots in the attic, just as they had been during the epidemic. A cook who worked for the hotel at the time used to help with the cleaning up there. I've heard from at least two sources that she saw the ghost of a woman in a white gown in the attic. It wasn't a formal gown, more like a white dress. She could see through her."

"That sounds similar to the white uniform nurses wore during the epidemic," I commented. "Perhaps one of the nursing staff died." Newspapers from that time period are hard to find, but research might reveal whether a local nurse had caught influenza from her patients and died.

"We keep things like baby cribs up there now where we can get at them easily," Schwartz continued, "things we need for guests. One of our guests brought his dog along one time. The dog was running around snooping, and he started up the stairs that go to the attic. All of a sudden he stopped and turned right around and came back down. He sat down by his owner and whined. He wouldn't go back up there. He wasn't scared, but he wasn't going up. We joked that 'Well, the spirits are active now.'

"Another night we had a couple of hunters who definitely weren't ghost believers. When they came down the next morning, one of them was absolutely convinced that something grabbed him by the toe in the middle of the night and kind of shook him a bit, in a humorous way. It woke him up and he knew something was there. He said, 'Look, I didn't believe in anything before, but there's a lot of things we don't know, and I know I was woken up when something grabbed my toe.'

"Sometimes we'll find lights turned on that aren't ever on. That happened again just a few days ago. Or we'll hear odd noises, especially from the attic or Rooms 18 or 29. A guy who was in Room 22 heard spurs jingling on two or three separate nights. It didn't make any sense, because nobody wears spurs inside any more, but he was an old cowboy and he knew what they sounded like. He had me convinced he heard it. He couldn't tell whether the sound was coming from the room or the attic above."

Given the hotel's lengthy history, the ghost with the jingling spurs might be almost any of its early guests, but Berney Kempton seems to be the most likely candidate. Kempton was a rodeo champion and roughrider. According to Tom Stout's *Montana: Its Story and Biography,* Volume 3 (1921), Kempton, who was half Sioux, joined Doc Carver's Wild West Show in the late 1880s. Not yet twenty, he performed before royalty and heads of state in most of the great capitals of Europe and, in Australia, even lassoed kangaroos. Berney Kempton died at the age of seventy-two in 1942, sitting in a chair in a corner of his own hotel. If Kempton's spirit lingers, it's probably because of a strong emotional attachment to the hotel.

Was Kempton also the prankster who once hid one of the hotel keys?

"We had a key go missing about five or six years ago," Schwartz told me. "It was the key to a door at the front desk. We kidded people about the ghosts taking the key but I was wondering how I could replace a key they don't make anymore. You can't even get those keys. Within about a month, Beth was walking near the desk in the back office, and the key was lying in the middle of the floor."

It takes a considerable amount of energy for spirits to move objects, and I was reminded of the high levels of electromagnetic energy in some of the rooms upstairs. "Beth told me that she often gets electrical shocks when she makes the beds in those rooms," I said to Schwartz. "Are there high-powered transmission lines nearby?" There were none, and he had already ruled out the heating system as a source. I asked him about the phantom sounds of dinner being served in the old restaurant.

"My mom said she'd heard about the sounds of dinner being served from Grandma," Schwartz replied. "Later she heard it herself on two occasions. The first time she thought someone had come into the lobby with a box of china. Both times it happened early in the evening, about dinner time. Guests talk a lot about strange noises, but it's an old hotel. If there are ghosts here," he added, "they're all friendly ones."

If you visit Terry, you'll find a wide variety of things to do, including hiking, wildlife photography, sightseeing and exploring the spectacular Terry Badlands Wilderness Area just three miles northwest of the town. The world-famous Evelyn Cameron Gallery is there too, and the Prairie County Museum.

If you feel a mite peckish, drop in at the retro-'50s Badlands Café and Scoop Shoppe, owned by Inger and Arline Koppenhaver, and meet jovial host "Badlands Bob" van der Valk. The chili's great!

And be sure to check out www.visitterrymontana.com for more suggestions.

THE GHOST IN THE GARDEN

CANYON FERRY MANSION
Highway 287 North, Milepost 74
Townsend, Montana 59644
Telephone: 406-266-3599
Webpage: www.canyonferrymansion.com

Ghostly Activity Level: High

HISTORY: The Canyon Ferry Mansion was built in 1914 by A.B. Cook, cattle rancher, railroad contractor and Montana state auditor. The house served as a summer home where A.B. and his wife, Mary Agnes Morgan Cook, often entertained. Cook's stepson, Franklin Hervey Cook, was murdered on the grounds in 1970 during a burglary. The present owners, Sandy and Steve Rose, bought the mansion in 1999, renovated it and now operate it as a bed-and-breakfast inn. The property covers five acres and includes Warm Springs Creek, mentioned in the journals of Lewis and Clark. Indians and traders once camped at the site. The Roses have added a renovated chapel used for weddings, a covered pavilion for receptions and a number of guest cabins.

PHENOMENA: Sandy and Steve Rose have identified seven ghosts and a poltergeist. The apparition of a man thought to be Hervey Cook has been seen by guests, while Sandy Rose has seen the ghost of former owner Mrs. Corrine Higgins in the garden. She has also seen antique automobiles presumably driven by Hervey Cook turn into the driveway but disappear before they reach the house. Piano music was heard when no piano was present. Cold spots are felt, objects are sometimes moved by unseen hands, and the aroma of fine cigars, much loved by A.B. Cook, has been noticed when no one was smoking. The figures of a weeping young girl followed by a dark male figure have been going up the main staircase.

When Sandy and Steve Rose bought the 12,750-square-foot mansion in 1999, they knew that it would take a lot of hard work to turn the home into the luxurious inn they envisioned. Nearly ninety windows needed to be replaced, the original maple flooring had to be carefully restored, wallpaper and paint chosen to match colors and patterns used when the house was new, and appropriate furnishings selected. Veterans of thirteen previous renovations, the Roses were undaunted by the huge task. Almost immediately the house let them know it wasn't quite sure of them.

"My husband runs a construction and renovation company," Sandy Rose told me. "He had hired a lot of extra men to do this restoration, and I came up from Manhattan that first weekend to cook for the crew. The first time I turned the stove on it smelled like a dead horse. It was the most awful smell I've ever experienced. The oven was clean, nothing inside or underneath. We took the stove out and replaced it immediately. The next weekend we turned a heater on in one of the many bathrooms, and the heater smelled like rotten onions. But the heater was clean, there was nothing caught in it. It was as if the house didn't like us because it didn't know us, as if it was afraid we were going to tear it down or hurt it in some way.

"I decided to put wallpaper samples and an antique piece of furniture in each room along with display boards like an interior designer would use. Then my husband took samples of paint from behind each door. It's a Colonial Revival house, so all the woodwork was light in color. We sprayed all the woodwork with paint that matched. And all the strange things quieted down. It seemed as if the spirits of the house finally realized that we were friendly and would do good things to the house."

Sandy Rose saw her first apparition a year later, at dusk one spring evening. "I was getting ready to turn the light on the front porch on as I do every evening," she said, "and I looked out into the yard. There is an old gate in the yard where Mrs. Higgins, the second owner of the mansion, had planted a garden. I saw a lady standing in front of the garden. She was dressed as if it were the 1950s. She had on a short sleeved white blouse with a Peter Pan collar, a midi-length A-line skirt, Oxford shoes and short, curly hair. She looked just like my next door neighbor, who had lived in the mansion as a girl, except my neighbor wears jeans and a jean jacket and cowboy boots and always waves at me. She didn't wave, she just stared at me. I called to her and waved. Then as I waited for a response, I realized that there was a very faint green glow around this person, and she started to dissipate. I was so taken aback that I turned my back on her and pinched myself, and then I made myself look again. I could see her fading away at that moment. I just broke out in goose-bumps.

"The next day we were entertaining the staff of the Charlie Bair Museum for luncheon. A.B. Cook had a ranch in Meagher County and there are several displays in their museum that featured Mr. Cook. After luncheon the ladies said, 'We want to hear the ghost stories,' so I told them about the woman I had seen the night before. They told me it was Corinne Higgins, who was the first owner after the Cooks. Corinne had been their best friend in high school and had given fabulous parties at the mansion. She had died in 1994. 'We really feel like Corinne knew we were coming and appeared to you so you would tell us this story,' they said. It was a very moving incident."

Another family also had eerie experiences while living at the mansion.

"The grandmother, the mother and the daughter all had the same experience in Little Gloria's room," Sandy Rose stated. "Little Gloria was A.B. Cook's daughter. She spent her summers there from birth until she was thirteen, when both her parents passed away within months of each other. The ladies would be lying in bed at night, unable to sleep, and an apparition would appear from the ceiling. It took the form of the top half of a handsome young man, and each woman reported that his arms reached down and held her in bed. They couldn't move, but none of them was frightened. They all said he seemed to be trying to talk to them or tell them something, and he had a very sorrowful face.

"Well, the daughter told her best friend at school and pretty soon five girls decided to have a slumber party at the mansion. Unbeknown to the parents, they brought in a Ouija board. That night the girls conjured up what we think was a poltergeist. Windows flew up, doors slammed shut, pillow, blankets and books went flying. The girls were really frightened, and they called their parents about one A.M. The parents told everybody and the story spread. Pretty soon everybody in the county knew about the haunted house."

Guests have also had experiences in the mansion. One red-haired lady has stayed several times in the third floor dorm. She told the Roses that whenever she puts on stockings, or dresses up, the lights flash on and off. She also claimed that Hervey Cook would sometimes talk to her. Cook was called the "Howard Hughes of Montana" because of his preference for showgirls.

A young couple who loved Halloween booked a Halloween theme wedding in the old chapel on the grounds. To add to the spooky atmosphere, the Roses suspended a doll dressed as a ghost with a wedding veil from the chandelier in the entry of the house. The doll had tiny skeletal hands and a Halloween mask. The newly-wed couple posed beneath the doll for a photo. In the photo, the *mask had eyes.* The young couple considered that photo worth the entire cost of the theme wedding.

Another engaged couple who were serious students of the paranormal asked Sandy Rose to tell them all the ghost stories about the mansion before they retired for the night. The young woman was bubbling over with enthusiasm, while her companion sat listening with apparent skepticism. When they came down in the morning, however, the young woman looked tired and red-eyed from lack of sleep, while her fiancé was definitely excited about something. When Rose asked the young woman why she looked so tired, she said that her fiancé had kept her up all night, poking her in the ribs and saying 'Did you see that? Did you hear that?" His skepticism had vanished overnight.

Visiting psychics have often seen a dark male figure following a young teenage girl up the steps. She is crying. Rose thinks that this is Gloria and W.D. Rankin, her guardian, bringing her home after her mother's funeral. Some have called Rankin an "unscrupulous lawyer," while others say he was A.B. Cook's best friend. He gained most of the 125,000 acres that once belonged to Cook and later profited from the sale of a major portion of it to the U.S. government for the present Canyon Ferry Lake.

I had been invited to the mansion to talk about ghosts with a group of students from a nearby school. My friend and researcher Cynthia Berst accompanied me on this trip. We stayed in Little Gloria's Room on the second floor, where the most recently ghostly activity had occurred. Most of the students stayed in the third floor dorm where the red-haired guest had reportedly encountered the ghost of Hervey Cook. All of us looked forward to an interesting evening and perhaps some thrills during the night as well.

It was a beautiful night, calm and cool, when we gathered around a huge bonfire for s'mores and ghost stories. Afterward, the students were still full of energy, so we decided on an impromptu ghost hunt, and Sandy Rose agreed to show us where the body of Franklin Hervey Cook has been found after the botched robbery in 1970.

Cook and his sister Mary Agnes Cook, nicknamed M.A.C., were the stepchildren of the original owner, A.B. Cook, whom they both adored. Hervey had a flamboyant personality in his younger days, and was often photographed with showgirls or Hollywood starlets on his arm. As he aged, however, he became reclusive and shy. One of his few pleasures was driving his antique automobiles along country roads. He sometimes delivered the payroll to his various businesses and always carried a loaded .38 caliber handgun in case anyone attempted to rob him.

Around midnight on November 21, 1970, three drunken young

men arrived at Cook's home. They had once worked for Cook, but had been fired that summer. They brutally beat the ranch manager, tied him up, and then drove the hundred yards or so to the mansion, where they parked on a ramp that led down to the underground garage beneath the house. They then broke into the house.

Cook apparently heard them enter, grabbed his dog, his pistol, and a shotgun and took refuge in the maid's closet on the second floor. The dog may have begun barking and given away Cook's hiding place or Cook may simply have decided to defend his property. He burst out of the closet and fired at one of the robbers as he fled back down the stairway. Badly wounded, the robber staggered out of the house and onto the grounds, pursued by the seventy-one-year-old Cook.

Meanwhile, the second robber tried to escape by jumping from a second-story window. He landed on the ramp below, breaking a leg and knocking himself out in the fall. The driver of the getaway car hauled the unconscious man into the car and took off around the back of the mansion, looking for the robber who had been shot by Cook. Just as he rounded the house, Cook ran out, firing. The driver gunned the car and knocked him down. According to the sheriff, it appeared that the men beat Cook severely. They then piled into the car and drove off, running over Cook as they left. He was dragged down the driveway about 100 yards before he dropped off.

Eventually, the injured ranch manager managed to struggle free of his bonds and crawled to the highway. A passing motorist took him into Townsend where the sheriff was notified. Cook's body was found later that morning. The sheriff estimated that he had died around 2 A.M. from the beating and internal injuries from being run over by the automobile. The three men were caught the next day by the Lewis and Clark County sheriff's deputies and Helena police and eventually were sent to prison.

We followed Sandy Rose down the moonlit driveway toward the site where Cook's body had been found. On the way she told us about the antique car she had seen several times. While seated at her desk, she would hear the buzz of the motion detector at the end of the driveway, and look out the window to see the car turning off the highway onto the driveway. It would come silently up the drive as far as the small building near which Hervey Cook's body was found, but never reappear on the other side of the building. Perhaps this is Hervey Cook's spirit returning home from taking one of his beloved automobiles out for a spin. More likely, it's a "place memory," a sort of psychic recording of past events that can occasionally be viewed by sensitive people.

We gathered around Sandy at the approximate location where Cook's body was found. I gave one of the students an EMF (electromagnetic field) meter and another student a spare tape recorder, just in case some emotional residue from the murder could still be detected. Other students were looking warily around just in case Cook's spirit had chosen to walk that night. All of a sudden they screamed and pointed toward the lawn, where something that resembled a person wearing a long gray cloak had just glided behind a tree. Whatever it was did not reappear on the other side of the tree.

Some of the bolder students ran over to the tree, only to discover that what we had all seen was the spray from the rotating sprinkler, backlit by lights from the house. I only glimpsed it for an instant and from my angle it certainly made a very realistic "ghost." Even though the "ghost" had quickly been debunked, the experience left most of the group shaken but thrilled.

Cynthia and I went up to Little Gloria's Room not long afterward. As we prepared for bed, we could still hear cautious footsteps and muffled giggles coming from the corridors. The students had gotten several "hits" with the EMF meter in the house earlier and were apparently eager for more. Meanwhile, Cynthia and I set up an infra-red video camera to cover most of our bedroom to see whether anything happened during the night. Nothing was caught on camera, however, except a few loud thuds and thumps that sounded as if they were actually inside our room. With so many people roaming the house that night, though, it would be impossible to prove that the noises were of paranormal origin.

The Roses call the spirits "Angels with Issues." When asked

why they don't have the spirits exorcised, Steve and Sandy say, "While we were first unbelievers, then frightened, now it's a love affair. We grew to like them and now feel protected by them—and so do our guests!"

We look forward to visiting the mansion again someday. After all, we weren't able to explain the cold spot in the second floor corridor near the maid's closet where Hervey Cook hid from the robbers, or the inexplicable scent of a lovely perfume that Cynthia noticed near Mrs. A.B. Cook's bedroom. The restored chapel is intriguing too, for orbs have been photographed there during weddings, and one of the students got a reaction from the EMF meter on the ramp where the second robber fell during that awful night in 1970. And I'd like to spend more time sitting on the porch, enjoying the warmth and contentment of this much-loved family home, just as A.B. Cook and his family must have done on warm summer evenings so long ago.

If you'd like to experience a murder mystery evening at a place where a murder was actually committed, feel free to contact Sandy Rose for reservations. This multi-talented lady can also help you arrange everything from a theme wedding to tours of local ghost towns. And after a busy day hiking, birding, or sightseeing in the vicinity, you can relax around an evening campfire or in the Jacuzzi. And who knows what the night may bring: hurried footsteps on the stairs, the scent of a fine cigar, perhaps the glimpse of a phantom lady in the garden. Relax and enjoy—you're in the most haunted house in Montana!

UNINVITED GUESTS

When you were a child, did you avoid walking past an abandoned house in your town that everyone "just knew" was haunted? Did your friends ever dare you to peek through the grimy windows? My friends certainly did. After I'd reluctantly accepted a few dares, I found that I'd somehow gained a reputation for being fearless. None of my friends knew that I actually lived in a haunted house, so perhaps that gave me an unfair advantage. Of course I was frightened, but I always tried not to let it show, and fear was always outweighed by my insatiable curiosity.

Nearly every inhabited place in Montana is rumored to have a "haunted" house. You probably know of one in your own neighborhood. You may even be *living* in one! These homes range from older houses with a rich history to doublewide trailers or cabins hidden away in the woods to newly-constructed homes in outlying subdivisions. There are even haunted farms and ranch houses, as well as a converted barn that hid a startling secret.

The owners of these properties are usually hard-working people who have experienced a variety of phenomena they can't rationally explain: a feeling of being watched; areas of intense cold that disappear after a few moments; footsteps, disembodied voices, or phantom scents like the tantalizing aroma of apple pie when no one has been baking. They may even feel a tap on the shoulder from an unseen hand.

Some of these phenomena may be what is called "residual energy." We all expend energy during our normal daily activities. Some paranormal researchers theorize that these energies can be somehow absorbed by and stored in the fabric of buildings, especially those built of stone or brick containing silica, which is used in computer chips. The more intense the energy, the greater the chance it will be stored.

Researchers also theorize that people who are sensitive to electromagnetic fields can detect these energies at times. There's strong evidence that the ability to sense ghosts is biological, and like the other senses, varies from one person to another. That's probably why some owners can live in a "haunted" house and not experience anything unusual, while others will be plagued by ghostly footsteps or other phenomena from the beginning.

Most of those who contacted me seem to view their uninvited guests with curiosity rather than fear. Some are intrigued enough to watch television programs about ghosts, or even do a bit of investigation on their own. Others find that having a ghost comes in handy at times. When my sister and I were very young, we blamed "George," our house ghost, whenever something broke or went missing. Our excuses must have sounded a bit unconvincing to our parents at times, but "George" never told on us!

Many people come to regard their ghosts as family members. In some instances, they *are* family. A young man who inherited his grandmother's small house near downtown Billings occasionally sees the spirit of his grandmother, rocking contentedly in her favorite chair as she used to do when she was alive. He is pleased that she still visits him occasionally, and always calls out a greeting to his grandmother when he comes home from work in the evenings.

In another case, a man bought a house in Billings Heights, only to discover that he was sharing the house with the spirit of the original owner's wife. When the wife died, her elderly husband had been forced to sell their beloved house and move to a retirement home. The new owner wasn't really bothered by the wife's ghost and figured that she would move on when her husband finally died. Eventually the husband did die, but his spirit moved back in to rejoin his wife—and brought with him the ghosts of their four Pomeranian dogs! The owner just shrugs. "They don't take up much room," he says.

The owner of a house near Montana State University–Billings sometimes hears a cough from the unoccupied guest bedroom, and occasionally the mouth-watering aroma of baking cookies fills the house, especially around the holidays. After talking to neighbors, she concluded that the ghost is the wife of the original owner, who always celebrated the holidays by baking lots of cookies. The owner doesn't mind sharing her house with the spirit of the former owner. "It would be nice if she'd leave me some cookies, though!" she says with a twinkle in her eye.

A small house in the historic district near downtown Billings has changed hands frequently over the years. Previous owners have reported seeing a young boy in their basement. The boy points at the concrete floor and then vanishes. So far no one has torn up the floor to see whether anything is under it. A local television crew that spent a Halloween night there experienced equipment malfunctions and saw the dial of a radio whiz back and forth by itself.

A large house on the south side of Billings was home to six generations of the same family. The last owner's children reported being "shushed" by an elderly man. He is thought to have been a long-dead uncle who disliked small children. When I visited, both the owner and I were startled to find that my tape recorder had picked up a man's voice saying crossly, "Be quiet." The owner recently moved to a larger home, and on moving day she courteously invited her deceased relatives to come along with her. So far there has been no paranormal activity in her new house, so perhaps her grumpy uncle decided to stay in what, for generations, had been his own home.

A ghost's personality doesn't change just because he or she had died, as one family found out to their dismay. A few years ago, they purchased a house from an elderly lady who had been widowed and could no longer afford to keep her house. She and her husband had lived there since the house had been built, and she was fiercely resentful of the new owners. She was killed in an automobile accident a few months later and her spirit promptly returned to her old home where she began to persecute the new owners and their teenage daughter. Both parents saw the ghosts of the elderly couple sitting on the sofa in the living room and the daughter was terrified by a menacing presence she sensed lurking outside her bedroom door at night. I suggested that the new owners speak firmly to the ghosts, explaining that the house no longer belonged to them and that if the ghosts wanted to stay, disruptive behaviors would not be tolerated. Apparently the ghosts understood, for things have reportedly quieted down.

The owner of a haunted barn in north-central Montana got quite a surprise when he decided to remodel an old barn into a bunkhouse for guests. The roof needed to be replaced, and in the process a previously hidden room in the hayloft was uncovered. An old leather suitcase lay on the dusty floor along with a few unused shotgun shells. The suitcase held tiny vials labeled "Essence of Rye" and "Essence of Bourbon" as well as packets of yellowed labels reading "Pride of Kansas." Apparently the barn had been used to produce illegal liquor during Prohibition. The owner had always felt uncomfortable whenever he stacked hay in the loft, as if he was being watched by something he couldn't see. His suspicions had been justified.

"Somebody must have stood guard up there with a shotgun," he told me. "After Prohibition ended, they didn't need the room anymore and just boarded it up."

Renovating a building has been known to trigger a haunting or, if renovations are extensive enough, even end a haunting. In this case, replacing the original roof apparently allowed the embedded energies to dissipate. The farmer no longer has the sensation of being watched.

"I kind of miss 'em," he admitted.

Of course, not everyone reacts calmly to a brush with the supernatural. A hired hand will never forget the night he spent alone in a haunted bunkhouse on a remote ranch north of Clyde Park. He woke to footsteps and moving shadows in the bunkhouse and at first thought he'd been joined by another of the crew. No one answered when he called out, however, so he got up and lit the kerosene lantern. A quick search proved that he was alone in the bunkhouse. A few minutes later the footsteps began again, this time heading directly toward him. Still no one was visible. He grabbed his boots, bolted from the bunkhouse and rattled off to the safety of the nearest town aboard the only transportation available, an old John Deere tractor.

I've always enjoyed going to "open houses" here in Billings, especially if the house is of historical or architectural interest, and I can usually tell as soon as I set foot inside whether I'd be comfortable living in that house. Some houses have felt welcoming, while a few have left me feeling very glad that I wasn't seriously in the market for a house. I can only hope, as I drive away, that whoever buys that particular house won't be sensitive to its uneasy atmosphere and will have no problems while living there.

Powerful emotions can sometimes linger for centuries. A couple of years ago my friend Pat Cody and I visited Mount Vernon in Virginia, home of George Washington and his wife Martha. We were familiar with Washington as the Revolutionary War general who became our first president and father of our country, of course, but knew little about him as a man. No sooner had Pat and I entered the grounds, however, than we were almost overcome by the powerful atmosphere of Mount Vernon. It was obvious to us that Washington had been a very great soul, a man who had accomplished his difficult life's tasks with grace and honor, and that his benign influence still lingered protectively over his estate. It was a very moving experience. I can't imagine anyone not being affected—in this case positively—by the powerfully benign atmosphere of Mount Vernon.

Unfortunately, negative emotions can also linger for centuries. One of the most fear-filled nights I have ever spent was at The Myrtles, a Louisiana plantation house built in the late 1790s. A number of murders are reputed to have occurred there, although only one has been historically verified. Pat and I are experienced paranormal researchers and it takes a lot to shake us, but the atmosphere that night was terrifying even though we saw nothing. I have to admit that I had nightmares about it for weeks afterward.

What's it like to live in a real haunted house? A couple I will call "Robert" and "Lola" moved into a brand-new house not far from the Canyon Creek Battlefield in 1999. According to old maps, their property lies not far from the route taken by Chief Joseph's band of Nez Perce as they fled from pursuing army troops back in 1877. Rob is partly of Blackfoot descent, and both he and his wife are extremely sensitive to the paranormal. Odd things began to happen soon after they moved into their new home. For several months Lola kept an account of what happened. It reads as follows:

August 1999: Felt something rub against my legs. Thought it was our cat, but she was asleep on our bed. Occurred several times until end of November.

October 1999: Around the third week, Rob saw the figure of a man. He appeared as all black with no facial features wearing a knee-length coat and what looked like a cavalry cap from 1870-1890.

October 1999: Saw what looked like a man wearing a yellow and black checkered vest. He had a large belly. Also smelled a very unpleasant odor behind my chair. Rob has also smelled the odor behind his chair.

March 2000: Rob was recording odd crackling sounds in the kitchen when something knocked the tape recorder out of his hand.

May 2000: Odor seemed to be following me as I was vacuuming. Smell lasted most of the day. Opened windows but smell stayed.

May 2000: I was reading in the living room when I heard very loud knocking on the bathroom wall, about 4 loud knocks. Shortly after that, I smelled something like formaldehyde behind my chair. It stung my nose.

May 2000: Rob and I were watching local TV when we both heard someone laugh. The laughter was so loud it blocked out the regular programming sounds. Rob left for work shortly afterward and I went into our bedroom. I turned on the small TV and again the HAHAHAHA sound came over the TV.

May 2000: While in bed, both Rob and I felt cool air brush over us. Later, I was in the kitchen when the whole lower half of my body got very cold as if something cold passed through me.

May 2000: Rob smelled cigarette smoke although neither of us smokes. The day before, I smelled campfire smoke.

October 2000: Heard pounding at the back door. Opened it and there was no one visible. Closed the door and the pounding began again. Opened the door and found the aluminum screen was bent from the force of the pounding.

The eerie events at that house continue to this day. Rob is convinced that some of the disturbances are related to the running battle between Chief Joseph band and the pursuing army, which may have crossed their property. Other phenomena, such as the apparition of an old man with a weathered face and a bushy white beard, may have more to do with an old sheep wagon Rob found at the edge of his property. In any case, Rob and Lola are resolved to stay in their dream home. They, like most of those who live in haunted houses, accept the unknown with courage and determination.

Could you?

THE LADY ON THE STAIRS

THE CASTLE MUSEUM
310 2nd Avenue Northeast
White Sulphur Springs, Montana 59645
Telephone: 406-547-2324

Ghostly Activity Level: Low

HISTORY: The natural hot springs that gave the town of White Sulphur Springs its name have long been known to Native Americans as a place of healing. In the 1870s and 1880s, people came from all over the world to take medicinal mineral baths. In 1890, wealthy stockman and mine owner Byron R. Sherman built a tall gray stone mansion on a hilltop overlooking the town. In 1905, the Sherman mansion was sold to Michael Donahoe, who lived there with his family until 1910. The building was divided into three apartments but later was vacated and had seriously deteriorated by 1960, when Donahoes' heirs gave the building to the Meagher County Historical Association. Usually referred to as The Castle, the mansion has been painstakingly restored and opened for tours as a house museum in 1968. It is open from May 15 to September 15.

PHENOMENA: A neighborhood youngster who peered in the window one day claimed to have seen a ghostly lady dressed in white floating up the main staircase. A woman living across the street witnessed what looked like a lantern being carried from one window to another window of the empty building. A deputy sheriff who searched the building after neighbors reported lights going on and off late one night found no one inside.

I first heard of a possible ghost in White Sulphur Springs from a friend who had toured the Castle while on vacation. At the end of the tour, she asked the docent whether the building was haunted.

The docent told her that a local boy, peering through a window at dusk one evening, claimed to have seen a lady in white float up the stairway with a candle in her hand.

"I was tempted to dress up in white myself on Halloween," the docent added, "and station myself on the stairs to give the youngsters a thrill. I decided against it, however. I was afraid that I might not be the only one on the stairs that night."

Chilling words, and irresistible to a ghost hunter! I drove up to White Sulphur Springs on a fine July morning with my friends Frank Stevens and Sue Tracy, eager to see whether there was any truth to the story. Mrs. Jean Reed, a docent at the Castle, met us when we arrived.

"Have you had any ghostly experiences here yourself?" I asked.

"I've been a docent here for eight years," Mrs. Reed replied, "and I've never heard of a ghost. Of course, I don't believe in them." The only odd occurrence that she could recall was a time when the security alarms kept going off at night. No one was ever found in the building, and there were no signs of forced entry. Eventually it was determined that bats roosting in the attic had somehow found a hole leading to the lower floors, and that the bats' swooping flight had triggered the motion-sensing alarms. Once the hole was repaired, the alarms stayed silent.

Mrs. Reed gave us an interesting commentary on the Sherman family as we began our tour. B.R. Sherman, who had made a fortune in mining and livestock, began construction of the gray stone Castle in 1890. The building was constructed of granite blocks hauled by ox teams from a quarry twelve miles away, and it was designed with the most modern conveniences, including a cistern in the attic that provided water for the house. There were twelve rooms, each furnished with the finest materials available.

Sherman, his wife Emeline and their children lived in the Castle from 1892 until 1905, when Sherman decided to retire. He sold the house to Seattle businessman Michael Donahoe and moved to California, where he divorced Emeline three years later. The Donohoe family occupied the Castle for about five years before moving back to Seattle. The Castle stood empty for a while, slowly deteriorating before it was subdivided into apartments. Eventually the Donohoe heirs donated the Castle to the Meagher County Historical Association. After extensive renovation, it opened as a historical museum in August of 1968. The antique furnishings are not original to the house but are on loan from local residents.

We followed Mrs. Reed up the ornate stairway at the front of the house. This was where a local boy, peering in through the windows one evening, had reportedly seen the ghost of a woman in a long white dress. There seemed to be nothing otherworldly about the stairway, at least in the bright light of day. The second floor contained several large bedrooms furnished just as they would have been in the early 1900s, and a charming nursery. We peered into the nursery, admiring the antique furnishings, and turned to follow Mrs. Reed to the next room. Suddenly both Sue and I heard a high-pitched infant's squeal of laughter coming from the nursery. It seemed to come from a point just inside the room and was definitely not a noise from outside. Oddly enough, neither Frank nor Mrs. Reed heard it, nor, when we played our tape recorders back, had the sound registered on tape. The nursery had been a bathroom when the Shermans lived there. Perhaps what we had heard was a baby enjoying a bath that had occurred over a century ago.

Emeline Sherman's last child, Emeline Genevieve, was the only baby actually born in the Castle. I'd heard of no rumors that a baby's spirit haunted the Castle, so perhaps what we had heard was merely the echo of a baby's happy laughter from long ago.

Is there really a ghost at the Castle? According to several witnesses, there are three: a lady in white, a man wearing an old-fashioned green suit who has been seen playing cards in the men's parlor, and a young girl in a white pinafore in the girls' room on the second floor.

Penny James Huffman grew up in White Sulphur Springs. She recalls that as a child in the late 1960s she was aware of rumors that the Castle was haunted. Once or twice she even saw what looked like the shadow of a woman drift slowly across a window. When she grew up, she left White Sulphur Springs, but returned in the spring of 1985. The Castle had become a museum by then, but the basement had not yet been renovated and the basement apartment was still available. Huffman rented the apartment, intending to bring over most of her belongings the next day. An uneasy night convinced her that she wasn't alone in the house.

"It was actually quite scary," she said. "I was twenty-three, and I had never been attuned to spirits, but I felt a presence there. It seemed to be focused in one room in particular, the little girl's room. I sensed a little girl in a pinafore." She moved out the next day.

Huffman isn't the only one who is convinced that life goes on at the Castle as it always has, mostly unseen and just beneath the surface of modern life. Shawn Dunkin, who lived across the street from the Castle for many years, often walked home late at night from her job at a local bar. Several times she saw a woman standing at an upper window of the empty building, looking out across the town.

"She was wearing a long white old fashioned dress high at the neck," she recalls, "and her hair was piled up on her head. When I would look up at her, she would look at me and then turn and move away."

On a number of occasions Dunkin saw what looked like a lantern moving from window to window of the darkened, deserted Castle. One night her children saw lights going on and off in the Castle, so Dunkin called the sheriff. The deputy met a representative from the Meagher County Historical Association at the building and they systematically checked every room of the

Castle. No one was found, but the deputy commented on the uncanny atmosphere in the building.

A young man who often visited the Castle as a teenager told his mother that he had seen a man wearing an old-fashioned green suit playing cards by himself in the men's parlor. The next moment the man had vanished. It's not known who the man may have been.

The identity of the female ghost may be easier to determine. The long white high-necked dress and the upswept hairdo described by eyewitnesses were fashionable from about 1900 to1905, when the Shermans were in residence. Emeline had married B.R. Sherman in 1882, when she was only eighteen. He divorced her in 1908 after twenty-six years of marriage. Perhaps the spirit of Emeline Sherman visits the Castle from time to time, nostalgically recalling her happiest years. If so, she is probably pleased that the building has been restored to its original grandeur and now attracts tourists from all over the world.

The Castle Museum is open from May 15 to September 1, from 10 A.M. to 5 P.M. The last tour begins at 4:30. And as you tour the mansion, be sure to glance into the men's parlor. Perhaps you too will glimpse the mysterious card player in a green suit. And if you shiver for no apparent reason on your way up the front stairs, you may have just brushed past the ghostly Lady in White.

GHOSTS OF THE REMINGTON HOTEL

REMINGTON BAR & CASINO
130 Central Avenue
Whitefish, Montana 59937
Telephone: 406-862-0017

Ghostly Activity Level: Low

HISTORY: The town of Whitefish was officially founded in 1904 when the Great Northern Railway arrived, although fur traders and loggers had been working in the area since the late 1800s. Today, this small town in the scenic Flathead Valley is a center for outdoor recreation, ranging from world-class skiing at nearby Big Mountain to hiking, fishing and biking in the summer months. The building that is now the Remington Bar was bought in 1908 by a Japanese businessman, Mokutaro Hori. Upscale dining was available in Hori's Café on the main floor and railroad crews rented rooms upstairs. The hotel eventually closed, and the Remington Bar and Casino now occupies the main floor.

PHENOMENA: Heavy footsteps are sometimes heard in the bathroom or an upstairs hallway when no one is visible. Inexplicable knockings and sweet odors were noted by a former manager. The figure of an elderly man wearing an old-fashioned long coat was seen by an employee moments before he vanished. Lipstick-smeared cigarettes are occasionally found still smoldering after the cleaners have finished for the night.

The Remington Hotel has long been rumored to be haunted. According to an article by Christine Hensleigh in the *Whitefish Pilot,* October 27, 2004, a former manager who had worked at the Remington from 1989 to 1999 claimed to have heard the sound of knocking when she was alone in the building. On frequent occasions she found lipstick-smeared cigarettes still burning after the bar had been cleaned and closed for the night. Employees who were openly skeptical about the existence of ghosts sometimes changed their minds when knives inexplicably fell from hooks on walls. A cloyingly sweet odor was occasionally noted at the top of the stairs, only to vanish shortly afterward. Its origin was never found.

One day, a visitor who had been watching his wife gamble was startled to find himself floating a foot above the floor. The incident was witnessed by an employee. A ghost the staff call "George" was blamed for that incident. George may not be the only spirit at the Remington, however. Ghost hunters who carried out an investigation there believe they detected the spirits of an older man, a woman, and a small boy as well.

A more recent article about the spooky doings at the Remington appeared in the *Flathead Beacon* of October 24, 2007. One of the bartenders told reporter Dan Testa that George still made his presence known by interfering with electrical equipment or "messing up" the kitchen. The bartender added that after closing one evening, the night manager heard heavy boots walking along the floor of the women's bathroom. No one was there and no one else was in the building. The footsteps have also been heard in an upstairs hallway. Again, no one was there.

Leslie Rule, daughter of best-selling crime writer Ann Rule, visited the Remington in 1998 while working on her book *Coast to Coast Ghosts* and interviewed a number of employees who claimed to have experienced paranormal activity. Chef Sean Thompson watched in disbelief as a kitchen clock flew across the room. A spare set of master keys disappeared one day, only to be found months later in an old dresser upstairs. Manager Joey Meyers actually saw the figure of an elderly man in a long dark coat standing smiling at the edge of a crowd during an employee party in mid-December.

"Meyers turned away for a second," Rule wrote, *"and when she looked back the old gentleman was gone. His appearance had been so out of place that she grabbed the bartender and asked if she had seen him. She had not, and helped Joey search for him. The two dashed outside and scanned the sidewalk, but the man had vanished."*

Rule was also told by a waitress that a third ghost, a man who wore a bowler hat and appeared to be in his thirties or forties, had appeared a few feet from her at the bar. Intrigued, Rule searched newspaper archives at the *Whitefish Pilot* and quickly found reports that identified three men whose violent deaths might have been reason enough for them to haunt the Remington.

The elderly man in the long coat who was seen by Meyers may have been Mark L. Prowse, who was struck and killed instantly by a train in mid-December, 1922, while making his way home from a Masonic Lodge meeting. He had celebrated his seventy-fifth birthday with his family earlier that day at Hori's Café. Rule speculates that Mr. Prowse may have briefly returned on what had been the anniversary of both his birthday and death, drawn somehow by the festive atmosphere of the holiday party.

The ghost in the bowler hat seen at the bar by the waitress may have been railroad conductor Ben Ramey, who was shot and killed by his son-in-law when an argument turned violent on December 1, 1922. Ramey's wife ran an upscale dress shop across the street from Hori's Café, and he would have been very familiar with the vicinity.

A female spirit who leaves lipstick-smeared cigarettes still burning may never be identified, but the "George" who seems to be the most active spirit may be George Winans, who was found dead in his room on November 14, 1919. His throat had been cut. The verdict was suicide due to ill health.

As she explored some of the original hotel rooms, Rule noticed that the roof of an adjoining building was only six feet below the windows, providing an easy escape route for a possible murderer.

At that moment, Rule wrote: "I was struck by a thought so powerful that it was nearly a voice. *'I didn't kill myself! I was murdered! Please tell my parents! Tell my sister! Tell Sarah!'*"

Impelled by that anguished plea, Rule set out to trace George's family. According to the newspaper account of George's death, they lived in Two Rivers, Washington. Despite extensive research, however, Rule was unable to trace a Sarah who might be connected to George.

When I contacted Leslie Rule to ask for permission to quote her findings, I was able to add some further information about George's family. Census records show he was born in 1888 in Illinois to a Norman and Celestia Winans. He did indeed have a sister, Helen. In 1920, his father Norman, now a widower, was living in Two Rivers, Walla Walla County, Washington, just as the article stated. As for "Sarah," census records list a younger Sarah Winans who lived in Walla Walla County in 1920. Research revealed that she was George's cousin.

The Remington's owner, Ted Sproul, told me that he'd experienced nothing unusual himself, but that some of his staff believed the building was haunted, and suggested that I talk with Dennis, a longtime employee. I met him in the casino just as he was finishing work for the day.

Dennis has had a number of odd experiences in the eleven years he's worked as a "swamper" at the bar. He's a quiet, well-spoken man who takes his encounters with the Remington's spectral visitors matter-of-factly. "I'd be walking or standing somewhere and all of a sudden I'd smell something really putrid, just for a split second. Or get a chill all of a sudden. That happened quite often. A couple of times I heard what sounded like someone banging on a pipe with a wrench off in the distance. And tools would come up missing. I'd find 'em, but I was pretty sure I hadn't moved them."

Most of the activity occurs in the front part of the bar. "That may be because George, the guy who's supposed to be the ghost, had his apartment in the front corner upstairs. He was a railroad man, and committed suicide by cutting his throat in that room.

I have no reason to go upstairs, but the few times I went up there, I never noticed anything."

The most dramatic event happened about four years ago, not long after a partition was put up dividing the casino from the main bar. "One day I was sitting here at a table," Dennis told me, "and I saw a dark figure, a silhouette like someone in a trench coat and hat float across the entryway. I never heard any noise. It was just floating above the floor. I walked out there and there was nothing."

"How tall was the figure?" I asked. Dennis thought for a moment. "I'd guess about five feet eight" he said, and added, "When there's some kind of change, activity really picks up. They don't like change. Things have been pretty quiet for a couple of years, but if we put up a wall or move something, things will start happening." It was an observation that I had heard many times from owners of haunted properties. Ghosts don't like changes to their environment, and sometimes make their objections quite clear.

The bar was now open, so I thanked Dennis and walked over to talk to bartender Patty, who has worked at the Remington for eleven years. She too had encountered something odd. It happened upstairs in the bookkeeper's office that Dennis stated had once belonged to George Winans.

"I was in the office upstairs one day," Patty said. "You can hear anyone walking down the hallway because the floor creaks. Well, I heard the floor creaking and waited for someone to open the door. No one did, so I got up and looked out the peephole. Nobody was there, so I opened the door and looked out. I couldn't see anyone, but the floor didn't creak as if anyone had left, either. Maybe that was paranormal."

Business was beginning to pick up, so I found a quiet place at the end of the long room and spoke to any spirits that might be present, hoping that my tape recorder would pick up EVP, or electronic voice phenomena, thought to be actual communications from spirits. First, I spoke to George Winans, who so desperately wanted his sister and his cousin Sarah to know that he hadn't committed suicide but had been murdered. I gently pointed out that since both women died long ago, he can finally deliver his message to them himself. Then I addressed Mokutaro Hori, whose granddaughter had recently contacted me by email. "Hori-san," I said quietly, using the Japanese term of respect, "Your granddaughter Judy would like me to greet you and present her respects."

There was no reply on the tape when I played it back, but something odd happened when my friend Pat and I stopped for lunch at Kwataqnuk Resort in Polson an hour later. On the way to the rest rooms, we happened to walk past several slot machines. One of them had colorful oriental characters at the top. Although I rarely gamble, I felt a strong urge to put a dollar bill in that machine. I didn't know how to play it, but I fed a dollar bill into it and randomly pushed some buttons. When the whizzing and whirring stopped, I was astonished to find that I had won $37!

My friend Pat suggested, only half-jokingly, that perhaps the spirit of Mr. Hori had chosen this way to thank me for passing on his granddaughter's greeting. Was my sudden urge to put a dollar into the only slot machine with oriental characters just a startling coincidence, spirit intervention, or completely random? I don't know, but I quietly thanked Mr. Hori—just in case.

Next time you're in Whitefish, why not take time from skiing or hiking to drop into the Remington Bar? At the very least, you'll enjoy a congenial evening with folks from all over the world. And if you spot an elderly man in a long coat who smiles reminiscently at the crowd before he vanishes, consider yourself lucky. You may just have caught a glimpse of Mark Prowse, who celebrated his seventy-fifth birthday in the hotel in 1922, just hours before he was struck by a train and killed.

YOUR QUESTIONS ANSWERED

Since *Haunted Montana: A Ghost Hunter's Guide to Haunted Places You Can Visit* was published in 2007, I've received e-mails from readers all over the United States and Canada. Many simply wanted to share their experiences with me but others asked serious questions about ghosts and paranormal research. Here are a few of the more frequently asked questions:

Q. *How did you become interested in ghosts?*
A. I grew up in a haunted house in Minneapolis and experienced a variety of phenomena during the nineteen years I lived there. While studying at the University of Minnesota, I became acquainted with a group of people who were interested in paranormal research. We spent many exciting and sometimes frightening evenings investigating haunted sites in the Twin Cities. Although many years have passed since then, I'm still fascinated by ghosts and have visited hundreds of haunted sites all over the United States and Britain.

Q. *What are ghosts, anyway?*
A. No one knows for sure. People have reported seeing ghosts at least as far back as the time of the ancient Greeks. Naturally, a lot of theories have been proposed to explain ghosts. Some say that ghosts are figments of the imagination, or that the phenomena attributed to ghosts are due to faulty observation. Others say that ghosts are a form of emotional energy given off in times of crisis and somehow absorbed by the surroundings. There is grow-

ing evidence that low-frequency sound waves that affect a certain portion of the brain can produce some of the phenomena attributed to ghosts. And of course, ghosts may be just what they've been assumed to be all along: spirits of those who have died. The ghostly voices captured on audiotape seem to point toward that conclusion, at least in some cases. Probably no one theory can adequately explain the different types of paranormal phenomena. If you'd like to learn more, log on to the website of the American Ghost Society at http://www.prairieghosts.com for lots of interesting information.

Q. *Why do some people become ghosts why they die?*
A. Apparently most people have no difficulty "crossing over." Only a very small percentage of people become what we call "ghosts." They may choose to linger for a variety of reasons: an emotional attachment to a home, an unwillingness to leave family members, particularly if there are young children; unfinished business of some sort, a fear of facing judgment, or lack of belief in an afterlife.

Those who are killed unexpectedly in accidents or die while heavily sedated in hospital beds may also linger briefly until they realize what has happened to them. For instance, my mother had been blind, deaf, senile and completely bedridden for several years before she died. The day before her funeral, my sister, brother-in-law, aunt and I went to her apartment to pack up her belongings. As I wrapped china, I heard Mom's distinctive hoarse voice say *"Karen!"* No one else appeared to hear her. I knew that Mom must be wondering what we were doing in her apartment, so I spoke aloud to her, explaining that she had died of pneumonia and that we had to clear her apartment for the next tenant, and assuring her that most of her treasured possessions would go to her granddaughter. I also told Mom about the funeral arrangements, and that we had chosen beautiful pink roses for the flower arrangements. When I finished, I heard Mom's voice again, this time just a brief *"Okay."* A few minutes later, Frank, my former husband, came into the apartment carrying more empty boxes. He set them down, commenting on the scent of perfume he'd noticed in the doorway. Mom's perfume had already been packed, and none of us was wearing perfume. He is convinced that Mom was standing in the doorway to greet him as he entered. I found it comforting to know that Mom's physical ills had been left behind with her worn-out body.

Q. *Are there ghostly animals?*
A. Certainly! Ghosts of many kinds of animals have been reported: dogs, cats, birds, horses, even wild animals, although those are less common. Ask anyone who has lost a beloved pet whether they have ever seen, heard or felt around them the house and chances are good that the answer will be a resounding "yes!" My mother used to hear her beloved canary singing in the sewing room where he died. Cat owners sometimes feel a ghostly cat winding itself around their legs or jumping up on their lap. Dog owners may hear a "thump" as if a large dog has just lain down next to their chair. Many times I have heard the unmistakable jingle of dog tags in the living room when my two living dogs were sound asleep in the bedroom. Once, I had just opened the back door to let my dogs out into the yard when another dog, hazy but recognizable as my long-dead dog Gryphon, bolted past me to follow the living dogs. Personally, I am sure that my beloved pets will be waiting to greet me when the time comes for me to cross the Rainbow Bridge.

Q. *Are ghosts evil?*
A. People's personalities don't change just because they are no longer in their bodies. Most living people are decent, caring folks. A few are nasty. The same thing is true for ghosts. If you ever feel uncomfortable or threatened in a haunted building, *leave.*

Q. *Do ghosts hurt people?*
A. Why would they want to? Most of the spirits you're likely to encounter will be your own deceased relatives and friends, dropping by to see how you're doing. I've never been hurt by a ghost

myself, although I've been touched by unseen hands on several occasions. That's not to say you couldn't run into one of the nasty types, although it's rare.

Stephen Weidner, a close friend of mine who is the founder of the American Association of Paranormal Investigators, told me about one such incident. He and his group were investigating an old cemetery in Colorado. The investigation appeared to be going well but Weidner became increasingly uneasy. He's learned to trust his instincts, so he called off the investigation and everyone headed back to their cars. Weidner's car was parked at a slant with the driver's door on the downhill side, so he would have to pull the door upward against the force of gravity to close it. When Weidner started to get into the car, the door slammed shut by itself, bruising his leg badly. At the same time his tape recorder picked up an angry male voice that ordered, "Get out." He left. If you run into one like that, the best thing to do is what Weidner did: *Leave!*

Q. *Do ghosts scare you?*
A. I'm not afraid of ghosts. It's the live ones you've got to watch out for. Seriously though, I've been in two haunted places that gave me a real fright. One was a Civil War-era bed and breakfast called the Weller Haus in Bellevue, Kentucky, just across the Ohio River from Cincinnati. The present owner told us that the previous owner had been found dead on the kitchen floor and supposedly haunted the building.

My friend Pat Cody and I had booked a room on the second floor at the top of the stairs. Since we were the only guests that night, we left the bedroom door open while getting ready for bed. While Pat was in the bathroom, I heard a loud shuffling noise from downstairs. It sounded as if someone was moving around the kitchen. I crept quietly down the stairs. The kitchen was dimly lit by an exit light and no one was there. I went back up, told Pat what I'd heard, and we both went down and took several photos. Nothing unusual showed up on camera, so we went upstairs again.

Pat went back into the bathroom to finish brushing her teeth and I sat on a chair looking through the open doorway down the brightly-lit stairs. Although nothing was visible, I became increasingly uneasy, and unease gradually turned to outright fear. When Pat came out of the bathroom, I told her emphatically, "If you weren't here with me tonight, I wouldn't stay in this house!"

"That's not like you," she replied, surprised. Now that she was nearby, though, the fear vanished, and I felt a little foolish. We closed the door and set up an infrared video camera that covered the doorway and most of the room. I climbed into the four-poster bed and quickly dropped off to sleep, but Pat decided to read for a while. A few minutes later, she heard two quick knocks on the bedroom door. There was a gap of about two inches between the floor and the bottom of the door, so Pat leaned over to see if she could see anyone's feet on the other side of the door. She saw nothing, and the knocks were not repeated. A little later, she turned out the light and went to sleep.

I reviewed the videotape the next morning. The knocks on the door were distinct, but there had been a third, much fainter knock that Pat had apparently not heard. As she leaned over to look for feet beneath the door, I slowed the tape. No feet were visible beneath the door. Not only that, but the videotape had later recorded men's voices speaking quietly, then what sounded like a fife and drums playing Civil War music. Odd light phenomena were also captured by the camera. They resembled sparkling bursts of light and moved quickly from one side of the room to the other.

At breakfast we told the owner what we had experienced. She was intrigued, and told us that the former owner had been accustomed to knocking on each of his daughters' doors when he went to bed. Although the daughters moved away many years ago, apparently the ghost is still knocking on their doors. And much to my surprise, there was indeed a Civil War connection with the property: a Confederate cavalry force had crossed the river in 1863 and raided the outskirts of Cincinnati before retreating. They had probably passed very close to the site of the present Weller Haus bed-and-breakfast.

Looking back to the events of that night, I'm certain that the ghost of the former owner had been standing on the landing just outside our door, watching us. Although I couldn't see him, I must have been aware of him on some level, causing uneasiness and actual fear. Next time, I'll grab a camera and see if anything unusual shows up.

The other incident that really frightened me happened in a supposedly haunted room at the Admiral Fell Inn in historic Baltimore. Pat and I had left the bathroom light on in case we needed to get up during the night. About 2 A.M. I was awakened by shuffling footsteps and thought Pat had gotten up. The bathroom light went off, and the shuffling footsteps approached my bed. I was lying on my side with my back toward the bathroom, and I could feel something staring intently at me, *willing* me to roll over. Ghost hunter or not, I simply could *not* force myself to turn around and look. I lay frozen, eyes squeezed tightly shut, and after what seemed like minutes, the footsteps receded toward the door. Oddly enough, I dropped off to sleep moments later. In the morning Pat asked me why I'd turned off the bathroom light and I told her what had happened. She hadn't gotten up at all during the night. We had apparently had a visit from the ghost who haunted that room. He was known to turn lights on or off and had also played tricks on previous guests. Fortunately, he left us alone for the remainder of our stay.

Q. *How can I tell if our house (or a house we want to buy) is haunted?*
A. If the realtor makes excuses to stay outside, the neighborhood dogs cross the street to avoid the house or the neighbors ask if you've "noticed anything" yet, there's a pretty good chance you've got a house ghost! Seriously—trust your instincts. If the house doesn't "feel right," be warned!

Some of the phenomena to watch for are unusual odors, such as the aroma of pipe tobacco when no one in the house smokes, the scent of perfume or perhaps the enticing fragrance of baking bread when the oven is cold. It's also quite common for people to catch glimpses of something moving when no one else is there, or feel watched by someone they can't see. Sometimes footsteps are heard when no one else is around, or televisions or water faucets will turn themselves on. You might notice cold spots that can't be explained as drafts or inadequate insulation. More rarely, you may hear a voice calling your name or notice that your pets are watching something move around that you can't see.

Q. *How can I get rid of a ghost?*
A. Let's back off a moment and try to see things from the ghost's point of view. Perhaps he (or she) doesn't realize he's died. He's confused, because people he doesn't know are living in what used to be his house and no one seems to be able to see or hear him. Naturally he's going to try to create noise or make things move in order to try to drive out what he sees as intruders. Wouldn't you?

If you really don't feel comfortable living with a house ghost and would like it to leave, try speaking aloud to the ghost. I always state the current date and explain that he is no longer living, and that he needs to move onward to wherever he's supposed to go. Then I suggest that he look around for a bright light and move toward it. Sometimes that's all it takes. I know of no way to force a ghost to leave if he's not ready. Even an exorcism, performed by trained clergy, is no guarantee that the phenomena will cease. If a ghost is disruptive and refuses to leave, explain what behaviors you will no longer tolerate. Be decisive and firm. Tell him that the house is no longer his and you will not allow him to frighten the children or pets. If he isn't ready to leave, he must behave in an appropriate manner, just as you would expect of a living guest. Usually things will quiet down after that. If not, you may need to call in clergy who will perform a house blessing, or contact a medium who will try to persuade the spirit to leave.

There's another type of phenomenon that is often mistaken for a true ghost, or spirit. It's called a "place memory" or "residual energy," and can be compared to a tape recording or video recording of events that have happened in the past. For instance, you might hear footsteps every night going up the stairs at ten, and find out that a former owner always went to bed at that exact time every night. That doesn't necessarily mean the former owner haunts the place. It's more likely that the energies of a repetitive action have somehow been absorbed by the surroundings. Unlike a true ghost or spirit, residual energy never reacts to a living observer. There's no way to communicate with it since no actual spirit is present. Eventually the energy will fade away, but it could take many years. This type of haunting seems to be far more common than an intelligent haunting, one that involves an actual spirit.

Q. *Have you ever encountered a "demonic" entity?*
A. I've heard lots of stories about "things with glowing red eyes" but the stories are always second or third-hand, the kind of tale that "happened to a friend of a friend of a friend of mine." In almost fifty years of investigating haunted sites, I've never encountered anything that could remotely be considered demonic. Frankly, I doubt they exist. There are certainly negative human spirits, and they are probably responsible for much if not all of the phenomena some investigators attribute to "demons." Most paranormal researchers do quietly ask for protection from a Higher Power before they go into a haunted place, however—just in case!

Q. *Why can some people see ghosts while others can't?*
A. Good question. Recent experiments have shown that people who report paranormal experiences are also unusually sensitive to electromagnetic fields, so the ability to sense ghosts may be biological, and, like the ability to see or hear, can vary considerably from person to person. It's possible that the "sixth sense" may even have been a survival mechanism. Think about it: in the days when small groups of people roamed the land hunting and gathering food, wouldn't it have been an advantage to be able to sense when hostile eyes were watching you? Perhaps you'd have avoided being eaten by wolves or ambushed by unfriendly hunters from another tribe. Over the centuries, as survival became easier, the "sixth sense" was no longer needed and began to fade away.

Q. *I don't believe in ghosts and anyone who does is crazy*!
A. Let's face it, ghosts defy logic. I probably wouldn't believe that ghosts exist either if I hadn't lived for nineteen years in a haunted house. Ghosts can't be dissected, distilled over a Bunsen burner or examined under a microscope and they certainly don't perform on demand, so their existence may never be "proven" to the satisfaction of scientists. If you have what you believe may have been a paranormal experience, always try to find a logical explanation for it. Only after you've ruled out normal causes should you conclude that it *may* have been paranormal.

Q. *How can I become a ghost hunter?*
A. Read. Study. Experiment. Experience.

Q. *Why haven't you written about a ghost in my town/city/area?*
A. This is probably the question most frequently asked! Actually, I have several tall file cabinets full of stories and more good leads come in almost every day. Someday soon, I hope to make it to your town. Meanwhile, keep the stories coming!

Q. *How can I contact you?*
A. I love to hear from readers, whether you have a question or would like to share your own eerie experiences. My e-mail address is kdstevens@bresnan.net. I do travel quite a bit so I may not be able to get back to you right away, but I always try to respond as quickly as possible. And do check out my new website at www.hauntedmontana.com for monthly updates on the most haunted places in Montana!